BIG LAUREL RISING

An Appalachian River Tale

N. David Clifton

Shore Publications

Big Laurel Rising, An Appalachian River Tale
N. David Clifton© 2006. All rights reserved.

ISBN: 978-0-938833-38-3

Published by Shore Publications
P. O Box 1801, Melbourne, FL 32902
www.ohiopyle.info

All inquiries, feedback, or information requests to:
shorepublications@yahoo.com
Online ordering: www.biglaurelrising.info

This and all Shore Publications books available at:
www.ohiopyle.info

Publisher's Note: This is a work of fiction. Names, characters, places and incidents are the product of the author's imagination or used fictitiously, and any resemblence to actual persons living or dead, business establishments, events, or locales is entirely coincidental.

Produced in the United States of America

DEDICATION

Sometimes the difference between accolade and ignominy (or heroism and villainy) is just a matter of timing or perspective. This book is dedicated to my friends who, guided by conscience, chose their own path.

N. David Clifton

About the Author...

N. David Clifton grew up in rural Appalachia. He has worn many labels over his lifetime including farmhand, steelworker, autoworker, truck driver, heavy equipment operator, whitewater raft guide, biker, kayaker, public servant, and small business owner. He calls northern West Virginia home, and now works for a local labor organization. His house is within sight of a free flowing mountain river.

PROLOGUE

J. Charles Robbins deftly folded the French cuffs of his medium starched Egyptian cotton dress shirt. Now a public servant, he had developed a taste for good tailoring and diamond cufflinks during a stint as the CEO of a successful coal mining company. After a series of convoluted and eventually rewarding mergers, he divested himself of the coal but kept the money. Shortly thereafter, he parlayed the financial backing of his energy business friends into a career in the public sector.

His political ambitions landed him the governorship on his first try. He had expected nothing less.

This was supposed to be a simple dedication. His Chief of Staff and Public Relations Director both promised a fluffy political photo-op at one of the most dramatic natural vistas in the state. On the carpeted corridor at the far end of the gubernatorial suite, a muffled moaning leaked softly from behind the locked door of the General Counsel's office. Silken powder-blue panties hung from a shapely ankle and draped over black Italian leather pumps. The moans were directed into the felt blotter atop a dark walnut executive desk. Carefully manicured fingernails clasped, white knuckled, the ornate edge trim beneath the center drawer of the desk. Auburn hair fell forward onto the desk. A fair-skinned and lithe body pulsed, shook briefly then went limp.

"Let's go, Eddie," he gestured to the state trooper who served as his chauffeur and bodyguard. It was a two hour drive to the desolate backwoods rock outcropping where he would make his announcement.

"Where's Deb?"

"I'm coming," came a feminine voice, cracking slightly, from the adjoining hallway. His Chief of Staff, Deborah Harlan, appeared from around the corner.

They left the capitol at 9:00 am. Two hours later the interstate was behind them. In forty more minutes so was pavement. It was nearly noon when they finally pulled over at a wide spot along a remote dirt track. Several dozen other vehicles were randomly strewn along the roadside and in the adjacent woods.

None of his staff had seen fit to mention the weather report.

1

Black clouds crowded out the sun within minutes after they stepped out of the black gubernatorial Suburban®. A damp chill enveloped them. The radio said that a fast moving springtime front was sweeping south across the Ohio River Valley. It was bringing severe heavy downpours. There were still occasional patches of blue between the clouds, but the wind was picking up and impolitely disturbing the Governor's two hundred dollar razor cut. Ahead lay half a mile of rough footpath. The trail, while dramatically sylvan and even beautiful to those who relish such natural things, was little more than a winding succession of sandstone slabs held together by tree roots. His political colleagues were probably not the only snakes between the car and the ceremony site. What an incredible clustered mess this might become if several hundred media minions and a multitude of minor state and local politicians decided to all run from a sudden downpour. These woods were not exactly an ideal place for a political gathering. The trail was narrow and brushy. Tall blackberry and multiflora rose bushes lined the trail with thorns that would occasionally pluck at the threads of his suit as he passed.

Deborah cursed softly under her breath. He found it oddly sexy. A blackberry cane had reached out and put a long run in her hose, right up the side of her leg.

"Governor, look at this. Will this show on camera?"

"Just face and upper torso, Deb," he replied, shaking his head. "I didn't hire her for her intellect," he thought to himself. It just did not matter. She showed him the runner on her thigh. He tried not to stare.

Her skirt was too short for the windy conditions. She had to keep one hand on the hem at all times. Her Gucci® pumps were scuffed and covered with mud. The artisans in Firenze hadn't designed them for wilderness use. She leaned against a boulder and, one at a time, lifted them high to check for damage. The Governor caught just a glimpse of blue lace.

"I think we are getting close," he remarked.

On either side they could see distant mountains and green forests that covered steep slopes to within a few hundred yards away, but nothing closer except narrow windows of light penetrating the thick brush and trees. They had been hiking onto a high and heavily forested promontory between two river canyons. The point was becoming narrower as they walked. Along the last five hundred feet of trail, short diverging paths led to small openings in the thick laurel. People were already buzzing that the bushes obscured a high cliff line. Several people stepped away from the group to stand at the edge of the dizzying drop-off and gaze awestruck over the canyon.

Debbie stepped towards the cliff, took a quick look over, wobbled insecurely on her heels, and quickly rejoined the group.

"Infreakingcredible," she stage whispered. "Why didn't someone tell us this was going to be a damn National Geographic expedition?"

Charles grinned weakly and looked down the path at the line of dignitaries and their entourage.

Suddenly the trail opened into a broad, windswept expanse of bare rock. On three sides of the exposed point, it was a long fall over sheer cliffs to the treetops. Standing in the open, even with all of the people around, was starkly intimidating. Below, tucked deep in a thickly forested sandstone chasm, two streams flowed together to form a single tumultuous mountain river. An uninterrupted view of dense forest and jagged cliffs stretched for fifteen miles down the main canyon. The gorge sides glistened in the emerald green of fresh foliage. The river reflected tones of gleaming white and dark muted gray wherever it was visible through the dense oak forest.

A red-tailed hawk surfed the wind less than a hundred feet from the crowd. Bold and curious, it watched the odd herd of creatures that had gathered on the rocks.

A dark line of thunderstorms slowly advanced upriver toward the high craggy point where they all stood. Someone yelled for the crowd to quiet down so the ceremony could begin. It was clear that they didn't have much time.

The tech people started a generator, well muffled but obviously not far away. They had engineered a simple public address system. Debbie handed the Governor a microphone as he strode to the highest point of the rock and faced the crowd.

"Thank you all for coming. Today is the effective date of the law that makes these rocks upon which you are standing, and all of the natural grandeur around you as far as your eyes can see, a new

National Recreation Area."

He spread his arms and held his hands high as he spoke. He felt oddly like a game show host describing the prize. Personally, he didn't care about this piece of ground. They could leave it for the bears, birds and backpacking nature freaks, as far as he was concerned. It was unlikely that he'd be back unless he needed to remind the Green voters in the next election that he was their friend.

The Governor's speech was short by gubernatorial standards. Thirty tedious minutes. His was the first of several bombastic proclamations by various duly elected representatives of the people. They basked like fat lizards in the warm sunshine of public attention.

No one would have guessed that he had originally opposed Federal protection of these lands on the grounds that it would prevent the mining of underlying coal deposits. Only after a series of strictly-off-the-record lunch meetings with Bill Mitchell, a close friend, campaign contributor, and the chairman of Monumental Resources, did he decide to support the designation. It seemed that the coal under these canyons contained far too much ash and sulfur, and lay in thin, broken seams that couldn't be mined profitably. Since the bill authorizing the Federal designation didn't give the governmental caretakers the right of eminent domain, they couldn't force anyone to sell their land. This enabled the mining company to work a trade with the Feds to ostensibly save it from mining. The Governor helped arrange for the coal company to acquire some federally owned land in the West that had profitable coal deposits under it.

Congressman Randall Young, who sponsored the bill in the House of Representatives, spoke next. An earnest, responsible man, he had spearheaded the effort to preserve the watershed of the Big Laurel River since the day, half a dozen years ago, when a country lawyer who lived along this river paid him a visit at his Washington D.C. office. That gentleman had impressed him with the story of uniquely wild and rugged country encompassing hundreds of thousands of acres, right in the congressman's own district. He had to admit at the time that, although he knew roughly the area in question, he had never appreciated that there was anything special about it. In fact, he had never been there despite the fact that it was within a two-hour drive of his hometown. This area was owned by several large land companies who had purchased it for the timber reserves on it and the coal and other mineral deposits under it. They had no desire to encourage its use for any other purpose, so it existed almost unnoticed.

The congressman soon visited the area. Accompanied by the lawyer and a somewhat colorful local farmer friend of the lawyer's, he hiked miles of rugged gorges and witnessed incredible sweeping views from places like the rock where the crowd stood today. The friend, a descendent of some of the early pioneers in the area, told stories of its history. He also provided insights into what life was like in this wilderness only a few decades ago. His family had been instrumental in keeping much of the countryside in its natural state.

The two locals made a common plea. They convinced the Honorable Mr. Young that, without an immediate and concerted effort to preserve this wilderness by some sort of federal protective designation, the mining and timber interests, as well as real estate developers and other opportunists, would slowly divide, exploit, and degrade it forever.

The developers had already made a few preliminary attempts. Only a year ago, possibly fueled by rumors that the area was being considered for Federal protection, the real estate speculators had moved in. On a parcel of land adjoining the lawyer's small valley farm, they built a rustic log cabin. A team of surveyors carved the land, a five hundred acre tract acquired from a local timber company, into ten and twenty acre "wilderness ranches." They advertised the project in the newspapers of the metropolitan Washington, D.C. area. Soon expensive SUVs began appearing in the nearby small town asking for directions to Big Laurel Glen.

Within days, the lawyer's nearest neighbor took countermeasures. A call went out to several dozen of his old friends. They were loud and powerful ghosts from an era in his past when he had traveled from his mountain home to find work in an ironworks just south of the Great Lakes. They arrived two days later as an extended family of several hundred, on big, dirty, thundering, uncivilized motorcycles piled high with camping gear. They were followed by old battered pickup trucks and vans full to the windows with supplies.

They roared into the tiny town in waves of five, ten, twenty, even fifty, looking like an invasion of neo-Mongols seeking new land to plunder. Suddenly the quiet village was full of rough-hewn, bearded, and tattooed people in black leather and dirty denim.

They set up a tent city, dubbed Smileyville after a fallen comrade, in a ten-acre field surrounded by tall hemlocks. It was directly across the narrow gravel road from the new log cabin real estate office. A five-foot tall poster of Smiley, a bearded leviathan of a man with a broad easy grim, graced an upturned picnic table at the eastern end of town. He wore a black t-shirt emblazoned with white letters proclaiming, "I'm a lesbian."

The summer became a season-long 24-7 party. The individual faces changed but the smoke, music and dust-raising revelry went on. Gasoline generators hummed in the woods, keeping the lights and amplifiers glowing. Bands played rock and roll. Topless women danced in the flickering light of blazing campfires.

Surprisingly, after the initial shock, the local people grew accustomed to the newcomers. While outwardly boisterous, they were generally very polite when they were in town. Business had never been better for the local diner. Ditto at the hardware store and the bait and tackle shop. Food and beer sales at the village grocery reflected the ravenous hungers of the visiting tribe.

One cool night in late July, when the census of Smileyville was at an all time high of about five hundred, the real estate office disappeared. All that was left the next morning was a toilet, sink, refrigerator, and some roofing shingles. They littered the little parking lot inside a pitiful square perimeter of concrete blocks that had once served as its foundation.

That evening several hundred happy campers partied all night around the warm incandescence of a roaring bonfire. They danced to the music of an outlaw country band that had driven in from somewhere south of Nashville to give a free concert in memory of Smiley. The local sheriff came out from town in the morning and dutifully inspected the empty building site. He spoke briefly with a guy known only as Lucky, self-proclaimed mayor of Smileyville. The sheriff never even ventured into the campground.

Not a single "ranch" was sold in Big Laurel Glen. The real estate company filed a lawsuit against the lawyer who owned the land upon which Smileyville was located, alleging intentional interference with its business. The attorney responded that the bikers had been trespassers. His defense was basically that no one in their right mind would run the risk of trying to evict several hundred obvious sociopaths from land where they really weren't hurting anything anyway.

The suit was later dropped when the lawyer was able to broker a sale of the parcel owned by the realty company to the Federal government. It was the first land acquired for the new recreation area. The office parking lot later became a trailhead for backpackers. The real estate people were able to get their money out of the project and moved on.

Today the Congressman extolled the virtues of wild country and the untold joy that this land and waters would provide to generations of hikers, campers, mountain bikers, hunters, fishermen, canoeists, kayakers, rock climbers, and others. As he spoke, the lawyer, his friend, and their families listened from the crowd. They watched the dark clouds march steadily toward the speaker. Sheets of rain obscured the mountains in the distance. For the Congressman, with his back to the drama, only a cool, damp breeze foretold what was about to happen.

A sudden sharp blast of wind welled up out of the canyon. It almost picked up the young red-haired child who was laying prone on the rock and dangling his head, upper chest, and arms over the cliff's edge. The force of the gust startled him. His up-close view of the sheer three hundred foot drop to the talus slope below had been exciting enough. He hadn't planned on the wind. Scooting away from the edge, he ran teary-eyed to his mother.

He had been hanging over the void because he thought he'd seen something far below on the churning river that poured along the bottom of the canyon. There had been brief flashes of color barely visible through the dense vegetation. But, stare as he might, they eluded him. He lost interest when the gust of wind hit him in the face. He was sure, for a moment, that it would flip him up and off the face of the rock.

After his mother comforted him and assured him that he was fine,

7

she turned him loose again to play in the woods. He strolled over toward his father. He was standing apart from the crowd on a broad ledge of sandstone that was separated from the mob scene by a two and a half foot wide fissure in the rock. Although narrower than a city sidewalk, the crack was probably fifty feet deep. It was more than deep enough to discourage most of those who had contemplated jumping over to the adjoining rock. The kid didn't trouble himself with assessing the depth of the cleft. He harbored no doubt that he could jump over it. His father turned to see him as he hung in the air, mid jump.

By the time the boy landed, it was a done deed. His father didn't scold him. He just checked to see whether the boy's mother was watching. The only threat now was that he'd be hearing from his wife about his failure to anticipate the boy's jump and do something to prevent it. Hopefully, she hadn't noticed.

The boy's father's name was Silas. He swept the lad up in his arms and placed him on his broad shoulders. The child, Aaron, instantly became a little lightheaded from the new perspective. If not for the unbending faith that he had in the power and presence of his father, he would surely have panicked and screamed. From this vantage point he seemed to soar over a wild green world that stretched before him to the distant horizon. Farther than he had ever seen before.

Suddenly, the red tailed hawk appeared again. It rode an updraft of air out of the canyon only to pause suspended just above their heads.

"Do you know what that is?" asked Silas.

"That's an eagle, like on your back," came the reply. The boy was referring to the large tattoo of an eagle in flight that spanned his father's back, shoulder to shoulder.

"It's like an eagle, Son, only smaller. That's a hawk."

"Its beautiful, Dad," he said. "Can I have it?"

Silas thought for a moment. The bird seemed almost close enough to grab. His boy obviously had that part of inborn human nature that wants to own what it finds beautiful. He turned a little so that, while keeping the hawk in view, the boy could also get a sweeping panoramic view of the canyon and the towering black clouds seemingly ready to engulf them.

"No, Son, the hawk is wild. People shouldn't try to own wild things. They need to be free to be happy."

He leaned forward ever so slightly. "See the river down there?" The boy looked down. His head was spinning. His fingers dug into his father's skin. Silas tightened his grip on the boy just a little. "That river is wild, too. We're here today because, once upon a time, some men tried to take away its freedom, ruin the river. People, including your Uncle Ian, stopped them. Now that hawk, the river, and all this country, as far as you can see, will always be free and wild."

He stood up straight and tall and spoke again to the boy.

"Now tell me what do you see?"

The boy looked out into space. The enormity of it was more than he could put into words.

"It's big, Dad," was all he could come up with.

"That's right son, it's real big. Bigger than you, bigger than me, bigger than all of the people over on that rock."

Silas turned briefly so that Aaron could see the crowd pressing around the Congressman.

"That's why we can never own it. That's also why some people want to destroy it. They are afraid of it. It is too big for them to control. They would cut it up so that they could make money from it. That is sad and very wrong. It isn't ours to cut up. It belongs to everyone, even to people who aren't born yet. We have to protect it from folks who are greedy or just don't understand, so that our children will have it for their children.

Some day you will have children. You will want to bring them out onto this rock and show them something big, bigger than yourself. This will still be here for you, and for them."

With that, Silas put the boy gently back on the ground. He reminded him to stay away from the edge. Except for another leap across the crevasse, the child followed his instructions implicitly.

No sooner had Aaron left than his mother appeared, seemingly out of nowhere. Silas stifled the urge to wince. She looked like she had something to say, as she so often did.

"What in the Hell were you doing out here with that boy up on your shoulders?"

"I wanted him to see the canyon."

9

"Why did he need to be on your shoulders? We're already on top of the goddamn world." Her hands were on her hips, never a good sign.

"I still remember what it felt like to be on my father's shoulders. I felt like I could see forever."

No response, just her special silence. And the soft moan of the rising wind.

"Kathleen," he pleaded calmly with just a twinge of frustration in his voice. "It's part of being a father, sharing what is important to you. Sometimes they pick up on it and sometimes they don't, but you have to try."

"There is no denying that you're his father." She shook her head in consternation.

"There's much more to being a father than DNA. He's a small bundle of raw fuel. All kids are. A father owes them at least an attempt to pass on a spark. Maybe it will ignite something in him that will give him purpose later in life. Purpose goes a long way toward guiding you after your kin are gone. That's what fatherhood is about."

"Lord God, he's a handful already. If he catches your fire I'll be one burnt-out old lady." She finally broke down and laughed to herself. Her Appalachian drawl softened slightly as she slowly shook her head. A small smile of warm resignation, a hint of mountain azalea sweetness.

"I'll go keep an eye on him."

She loved that she had found the one man in the world she couldn't rattle.

Only minutes after the boy's release, nature took control of the agenda. Sheets of cold, wind-driven rain, pressure-washed the exposed rock platform. People scattered for the less than adequate shelter of the forest. The microphone went dead within seconds of the start of the deluge. Everyone assumed that the rain had shorted out the electronics.

Actually, Aaron had pulled the plug.

The crowd streamed down the trail toward the shelter of the cars parked half a mile away. Small sticks shook loose from the branches overhead to bombard the soaked politicians and reporters to remind them that time was of the essence. They rushed back to their shiny metal boxes. Debbie fell three times on the slick clay spots between the rocks. Her shoes and hose were total losses. Safely back in the limo, Charles wiped his face and hands dry with the towel Bennie handed to him. Then he handed it to Debbie. "You're soaked," he noted. "And shivering."

Her clothes stuck to her trembling body, erect nipples protruded noticeably. He wrapped the towel around her to pat the water out of her now shear and clinging white blouse. If his wife ever found out about the two of them, there would be personal and public Hell to pay.

Fifty yards down the road the lawyer, his friend, Silas, their wives, and Aaron piled into the lawyer's club-cab pickup truck. Their hair was dripping water and they were laughing. Aaron shook his head, flinging water onto his mother. She placed him in a gentle head-lock. The lawyer's wife carefully unwrapped fleece blankets from around the face of the baby boy she had been cradling in her arms. He was sound asleep.

"Amazing, does anything upset this child?" she asked.

Silas, in the back seat staring out the window at the pouring rain, wore a large grin. Water ran down the side of his face.

"Mountain weather." was all he said.

This land refused to be deferential, even to those who claimed to be its protectors. Ian, the lawyer, turned on the truck's defroster and put the transmission into gear.

A thousand feet below the soaked masses, the rain beat down on three other men celebrating the newly designated recreation area. The three kayakers had started their river trip where a hiking trail intersected Sugar Branch, a tributary of the Big Laurel Fork, well above its confluence with the main river. They carried their brightly colored plastic boats to the stream a mile and a half from the nearest dirt road.

Sugar Branch was running full and pushy from a week of spring rain. It was a steep, technical whitewater run. The three boaters had barely time to catch their breath. After each move, there was another rock to miss, another boulder pile to maneuver around, or another ledge to line up for. It was like skiing a huge moving mogul field that never stopped. At the confluence, they eddied-out to rest and have a drink of water. The hike in, and the miles of

11

constant strenuous paddling, had already taken a toll on their strength and reaction time.

As they took off again, they all harbored mild misgivings about the dozen miles of whitewater ahead of them. The water carried a class IV to class V rating on the international whitewater rating scale. A very serious river by anyone's standards, it was quite capable of administering a serious, even fatal, beating to the unlucky or unprepared. To make matters worse, it was clear to them that the skies were going to open up at any time. Any increase in water level would make the river even more difficult and dangerous. They would have to keep stroking relentlessly toward the takeout. Any time they spent resting was time the river might use to rise to an unrunnable level.

Minutes before the rain began, immediately below the prying eyes of a red-haired boy far above them, they entered a rapid known in the paddling community as "Fang." Here the entire riverbed consisted of a smooth slab of brown sandstone. It tilted downstream at a twenty-degree angle.

The polished, almost frictionless, riverbed and steep pitch caused the water to accelerate to incredible speed. At the bottom of this fifty-yard long natural slide, the river piled into deep water backed by a boxcar-sized chunk of the same ageless sandstone. The whole river then folded backwards upon itself in a seething white mass. It poured, still a white froth, around the right side of the boulder corkscrewing downstream. Then it was immediately split by a tall pointed rock, the Fang. Plumes of river ricocheted off the sides of the Fang to finally find ten yards of peace in the pool below. Fang was a solid class V rapid, even at reasonable water levels.

The first kayaker, Ed, was a dedicated river bum and professional raft guide. He entered the rapid exactly where he had intended. His paddle strokes were strong, controlled, and steady. He accelerated with the river and plowed into the huge foam pile about thirty feet from its right terminus. The boat rode up on the crashing wave, standing vertically on its stern end. It surfed toward the right side of the river with the bow pointed at the sky, then flopped back to a horizontal position. The river hurled the boat at Fang Rock. Ed leaned on his paddle blade in a deep brace, and rode a surge of current off the left side of the rock into the pool below. All smiles, he flashed a thumbs-up to the two boats waiting in the eddy above the rapid.

Next boat down was piloted by the youngest of the boaters, John. He was a second year law student who had discovered the lure of wild rivers through a friend at school. Although he had been kayaking for only about a year, he was competitively driven, naturally athletic, and fearless. Obsessed with the sport, he boated almost daily after apprenticing with some of the most technically proficient paddlers in the state. Ed's lingering concern about John was that he had not yet amassed the experience, and the caution that comes with it, that can only be developed through years on the river. John had yet to develop a true respect for the power of the water. Ed's own reverence had come at great expense. Over the past ten years he had watched several friends drown in river accidents spawned by seemingly minor misjudgments. He knew young John had not yet internalized that he was quite mortal.

John's line began about where Ed's had, but he either underestimated the strength of the current, which was moving slightly right-to-left down the slide, or was perhaps a little fatigued from the first five miles of constant paddling. The river swept him left, into the heart of the white water. His boat reared up like a bronco, flipped over backward, then did it all again, flipping end-for-end twice. John and his kayak were swept to the right and around the end of the first huge boulders.

John had tucked-in tightly against the deck of his boat. When the violent thrashing subsided for a moment, he executed a perfect Eskimo roll. As the water sheeted off of his eyes he turned to see Fang Rock rushing at him. Though his reflexes and boat handling skills were superb, he was simply not fast enough to avoid the imminent collision. The rock caught his boat broadside, right at the cockpit rim. John made the appropriate countermove, throwing his weight forward and against the rock, hoping he would ride the surging currents to safety. It wasn't enough.

The force of the water crushed his boat and wrapped it solidly around the rock. Pain shot up his side as his legs, trapped in the boat, were bent by the force of the water. He couldn't move. The cold river swirled within inches of his nose.

John's luck had held in two respects. First, as uncomfortable as he

13

was, his legs had not been broken by the force of the water when he pinned. Second, he could still breathe. This was tenuous good fortune at best because any rise in the river level, or even the regular surges in the current, could work the boat down the rock, and pull him under water.

He fought the urge to panic. It was impossible to call for help with water swirling around his chin and mouth. He knew his predicament would be obvious to the other guys and prayed that they would be able to rescue him. He was captured by a very violent river, essentially paralyzed by the force of thousands of pounds of frigid water. Soon the cold would overwhelm him and he would no longer be able to hold his head above water.

He felt the boat shudder briefly and begin to move. The current pulses were working it down the rock. Shit. Now he was breathing half air, half water from a pocket in front of his face as more water poured around his head. Time slowed as his panic took on a strange, calmly detached, dimension. He wondered whether hypothermia or drowning was the better death.

Ed was streaking up the shoreline with the coiled rescue rope that he carried in his boat. His first toss landed squarely across John's shoulders. John clutched it with all his strength. The rope helped slightly in keeping his head out of the water, but the angle was wrong. There was no way that Ed could get enough leverage to pull him free from the rock.

While Ed had been getting in position to throw a rope, the third kayaker, Daniel, (another long time waterdog and de facto brother to Ed) ran his boat up onto the rocks just upstream from John and jumped out. He was now sprinting across the top of the huge boulder that backed up the churning hole at the bottom of the slide. Running full speed, he dove across the worst of the twisting currents nearest the rock, out into the green flume that headed straight for Fang Rock. He surfaced on his back, floating feet first toward the rock.

In an instant he was there, feet against the Fang and hands firmly clasped on the pointed bow of John's kayak.

Putting every ounce of muscle at his disposal into one great upward movement, he was able to pry the boat up and out into the jet of water accelerating around the rock. The current immediately peeled the boat and John away from the boulder, and sent it spinning, bottom up, downstream. In a few seconds John bailed out of the crushed boat and swam it to shore.

He dragged its bent hull up onto the rocks and collapsed beside it gagging and gasping for breath. His side and legs were badly bruised but nothing seemed broken. Dan rode Ed's throw rope to safety, sweeping like a fifty-foot pendulum across the current to the relative safety of the downstream pool.

Ed slapped him on the back as he retrieved his rope. "Gnarly rescue, Dude."

Dan knew he had taken a questionable gamble, had violated multiple rules of whitewater safety, but he probably saved his buddy's life. They retrieved John's paddle a few yards downstream where it was circling lazily in the eddy. Its shaft was nicked but it was still useable.

As they kicked John's kayak back into shape, and repositioned the interior reinforcements that were supposed to help keep it from collapsing in situations such as this, they shared a collective sense of relief. John had experienced his first real dance with the River Gods and lived to tell about it. That evening, after they got off the river and were warm and dry in Ed's truck, they toasted their good fortune with cold beers from his cooler. Aside from John's boat getting all crunched like that, it had been a primo run.

They drove into Elton for dinner. Ed shook his head when he saw the parking lot of the Riverside Diner. The only vehicle that did not carry a load of kayaks or mountain bikes, from the mountaineering equipment decals plastered all over its windows and bumper, obviously belonged to a group of rock climbers. In years gone by, the only patrons in this little place were loggers, miners, workers from the sawmill and other businesses around town, and an occasional trout fisherman. Now, in the last decade of the twentieth century, the Riverside had been discovered. Inside they were greeted by the owner, Lori, with a fresh pot of coffee.

Maybe it was the afterglow from a dramatic day on the river, or euphoria arising out of the imperfect realization that he had temporarily postponed dealing with his mortality, but John was feeling full of himself. It was probably just the effects of four cups of coffee on top of four beers. As Lori was walking away after his

15

fifth coffee refill, he commented to Dan a little too loudly that, for a mature woman, she was a babe.

She never broke stride. Her eyes glistened just a bit as she fought to hide her facial expression.

After the restaurant closed for the evening, Lori walked down the town's single main street to the long white frame building that housed the town's hardware store, law office, and motorcycle shop. The lights were still on in the bike shop. Inside she found her husband, Ian, her best friend, Kathleen, and Kathleen's husband, Silas. Silas was deftly installing a new camshaft in a somewhat ratted-out shovelhead Harley Davidson®.

She told the story of the young kayaker's comment to Kathleen, whose response was one raised eyebrow and the simple question, "How old?"

"Early 20's, I suppose."

"Young, dumb, and full of cum," was her blasé appraisal.

Silas looked up briefly from the motorcycle and shook his head. The four of them sipped beers from the shop refrigerator and made comfortable small talk. Lori's husband rocked their baby in the little plastic backpack carrier that the child had been sleeping in for most of the day. She took the infant from him and stepped through the back door of the shop onto the sloping lawn that gradually fell away to the river.

She held the hungry infant to her breast and looked out across the rippled water. The full moon turned it into a sea of moving sparkles. Spring peepers chirped from the weeds along the banks. A soft breeze carried the clean coolness of the river past her and into the shop.

When she stepped back into the building, Ian was being nostalgic. He had been in that mood all day, was musing over the changes in his life that had brought him to this place.

The mechanic, generally a man of few words, looked up from the bike and shrugged knowingly. Putting down his wrenches, holding up his beer, he made the summation.

"Thank you, God, for leading us home to this valley."

16

CHAPTER ONE

"Justice is incidental to law and order."   J. Edgar Hoover

"There is nothing so powerful as truth-and often nothing so
strange."   Daniel Webster

" Fuck'em if they can't take a joke." ·   Panhead Joe

Cool gray daylight penetrated the tinted glass of the long windows
lining the corridor outside the fourth floor courtrooms. Judge
Aaron Guthrie stepped off the elevator of the new judicial annex
building. After fourteen years of doling out justice under stained
ceilings and chipped paint, he finally had a new office and a
sparkling modern courtroom. Best of all, he had his own reserved
parking space in the new city parking garage.
Loitering among the benches that lined the hallway between the
judge and his office door, was the usual entourage of winners and
losers. Many were officers of the court. Some were its victims.
Oftentimes it was hard to tell who fell into which category. Ten
paces from the door, a county sheriff's deputy turned and nodded
a reserved greeting to Aaron.
"Mornin,' Judge."
Aaron nodded back, trying to look hurried. He really did not feel
like howdying it up in the hallways first thing in the morning. He
could never be sure who was standing around and whether his
actions would be interpreted by someone as a sign of familiarity, or
worse yet, bias.
He recognized the gentleman who the deputy accompanied to his
court. The man stood tall and relaxed. Long brown hair spilled in
loose waves to well below his shoulders. He seemed oddly at ease,
even in leg irons. The judge first noticed his arms, bound in front
of him by plastic zip-tie restraints. An intricate tapestry of red,
black and green artwork, indelibly etched into the prisoner's skin by
thousands of ink-soaked needle points, protruded from the blaze
orange sleeves of the county issue jumpsuit.
"How you doing, Lucky?" crossed his lips before he thought to be
more judicious.

The prisoner calmly responded in a soft drawl that echoed of the hollows of southern West Virginia.

"Not too bad, all considered." A brief pause. "How's it hangin' yerhonor?"

The deputy poked the prisoner in the ribs.

"That's no way to talk to the Judge!" he whispered, shaking his head. Aaron, turned his back to them both as he opened the door to his new office suite, smiling broadly.

Later, in the courtroom, Stephan "Lucky" Sonovich sat at a front row table with his court-appointed counsel. The lawyer stiffly modeling a new J.C. Penney® suit, was clearly a Public Defender, and as bright green as fresh April leaves. The Prosecutor's Office representative, sitting at the other front table, was Assistant Prosecutor "Maximum Max" Chandron. The Prosecutor's Office was sending the message that it wanted Lucky put away.

"Your Honor," Max began. "We have a plea to present to the court." He had spent the early morning badgering the young Defender into an agreement. Lucky Sonovich was a repeat offender. To Max he was biker trash; just another incorrigible redneck brawler and trouble-maker. This was the latest of a string of arrests for assault and various public disturbances.

"Approach the bench, Counsel," Judge Guthrie directed in his trademark paternal tone. Max strolled forward. The Public Defender stood behind his table at attention.

"You too," the judge lip-synched, raising his eyebrows, and gesturing toward him.

When they were both standing before the bench, speaking in tones inaudible to the rest of the room except for the court reporter, the young Defender's nervousness became too obvious to ignore. Aaron tried to break the ice with small talk.

"I've never seen you in my court before," he remarked.

"This is my first case Your Honor," he admitted, his voice breaking from the stress. "I just got admitted to the bar last week."

"Well, welcome to the profession." The judge said it with relaxed and unrehearsed sincerity. He had never become as cynical about the law business as many of his colleagues.

"Gentlemen," he continued, "let's hear what you've agreed upon."

Max quickly interjected his two cents. "Well, Your Honor, as you

18

already know, Mr. Sonovich is a violent and unrepentant individual and a repeat offender."

The Judge was not impressed, and summarily ended Max's presentation.

"I am aware that Mr. Sonovich has been in my court many times, Counsel. Please get to the point. Have you two reached an understanding?"

"Yes, Your Honor. On the charge of Destruction of Property, Defendant has agreed to plead guilty. He will serve six months incarceration and provide restitution to the property owner. On the charge of Assault and Battery he has agreed to plead guilty and serve one to three years at the state medium security facility." Max seemed satisfied with that result. Frankly, it was pretty reasonable for Max. He felt he had gone a bit easy on the young Defender.

"Is that an accurate recital of your agreement?" the judge asked the Defender.

"Yes sir it is," he responded.

"Will the defendant please approach the bench?" Aaron motioned to Lucky to rise from the wide oak table where he was seated, and come up to the front of the room where counsel and the court reporter could hear him enter his plea. Lucky obliged, shuffling up to the attorneys with the length of steel chain that bound his ankles dragging across the hardwood floor.

Everyone except Judge Guthrie expected the usual litany of questions to affirm that the plea was entered willingly and knowingly. Instead, the exchange was informal and hardly judicial.

"Good morning once again, Lucky."

"Good morning, Your Honor."

"Why are you here, Lucky?"

Lucky shot a quizzical glance at his attorney. The Defender blushed red.

The Judge leaned forward across the broad surface of the bench and looked straight into the eyes of the Defendant. His voice was almost gentle, more like that of a father talking to his son than a judge questioning a prisoner.

"No, I mean in your own words. What happened that got you arrested?"

Lucky shifted his weight foot to foot until he found a stance that was comfortable. The Deputy that accompanied him watched him intently from his spot a few paces away. Lucky clasped his tattooed left wrist firmly in his right hand and leaned back onto his heels. "Well, it happened like this, Your Honor." He began. "I was out on the town with Tina Hall. We were having a drink at Rudy's, that little place down by the river."

Aaron felt like he knew Rudy's well, although he had never been there. Lucky was not the first defendant to present a story somehow connected to Rudy's. It was the most notorious biker bar in three counties, but its owner, Bud Thomas, kept its clientele on a fairly tight leash inside its walls. The parking lot was quite another story.

To his credit, Bud was one of the few local tavern owners who religiously checked ID of suspected underage drinkers. He occasionally turned away even those with apparently valid ID because he just did not believe them. One such baby-faced would-be perpetrator was the Judge's youngest son. Bud tipped Aaron off. He met the boy at the door when he got home.

Aaron also knew Lucky Sonovich quite well. He had appeared in his courtroom more than the judge cared to recall. Almost incredibly, every time that Lucky appeared he had a plausible, sometimes even heroic, explanation for the action that landed him in jail. Lucky's heart seemed to be in the right place. Unfortunately, the location of the rest of his body was often problematic, especially considering his timing.

The judge secretly enjoyed listening to the Biker's explanations as to why he was in custody. Lucky was always willing to share the blow-by-blow details of his infractions. He never displayed guilt, shame, or remorse. In fact, he apparently lacked much of the innate appreciation and respect for rules that guides most people through the gauntlet of life. He was undeniably a brawler and wild child, although oddly without malice. Aaron was actually a little impressed that, while he wrecked havoc on some more mundane sections of the penal code, he was able to do so without significant violation of any of the Ten Commandments.

Lucky continued. "I had just finished shooting a game of pool, which I lost, and was standing at the bar with Tina. We were both just talking and having a beer. This big drunk guy sitting near Tina kept staring at her. We were trying to ignore him but he kept right on staring. Finally he reached out and put a hand on her, well, you know… *boob*." He slowly drew a deep breath.

"So Tina slapped him. Pretty hard. Rang his chimes just a little." Lucky shrugged. "It didn't seem like an unreasonable response to me at the time. But then this joker gets all agitated and grabs Tina by the arm, so I put one hand on Tina and pushed him off with the other. He hangs back for a minute and makes some remarks about her being a fat slut."

Lucky paused to let that information sink in, or maybe just to collect his thoughts. He wrinkled his face as if tortured by what he was to say next and continued haltingly.

The judge never took his gaze off the defendant's eyes.

"Now, if you know Tina, you know she is *very* sensitive about her weight, so she starts crying immediately. This guy, he just won't back off. In a few seconds he gets this real crazy look on his face, pulls back his arm and rushes at her again. Fast. Like he intended to either hit her real hard or to jump on her. So I was forced to punch him."

"Did you hit him hard Lucky?"

"Sure, I wanted to hit him hard enough to stop him. And he was coming at us pretty fast, so that added to the force of my shot."

"Your Honor," interjected Max, "he broke the victim's jaw in three places."

"How many times did you hit him, Lucky?"

"Just the once, Judge."

Aaron turned toward Max. "How is the victim now?"

Max looked peeved. "We don't know, Your Honor. He disappeared."

"He gave the emergency room a fake name and false insurance information," added the Public Defender.

The Judge looked down at the papers in front of him. His brow furrowed, then relaxed as he looked back up.

"I don't know, gentlemen," began the judge, shaking his head slowly, "this sounds a lot like mitigation, maybe even self-defense or defense-of-another. Maybe you should talk over your plea arrangement some more."

"Your Honor," Max protested, his voice shrill with frustration at seeing his plea bargain wither before his eyes, "he broke that man's jaw *in three places.*"

"Max, you know that might factor into damages in a civil action, but it doesn't prove much here. And, it sounds like you don't have the victim to testify."

"But he's pleading *guilty.* And doing it knowingly with the assistance of counsel," Max insisted. His eyes narrowed. He clenched his teeth until his jaw muscles flexed.

The Judge was becoming visibly annoyed.

"Five minutes. You two go out in the hall and talk," Aaron directed, pointing toward the door. "And take Mr. Sonovich with you. I'll be right here when you get done."

Six minutes later, the attorneys returned. Lucky presented a plea for misdemeanor disturbing of the peace.

Aaron Guthrie sentenced him to the time he had already spent in the county correctional facility and sent him on his way to reclaim his impounded motorcycle and get on with his life. His public defender, beaming, shook his hand heartily and bid him farewell. Max turned away, picked up his briefcase, and left the courtroom shaking his head slowly in disgust.

Lucky, who had fully expected to return to a lonely, cacophonous world of drab pastel green cement and iron, walked back to the sheriff's office a free man. He quickly changed clothes and soon had his wheels back under him. It was a sad testimony to a haphazard existence that all he had to his name was six hundred and fifty pounds of aluminum and steel and whatever tools and clothes his saddlebags would hold.

Prior to his incarceration, he had been staying at Tina's trailer, but suspected that he would not be welcome back there. Even though he had been arrested defending her honor, they had been arguing all that evening. She said she was tired of rowdy rednecks and living day to day.

Her exact words were "I just want a man who knows how to do more than fuck and work on motorcycles."

"Ain't that just like a woman," spoke his inner voice. "The very things that attract them to you in the first place become the reason they eventually leave you."

It was a dirty and tired looking shovelhead Superglide. After over a dozen years on the road, it was still ran strong. It usually started at the touch of a button, but had a kick-start lever just in case. Soon the wind was in his face and he was gone. This was just another brief flash in his odd life of disjointed video episodes. He headed south. It seemed like a good direction. The office buildings that ringed the old city-county building were replaced with strip malls. They eventually faded into random bars, auto repair shops, and convenience stores. Finally, the road stretched out into green farmlands and patches of woods. The wind in his face became cooler.

His engine sputtered, then cut out. Instinctively, Lucky reached down under the tank and flipped the lever on the petcock to Reserve. He had fifteen or twenty miles to find a gas station. No big deal, he was not that far into the boonies. The blacktop he was riding was fairly well traveled and passed through numerous little crossroad towns. Sure enough, it was only a few miles to a dusty gravel parking lot graced with a large yellow and red sign promising gas, beer and lottery tickets.

Lucky pulled in against the hi-test pump. He believed in taking good care of the important things, like his scooter. He noticed a dozen other bikes standing off to the side of the lot on the edge of a field of ankle-high corn sprouts. Sun baked bikers loaded beer and junk food into a battered Ford® van parked in front of the equally weathered and dirty convenience store.

Lucky filled the Shovelhead's tank with gas. He went inside to pay and get a cup of thick, harsh, scalded coffee. He preferred his coffee, like his women, hot, strong and a bit bitter. When he came outside, he pushed the bike to a corner of the lot. Opening one dusty leather saddlebag, he noticed his cell phone. It was his single concession to modern gadgetry. It was his only connection to those who might want to find him, although he spent most of his time in places with no cell service. Turning it on, it showed one missed call. The message was three days old. It was from a man who was the closest thing to a mentor Lucky had ever known. The voice said there was a job waiting for Lucky up in the hills.

Next to the cell phone Lucky found a crumpled cigarette. A home-made one. How had the police at the impound lot missed that? Like his ex-wife used to say, "Some days it is better to be Lucky than smart."

He put flame to it and sat back in the saddle watching the bikers load up. One of them noticed him looking.

"Where you headed Bro?" came the greeting.

"South." Even as he spoke the word, Lucky felt his response was too laconic. Not wanting to appear unfriendly, he elaborated. "I was thinking Tennessee, but I might have to take a job somewhere closer."

"Just out for a putt, eh?" came the acknowledgment. The biker hadn't really heard what Lucky said, but noticed a familiar smell in the air.

"Toke?" He asked, pointing at Lucky's hand.

"Sure,." Lucky grinned. "Mother always told me to share." He handed the joint to the stranger.

"Yup, nice day for some wind and some miles," the stranger noted. He took a long hit while looking at the sky. He seemed a friendly sort, but not a guy Lucky would turn his back on.

"If you're flexible as to where you end up, you're welcome to ride with us," the stranger offered. "We're heading west toward Chicago. There's a week-long get-together on the shore of Lake Michigan. It's in memory of a Bro killed by a cager up in Detroit. We have some friends up on the lake that said we can use their land to camp and party."

"Was this guy who was killed one of yours?"

"No, he belonged to another club. This is a nondenominational memorial celebration." The biker smiled, he knew perfectly why Lucky had hesitated. A solo tagalong on a club ride could easily wake up one morning alone and without his bike and belongings. "This is a completely cool ride." The biker seemed to be genuine enough, but was trying a little too hard to be reassuring. "Everyone is welcome."

Lucky took a last hit and thanked him for the invitation. "Sounds nice, but I best take care of business before I play. You have a good ride." He reached down and turned on the ignition. "Keep the rubber side down."

He crushed the still burning roach between his fingers and put its remains in his jacket pocket. One tall jump on the kicker fired up the bike. Lucky saluted the others and tractored out of the lot.

CHAPTER TWO

"The whole head is sick, and the whole heart faint." ·Isaiah i. 5.

"The Lord gave, and the Lord hath taken away; blessed be the name of the Lord." · Job i. 21.

Silas McGraw sat uncomfortably alone in a row of chrome and vinyl chairs, staring at the bare pale blue wall across from him. He hated hospitals. The air of sterile foreboding. The faint odor of disinfectant, floor polish, alcohol. You could smell the pain.
It had only been forty minutes since he said good-bye to his wife as she lay on a metal stretcher, being wheeled through the double doors into the operating suite. He did not like medical, especially surgical, solutions to what he saw as personal problems. She insisted, however, on knowing why two seemingly healthy young (although he was painfully aware of the stray gray hairs in his beard) people could try like hell for over a year and still not conceive a child. Her frustration had taken her to several OB-GYNs and finally, to this hospital. Today they would insert a scope into a small slit in her abdominal wall and peer around at her internal female parts for a possible explanation.
Linda was a fair-haired urban angel who had become Silas's main reason for living. He met her only eighteen months ago. For years prior to that, he had been going through the motions of survival, but was sorely lacking a life. That past already seemed very distant.
The youngest of six sisters, Linda grew up mere blocks from the mills that lined Railroad Avenue. They lived in a simple two-story frame house. It was sided in the red brick-look asbestos shingle siding that used to be common in Midwestern factory towns. From the second story, she could watch an unending brown plume rise from the smokestacks down by the river. Thick black dust on the windowsill was as much a childhood memory to her as the smell of blooming lilacs and fresh cut grass is to the kids in the suburbs.
Her father was a tall, handsome man who never stayed at a job long enough to get the seniority necessary to earn day shift. Most of his life he went to work late in the afternoon and came home

either while she was sleeping, or as she got ready to go to school in the morning.

Her mom was a sullen, hardworking woman. Lack of education relegated her to the service sector in the days before the media learned to call it that. She cleaned peoples' houses during the day. At night, alone in the house with her daughters, she drank. She usually worked several jobs, even within days of delivering each daughter. The older children looked after the younger ones, and the young ones grew into responsibility quickly.

When Linda was in high school, her mother became very ill. They said it was her liver, but it was never clear whether it was infectious hepatitis or cirrhosis from lifelong alcoholism. Although Linda wanted to stay home and care for her, her mother insisted Linda go to school each morning. Eventually she became very yellow and weak.

One afternoon in late spring, when the days were finally breaking out of the eight-month grayness of a Great Lakes' winter, she died. Her refusal to go to the hospital had probably hastened the process.

When Linda came home from school, she called her to her room. Taking Linda's hand, she held it to her face.

"I just want you to know that I love you," she said, closing her eyes. When their father came home from the mill late that evening, he found her dead.

Within days of Linda's high school graduation he disappeared. Rumor was that he was living in Florida. Perhaps he felt his fatherly mission had been completed by raising six daughters to biological, if not legal, adulthood.

At seventeen, Linda was much more self sufficient than most recent high school graduates. She soon found work in a factory that manufactured water pumps. It was there that she met Paul. He was tall like her father, and very worldly and charming. They were married three months later. Of the six years that they were married, he worked two, but maintained a serious cocaine habit for five.

The coke made him paranoid, exaggerating his already controlling nature. Eventually he began shadowing her every movement. When he began paying her random surprise visits at work, it cost her the job. The night she was fired, she returned home to find the apartment in shambles. Paul had decided that she was hiding money from him and had turned the place inside out looking for it. Linda put her toothbrush, hairbrush, and some makeup in her purse and left. She stayed with various friends for several weeks, always a step ahead of Paul. Finally, a Legal Aid attorney got her a protective order and a divorce.

Soon she found a job as a barmaid in a little dive not far from her old neighborhood. The bar owner had been a friend of her mother. It was not a very busy place, but most of the customers were regulars who treated her with respect and tipped adequately, if not lavishly.

One night a guy walked in alone. She had never seen him in the place before. He was a good bit older than she, but still carried the power and confidence of youth. He was a big guy, and a little on the rough-looking side, yet polite and soft spoken. She somehow felt comfortable, even safe, around him. And he was a good tipper. Over the next few months she learned that his name was Silas. He worked as a shakeout man at a nearby iron foundry. His job was to split the sand-lined molds from around the glowing orange castings as soon as the freshly poured metal cooled and hardened enough to be removed. With yard long steel hooks, he drug the barely solid metal across a thumping shakeout floor, which knocked the thick hot foundry sand from the castings. A conveyor took them to a shot blaster to be cleaned. Each regular eight-hour shift left him coated with black foundry sand and clinically dehydrated. His arms and legs bore the scars of countless forgotten minor encounters with the raw metal. There were round scars caused by the splash of liquid iron from being too near the furnaces while the molds were being poured full. The longer scars were from contact with the edge of hot castings recently freed from the molds. Time had taught him to be reasonably cautious, but he was never afraid of honest, hot, dirty, even brutal, work.

She was not surprised to learn that he had grown up way back in the hills of Appalachia on a hardscrabble farm, the son of a coal miner. That history was consistent with his stoic demeanor regarding the rigors of his current profession. She sensed that what some may see as a bucolic or even serene childhood was not so romantic for those who actually had to live it.

27

There was something else about him, an intelligence and awareness that she had not seen in the regular crowd. It was obvious that he read a lot. She asked him about that once. He told her that he began reading in Vietnam to help pass interminable expanses of time that separated moments of exquisite terror. Any book that he could get his hands on would suffice. He lost himself in print for hours on end. Linda first noticed it when he quoted, fairly regularly, famous people who she had never heard of. She would make him explain who they were and why they were wise enough for him to want to use their words rather than his own.

They had known each other casually for months when he finally, almost shyly, asked her to a movie. She had not been on a real date since leaving Paul. On some level she was afraid of what Paul might do if he found out that she was dating, either to her or the guy. This man, Silas, would not be intimidated either by the situation or by Paul. She said, "Yes."

Within a week, she was introducing Silas to her sisters. In a month, she was moved into his house. In two months, they were married. It was a symbiotic relationship. Yin and Yang. He was the rock she had never been able to find to moor to and the protector she had never had. She was the softness and grace that had always eluded him and the tranquility he had finally found.

Linda was right about his strength. Silas was a survivor, although during the several years immediately before he met her, he sometimes wondered what he had been surviving *for*. A quiet and generally kind man, his senses had been honed to a keen and primal edge by a lifetime of harsh reality and stark brutality.

She was his proof that life could be filled with love and warmth. The walls he built between himself and the rest of the world melted whenever she was around. He felt emotions that he had not known since his mother died when he was eight years old.

They had taken his mother to the hospital shaking and crying uncontrollably. A few days later, she succumbed to rabies contracted while skinning a fox that his father caught in his trap line. She was twenty-six years old, still too young to have become hardened by the mountain lifestyle. Silas remembered her singing him to sleep. Her daddy had been a bluegrass fiddler so she knew all of the old traditional songs. The hymns she knew from church choir. Her voice was sweet and softly southern. Even now, certain southern accents made him feel oddly peaceful, like he was back at the home place.

Whatever Linda wanted, Silas wanted her to have. What Linda wanted most was children. Silas had some doubts as to his own parental aptitude but he knew without reservation that she would make a superb mother. Children loved her and it was mutual. They would seek her out on the street, in restaurants, in crowds. Wherever people gathered, they seemed to magically appear, looking up at her with outstretched arms. She would take them by their little hands and talk kid things with them until their parents politely explained that they had to go.

Hours passed. Silas read every magazine in the waiting area. He retraced every day of his life since meeting Linda.

Motion in the room caused Silas to look up from his daydream. Dr. Elliot Hamstead, Linda's gynecologist, had just opened the door from the operating suite. He had an odd air about him. His eyes moved rapidly about the room but did not make contact with Silas. Even if the doctor's eyes had been *closed*, Silas would have recognized the emotion.

Almost before he left infancy his parents had noted that Silas was just a tad feral. They discussed this with his mother's parents, the child's granpaw and mamaw, who diagnosed that he was born with a little bit of the wolf in him, probably from his father's side of the family. Curious but quiet, he was nearly always aware of the adults before they were aware of him. They had never seen a child so comfortable in the dark, even alone. And they swore he could smell fear.

Why was the doctor so uncomfortable? Had they found something that they did not want to tell him about? Would she be forever sterile? Was it a tumor? Silas began to feel weak and cold.

Elliot Hamstead was not without reason for concern. Silas, though not generally violent by nature, presented an intimidating countenance. He was a large man with a full beard. A long braid hung down his wide back. He sported numerous visible tattoos and a small gold earring in his left ear. Foundryman, ex-USMC, ex-dynamite handler, ex-con (a very short stay for a post war indiscretion that left a biker with a permanent limp from a badly-mended knee), the potential realities very nearly matched the imagined dangers.

Admittedly never an easygoing man, Silas had been trained by Uncle Sam's military to be a Warrior. He had not needed much coaching, but the lessons served him well and helped him stay alive through twenty-four months in the Mekong Delta. He internalized them deep into his brain and bowels, well beyond the reach of contemporary military or civilian extraction therapies. Unlike most folk, he knew how it felt to take a human life without mechanized assistance. Fortunately, he also recognized he could never again use that knowledge. Just having it, made him vaguely uncomfortable. He knew guys in 'Nam that spoke of the power they felt from carrying the knowledge. For him it was a constant reminder of the fragility of an individual life and how easily such a precious thing can disappear into nothing. He was aware that his experiences made him different from most people.

Maybe it showed.

Elliot had come back through the operating suite after calling the hospital attorney from the anesthesia office. The two of them had prepared and rehearsed what was to be said to Silas. Beyond that carefully rehearsed statement, there was to be no discussion of what had transpired in the operating room that morning.

"Mr. McGraw," he began, hoping to get the words out before all the blood ran out of his face.

"I have some very bad news." Silas now too felt flushed, but only for a moment, as fear and puzzlement began to inexplicably turn to anger.

"There was a terrible accident in the operating room this morning. The machine that breathes for the patient while they are under anesthesia malfunctioned."

Suddenly there was a reason and focus for the anger. The *patient* was Linda. Beautiful, gentle, guileless, innocent. trusting Linda. His Linda. His wife.

"We tried by every means at our disposal but we were unable to save your wife's life."

Silas was reeling inside but forced a cold composure. He knew his anger was *supposed* to be muted by the portrayal of heroic efforts by Linda's medical care team in response to the tragic and arbitrary

30

attack on her by the faceless, blood-thirsty, and evil machine.

Silas did not buy it. His right arm rose from the arm of the chair as if of its own initiative. Slowly and deliberately, it planted a large callused hand on the collar of Dr. Hamstead's shirt. Silas drew him close and looked squarely into his eyes. The Doctor cast a quick apprehensive glance around the waiting area. They were alone. He was very afraid.

Silas spoke slowly and softly, with the calmly threatening resolve of an already dangerous man with nothing left to lose.

"I want to know *exactly* what happened. Don't spare me any of the details. Tell me now."

He loosened his grip enough to let the Doctor settle into the chair next to him. Between the fear and his own need to talk himself through a personally and professionally tragic and disturbing event, Elliot knew immediately that he was going to spill his guts. "Fucking lawyers," he thought to himself.

Linda's surgery was to be as routine and simple as they come. The surgical team was well trained and experienced. Dr. Hamstead had done what seemed like a thousand exploratory laparoscopies in his medical career. Simple...anesthetize, inflate the abdomen, blind trocar stab, insert the scope, visualize the various structures, remove the instruments, a couple of stitches, patient to recovery. If anything tripped up the doctors and nurses that morning, it was the lack of something special to demand their attention.

The anesthesiologist began the process of preparing Linda for surgery by sedating and then chemically paralyzing ("relaxing," they like to say) her with a powerful drug related to the compound South American native hunters once used on their blow-darts. Since this relaxation effects even the muscles that help the lungs inflate and deflate, it prevents a patient from breathing on their own. The patient must be hooked-up to a ventilator, a machine that pumps air into and out of their lungs. Before Linda could be hooked up to the breathing machine, she had to be *intubated*. He explained that the intubation process consisted basically of placing a plastic tube down her throat and into her windpipe, then sealing it into place by inflating the plastic collar encircling the tube. The procedure was carried out uneventfully.

Unfortunately, Linda was the first OR patient on Monday morning.

Doctors and nurses are not immune to the condition that afflicts some working folks on Monday mornings and Friday afternoons. Many people maintain that they do not want a car built on Monday, Friday, or right before or after a big holiday. Those same people would probably not want surgery then either.

The anesthesiologist was a young man named Jim. The nurses all agreed that he was quite handsome and smart. He had graduated near the top of his medical school class and had completed his residency at a highly respected teaching hospital. By the time he finished his post-graduate training, he had already been offered a position in the most prosperous anesthesiology group practice in the city.

The Saturday before Linda's surgery, he had closed the deal on a new Porsche®. The model with the "whale tail" rear spoiler. He saw it as his "I have arrived" proclamation to the world.

Saturday also found Billy Tinchell, Respiratory Therapy Assistant, working late hours to clean and prepare various pieces of respiratory therapy equipment, including ventilators, for use during the busy week ahead. Billy had worked in his job for many years. The pay was meager but the benefits were good. Health insurance was absolutely critical to a man with a chronically ill wife and five kids. He was a dedicated and dependable guy, although he had little formal education.

Billy was not intimately familiar with the new ventilators, but they did not differ markedly from other brands he had been servicing for years. He stripped the machines down, removed all the hoses, cleaned everything in disinfectant, and reassembled them for use. The finished machines were inspected by his supervisor, and tagged for return to service.

Come Monday morning, Jim was in the operating room with Linda McGraw supine and unconscious on the table before him. He was animatedly describing the attributes of his new car to Susan, the new circulating nurse, who was apparently interested. Susan was fresh out of nursing school, twenty-two years old, blonde, size five, and even in scrub clothes, very, very attractive.

"It is a flat, opposed high-compression air-cooled six, and it will do zero to sixty in five seconds," he noted. She nodded approval, not appreciating a single substantive thing he said, but clearly getting his message.

No one in the room gave any thought to, or was even aware of, the fact that under the ventilator there was an air routing valve with multiple ports. Plastic hoses emanated from each port. Back at the ventilator company the engineers had recently determined that if the hoses were attached to the wrong inlets/outlets of this valve "harm to a patient is a possibility." They would soon redesign the valve with ports and tubing of varying sizes so that the machine could not be accidentally misassembled. A product recall notice would be issued and the new valve provided free of charge to all hospitals with that model of ventilator.

This would, however, come too late for Linda McGraw. As she lay on the operating table, deep in the sound dreamless sleep of a surgical patient, the ventilator cycled its bellows over and over again. Each stroke drove a fresh breath of air deep into her lungs. Jim, per his anesthesiologist training, had listened briefly with his stethoscope when she was first placed on the ventilator. He heard the requisite "breath sounds." Typically, these would be a sign that the intubation had been done properly, that air was going into the trachea and not the esophagus, and that the patient was ready for their procedure. What Jim missed on his quick check was that those sounds were really only the whoosh of air going *into* Linda's lungs. He could not have heard air being exhaled because the routing of the ventilator hoses did not allow her breaths to be vented to the outside air.

As she lay calmly on the table, Linda's lungs swelled and burst. Air filled her chest and abdomen. It infiltrated her chest wall, bloodstream and muscles. When Dr. Hamstead touched her abdomen to make his initial incision, the skin crackled audibly.

"What the Hell...?" was all he could manage to express upon discovering it.

Air had already worked its way under her skin. Subcutaneous emphysema. All of her vital signs crashed immediately. He looked up at the anesthesiologist with panic in his eyes.

"I need help here now!" he pleaded. Everyone else in the room only mirrored his anguish.

A nurse rushed out of the room to find additional help. She returned with Don Gravis, a trauma surgeon who was just leaving another operating room. Within minutes, Linda's chest had been split open and Dr. Gravis held her motionless heart in his hands in a valiant attempt to massage life back into her young body. Remarkably, probably because she was young and strong, he was temporarily successful. Her heart struggled for life for several hours. Long enough for the medical team to put her through multiple other therapeutic indignities. In a short while, however, the insult proved too great to withstand.

Death's empty tranquility eclipsed the unshakable serenity that characterized her life.

When Dr. Hamstead had finished relating the story, Silas McGraw placed his hand on the Doctor's shoulder.

"Thank you, Doc," He whispered calmly.

They both hung their heads. Tears filled their eyes and ran down their cheeks.

CHAPTER THREE

"No greater grief than to remember days
Of joy when misery is at hand." · Dante Alighieri

"Man is born unto trouble, as the sparks fly upward."
Job v. 7.

Silas McGraw had a very bad day. The county Medical Examiner had taken his wife's body because it was an "unnatural death of a young healthy person," and would not let him see it until an autopsy was performed. This morning he said goodbye to his life's love for what was to be less than an hour. He had not seen her since. In the meantime, she was violated in almost every conceivable way. Yet none of the perpetrators had committed any act which society would consider even remotely criminal. This did not mean, to Silas's way of thinking, that no one was going to pay for these events. It was just a matter of determining how to exact the revenge.

The empty apartment echoed with memories of Linda. He could hear her voice with every gust of wind off the lake. The king size bed remained unmade from this morning's hasty departure. It would remain unbearably big and empty for a long time to come. Silas wished they had taken more time before leaving, and that he had told her how much he loved her.

Grabbing his leather jacket, he headed out into the blustery night. The wind tugged at his sleeves and poured down his neck. Not a night for a long walk. He made it about four blocks to Tiny's, a hole-in-the-wall tavern on Madison Street.

Tiny's was a ruggedly comfortable, somewhat dingy, little establishment. The place smelled of spilled beer, mildew and other mustiness, probably old sweat. Its most prominent feature was a long, dark Formica bar chipped in a million places by a generation of careless, drunk, or unruly patrons. There was one row of barstools, most with portions of the stuffing missing from their upholstered tops. Six booths. Six tables, all with enough pocketknife carvings on their tops to be someday archeologically significant. And a nearly-level pool table covered in mostly-intact green felt.

The proprietor, Tiny, was six foot five, two hundred and eighty-five pounds. His presence discouraged alcohol-induced antisocial acts in general and acts which might damage his property in particular. His clientele were a colorful potpourri of local alcoholics, drifters, unemployed and employed mill workers, and bikers. Lots of bikers. Tiny nearly always wore a black Harley Davidson® t-shirt or leather cap to assure his patrons that this was a biker-friendly establishment. Tonight all of the dozen-odd people in the bar belonged to the local chapter of a motorcycle club of particularly ignoble, some might say nasty, reputation. Each was a "patch holder." They wore the colors of the club, large sweeping embroidered patches with the club name and chapter, on dirty, tattered denim vests pulled over their black leather jackets.

Silas noticed the colors and the 1%er patches, references to a statement made years ago by a representative of the Harley Davidson Motor Company® that only one percent of motorcyclists were the stereotypical bad bikers of popular folklore. Silas did not give the display a second thought. He had grown up around motorcycles and motorcyclists. As a boy it was the sound of his father's knucklehead Harley filtering through the trees and up the hollow that brought him out of the woods, or in from the fields, at the end of each workday.

His father had been a blaster in the mines, a man who could light a too-short dynamite fuse with his burning cigarette and calmly walk away calling "fire in the hole" while all Hell broke loose behind him. He rode a Harley back when that sound was as rare in those hills as the growl of a wildcat is there today.

Silas himself rode a thirty-year-old pan-head that he bought used when he came back from Vietnam, just before he followed his father into the mines. It had been rebuilt and repainted many times, but he would not consider ever parting with it. He had held and massaged every piece of that bike over and over again until it became part of him and he part of it. He knew every specification, every torque setting, by heart. His scooter was a cast iron constant in an otherwise chaotic and transient life. Like him, it felt no need to be pretty. Strong was good enough. Like any machine of its vintage, it got temperamental occasionally, but he knew it would never abandon him.

The bar was warm and smoky. Except for the bright light over the pool table, it was dusky at best. For some reason this felt calming to Silas. The day's brilliantly harsh reality had shredded his nerves. There were only four people sitting at the bar. Silas pulled up a stool and made himself as comfortable as his circumstances would allow. He ordered a beer. Then another one. Each cold draft helped dull the pain just a little bit.

A woman at the bar asked for a light. He pulled a plastic lighter from his pocket and held the flame to her cigarette. Her name was Dee. Her "old man" was the club sergeant-at-arms.

"You riding tonight stranger?" she asked. It was a foolish question. There were no bikes outside, it was forty degrees, and the wind was hustling random pieces of paper trash past the window.

"Not tonight ma'am," he replied. "I'm on foot."

"So you live around here," She observed.

"Couple of blocks."

"Shitty neighborhood," she volunteered, casually blowing out a lungful of smoke. It hung in a billowing cloud over the bar.

"It's like anywhere else. The people who live here make it what it is." He took a long slow drink from his glass. Silas was not in the mood for small talk. He was wearing his depression like club colors.

"You got a problem big guy?" Dee asked.

It might have sounded a little flippant, even confrontational, but she meant it compassionately. A very perceptive and streetwise woman, Dee prided herself on her ability to read people. This guy had pain and torment written all over him like a bad tattoo.

Silas looked at her. Her face seemed kind. He pulled his wallet out of his back pocket by its chrome chain. Opening it up, he pulled out a weathered color snapshot of Linda. He slid it across the bar to Dee.

"Her name is Linda, she is, or was, my wife. She died today."

Dee looked at the photograph. She could see the joy and innocence in Linda's eyes, even in a time-worn picture.

"She was so young, and very beautiful."

Silas nodded in agreement, his eyes filling with tears. He fought them back and starred across the bar at the bizarre accumulation of junk Tiny had collected over the years. It all graced the mantle beneath a sign that proclaimed "We don't serve women here, you have to bring your own."

The only criteria for inclusion in the bar décor was that the item caught Tiny's eye or tweaked his imagination. A jackalope stared at a large stuffed rattlesnake next to a loaded "inoperable replica" of a 9mm automatic weapon. There were Elvis busts, and plastic molded breasts, four (count 'em) lava lamps, Harley parts, pins, shot glasses, and posters from Sturgis, Laconia, Laughlin, and Daytona Beach, a collection of shiny and not-so-shiny panties, and photographs of all sizes, some suitable for public display and some not.

Dee walked around to behind Silas and placed a comforting arm across his broad shoulders. She pressed against him and whispered. "Life is full of pain, Big Guy. You should try to let yourself cry. You don't have to do it here, but definitely tonight. Don't waste your energy trying to put off the inevitable. It will only be unbearable for a little while. Then the pain will slowly begin to pass. The scars will begin to fade. God has a reason for everything. Don't keep it locked up inside because it is your proof that you are still alive, living, breathing, feeling. In the long run it will make you stronger. Maybe someday you will put that strength to good use. But always keep her memory. That too defines you. Even now she can help keep you from becoming a wild animal."

Dee moved over and sat down on the stool next to him. They talked for a long while. Eventually he became aware that the beers had worked their way through to his bladder. He placed a hand gently on her thigh. It was meant only as a gesture of warmth. Silas surprised himself at how deeply he appreciated the comfort she had taken the time to offer a total stranger. He rose from his seat and turned toward the restroom.

The restrooms were in the far corner of the bar, back behind the pool table. He waited briefly out of courtesy as a smallish, balding club member carefully lined up a shot. After the guy took his shot and missed, he stood up straight to block Silas's way to the men's room.

"Excuse me, Friend" Silas offered as he attempted to step around. "I don't think so," the little guy challenged, puffing himself up but still a head shorter than Silas.

"Shit," thought Silas, "it's always the little ones who pull this kind of crap." He was in no mood to play.

Silas just moved him aside with a slow sweep of his right arm and started toward the can. He felt the sharp sting of the cue stick as it broke across his back. The physical pain was muted by his mental preoccupation and alcohol. The adrenaline burst generated by the attack, however, unlocked a Pandora's box of repressed rage.

He turned to see the guy coming at him with the butt-half of the cue held high. Silas grabbed the arm holding the stick and gave it a twist. His attacker spun around in a futile attempt to avoid the inevitable pain of having his shoulder wrenched out of its socket, only to have Silas plant one large boot in the middle of his back and rocket him across the barroom. He fell into a front table, which he shoved into the bar's plate glass front window. Shards of glass rained down on the sidewalk. Luckily, there were no pedestrians outside to be injured.

Suddenly, the biggest guy in the place appeared in front of Silas. He was a hulking three hundred plus pound monolith. A living sphinx with a huge hairy face.

"Oh shit, *Big Dude*," Silas thought, and winced visibly.

The Sphinx grabbed Silas around the chest in a bear hug, lifting his feet off of the ground and pinning his arms. Sliding his arms upward and free, Silas leaned forward against the weight of his attacker. He reached behind and got a firm grasp on the Sphinx's ears and snapped his head up hard. The back of his skull crushed the big man's nose. Blood gushed as he crumpled to the floor. Then the real action began.

The bar became a swirling flurry of fists, feet, and furniture. Silas would later vaguely remember driving someone into a wall with his head. What made it stand out was the clear sound of ribs breaking and air rushing out of the guy's chest. At one point, he was on the ground with someone kicking him. He grabbed the foot, gave it a twist, then gator-rolled. Someone screamed in pain. That same move had spiral fractured a man's femur in another fight years ago. In the background, Silas could hear a female voice cursing someone or everyone.

Soon everything was quiet. Silas looked up from the floor to see at least four police, guns drawn, looking down at him. There was blood in his eyes and the adrenaline had largely burned off, leaving him weak and exhausted. He just groaned and laid there.

He was loaded into an ambulance. The EMT was young and exuded inexperience, but looked nice in her navy blue jumpsuit. They were alone in the back of the vehicle, which rocked softly. There was no siren. Her voice was comforting as she offered him water. He declined, but was comfortable enough to fall asleep within minutes. After a short nap, he awoke in the emergency room to see the bald guy and the sphinx on stretchers ahead of him. Nurses were taking his blood pressure and asking questions like "did you lose consciousness?"

"Only on my terms," he responded.

He was tired and depressed, not really physically damaged. He had been lucky. His injuries were limited to a few bruises, cuts around his eyes and forehead, and a killer headache. He went back to sleep. Strapped to a stainless steel cart, he received an odd half-conscious tour of the hospital. He would occasionally awaken to find that he was in x-ray, or to see a doctor stitching his facial wounds.

They wheeled him to a large room and pulled a curtain around him. Finally, sleep came undisturbed. There were pain meds involved.

When he awoke this time there was a large cop sitting next to him. "Who the hell are you?" Silas asked, not in the mood for social niceties.

"I'm your babysitter, buddy," came the reply.

Groggy from sleep and narcotics, the place looked unfamiliar to Silas. He was once again vaguely aware of a throbbing pain in his head and another in his back near his left kidney.

"Where am I?"

"Emergency Department, Saint Helen's"

"Did you see the bus that hit me?"

"The way I hear it you're the one who should have a greyhound tattooed on his side"

Silas just winced. The light was way too bright. The night before was coming back to him as he became reoriented. "How are the other guys?"

"Lucky for you, no one got killed. I hear that there were a couple of concussions and some broken ribs."

"I was just defending myself."

"I don't want to hear anything until you've been Mirandized."

"You arresting me?"

"Probably, I just don't want to start the process if everyone else involved is going to go deaf, blind, and ignorant on us." The cop looked down at Silas. "Why don't you go back to sleep for a while?"

Silas did just that. No need to ask twice.

The next time Silas woke up the cop was gone and Dee was sitting in his chair, smoking a cigarette. Sun was streaming through the window.

"Good morning" he offered.

"Good morning, Honey. How are you feeling?"

"Not too bad considering. How's everyone else? What happened to The Law?"

"The rest of them are ok, except for the ass-chewing that I gave Critter for picking a fight with you last night. He thought he was protecting my honor or something. I think he was just compensating for the size of his dick. He's got two broken ribs and a sprained back to remind him to stay cool next time.

Let's see, there's also two other guys with broken ribs, and one with a dislocated hip, and my old man, Smiley, has a broken nose and a mild concussion. They told him to avoid any more blows to the head for a while. He told them that he would make an effort to get blown elsewhere instead." She smiled tolerantly.

Silas just covered his eyes with his arm to block out the rude sunlight.

"Come on, you're going home with us. The doctors told me that you were ready to go." She moved his arm and motioned toward the door with her head. "I told them that I was your sister."

Throwing the spent cigarette on the floor, she stood up and leaned over to help him up from the stretcher.

Silas gave her a sideways glance. "I got my own home."

"You can't walk there from here Cowboy, and you got no good reason to go there anyway."

Silas looked quizzical.

"Remember, you spilled your guts to me last night."

She continued. "The cops finally left in frustration half an hour

41

ago." A slow wink. "No one saw anything."

"We told Tiny that we would fix the place back up and replace anything that got damaged. Smiley sent two bro's over there already to replace the glass. Tiny declared you the winner of the bout by a decision and says that he's got a trophy for you next time you come around."

She smiled again. It was a broad, easy, knowing smile. The smile a mother gives a scared child resisting the first day at a strange new school. "Now, come on, let's get out of here."

The rest of the crew was waiting for Silas at the ER door. At first he wondered if he wasn't being set up to finish the previous evening's fight, but Smiley, the sphinx, put a big paw on his shoulder and said, "We're really sorry man, Dee told us all about your old lady and all." His nose was packed with gauze and his voice soft and almost comical.

We've been talking this out among ourselves and with Tiny. He says you've been coming in for several years and that you ride a Pan. He says that as far as he can tell, you are solid. You are welcome to ride with us."

Silas had never been the club type, but he knew the significance of the offer. It was the greatest gift they could offer him. Still, in his experience, clubs had too many rules and social obligations. And then there were the initiations. They varied from stupid to criminal. "No initiation?" he asked.

"Well, we thought about that," Smiley responded, "but we couldn't come up with anything tougher than what you've already been through." He shrugged his shoulders and added, "Besides, we didn't want to risk pissing you off again."

So Silas became a one-percenter. He accepted the other members of the group as his brothers and sisters. They helped fill a hole that Linda's loss had left in his life. When the club members turned out en mass for Linda's funeral her sisters were at first apprehensive about all the tattoos and leather, but were soon won over by the respect that they showed for Linda's husband, her family, and her memory.

The events at Tiny's that night were never mentioned again, except for one day at the mill when the foreman asked Silas if he had been in a car crash. He said that the Human Resources officer had told him about an ER bill for exam, suturing, x-rays, and observation for injuries consistent with a motor vehicle accident.

"I'm ok, thanks for asking," was the extent of Silas's reply.

CHAPTER FOUR

"Put not your trust in princes." Proverbs xxvi. 5.

"Bury me on my face, Because in a little while everything will
be turned upside down." Diogenes

Ian decided that after the events of the morning he should probably go home for lunch. The traffic on the freeway was light. In
less than twenty-five minutes the guard was waving him through
the front gate to the condo complex.
Cynthia's Jaguar sat in its usual spot in the parking garage. Either
she was at home or had left with someone else. The answer came
when Ian entered the deserted condo. He checked the refrigerator,
but chose to ignore the two-day-old paper bucket of fried chicken
in favor of a can of soup. He poured it into a cup, nuked it, and
drank it down.
He stood before the living room window peering into the wind-
driven sheets of rain. The condo was paid for, so were both cars.
No kids. His conscience would be clear.
Grabbing a suitcase and a large duffel bag from the hall closet Ian
selected his favorite four suits. He carefully folded the suits and
placed them in the suitcase along with his dress shoes, neckties,
belts, etc. His professional kit. Important papers went into the
briefcase. Everything else went into the duffel bag. He lugged them
to the elevator and hit the down button. As he began loading them
into the Toyota®, he had a minor epiphany.
Back upstairs, he found the keys to the Jag.
"I paid for a Jaguar®, I'm driving a Jaguar," he thought as he
turned out of the complex. A quick stop at the bank for a large
cash withdrawal (How much is in there? Give it to me.) and he
would be gone.
The highway beckoned. Forget the scenic route, this was no
Sunday pleasure cruise. This had to be a major road trip, perhaps a
trip of no return. It occurred to him that if he went beyond the
boundaries of his home state he would no longer be licensed to
practice law. Big Damn Deal. Once Blackburn figured out that he
had just bailed out with no notice, he could forget about getting a

45

glowing reference from the firm.

Clients who called for him would be given the evasive "he's not with this firm anymore, can I direct your call to Mr. Blackburn?" No, this would be a road trip to *somewhere*. Somewhere real. Somewhere different. Maybe somewhere worthy of building a whole new life around.

As Ian headed for the interstate, he thought about his mother. It seemed odd, even to him. He had not seen his mother in twenty years. But then again, he had not seen his father in ten, and he lived only twenty minutes away.

His father was a real estate developer and an end-stage workaholic. Even in Ian's childhood, his dad's life had become so one dimensional that there was nothing to talk about with him. There were none of the father-son moments that color a young boys life. No little league. No fishing. No trips to the park. Instead, there was a constantly expounded and vigilantly enforced work ethic.

His father's first words upon arriving home from work were "what have you *accomplished* today?" Catching a fish or hitting a home run did not count as an accomplishment. You had better have cleaned-up, or mowed, or painted, or hauled something.

Ian's mom, not surprisingly, had met his father where he spent most of his time. In his office. She had started out as his girl Friday then acquired various managerial and executive titles as his infatuation with her grew over the years. When she became pregnant, he dutifully married her and allowed her to quit the office to become a full time mother to Ian. He never quite respected her after that. She had become unproductive. On the other hand, it freed him to devote himself to the business without being distracted by the demands of raising a son.

Ian suspected that the obsessive career focus that brought him to today's events grew out of the example set by his father.

His mother eventually left, but not until Ian was out of the house. He came home from college for Christmas his freshman year to find his father sitting alone in the house smoking a cigar. There was not a sign or artifact to suggest that his mother had ever been there. When he asked what had become of her his father simply said that she had gone home to the hills. He had suggested that it was for the best and that she had never been happy with city life.

Once a hillbilly, always a hillbilly.

His father could be extremely condescending.

Ian went back to school from Christmas break early that year. He realized that he was just in the old man's way. Besides, he did not feel like doing petty chores around the house.

While he was unsure exactly where his mother was from, he had a basic idea. Maybe there was something special about that countryside. Maybe there was no time like the present to find out.

The Jag found the interstate and he pointed it south. He smiled at the thought that the Hillbilly Highway was a two way street. The heavy gravitational pull of the Appalachian Mountains was a constant, even where it might take a generation to kick in. He need not have been surprised. They are very ancient mountains, and very patient.

Ian had gotten a late start, even though he had forgone the drafting of resignation letters and goodbye notes to save time in his getaway. In a few days, when his head cleared, he would stop by a public library and write and fax those letters to whoever was in need of them. By then Blackburn would have pulled the rest of his hair out and Cynthia would probably have met with her divorce attorney. It was well after sunset by the time Ian crossed the broad, darkly reflective waters of the Ohio River.

He stopped for dinner at a greasy little restaurant in a dingy river bottom town. Even in his casual clothes, he felt overdressed. The tall blond waitress was captivatingly ditzy. She poured half a cup of coffee in his lap then gave him unintelligible directions to the local Wal Mart®. He over-tipped her anyway.

Three pairs of pre-faded blue jeans, two sweatshirts, a canvas coat, and some real lace-up work boots later, Ian was back on his way. There were lots of miles left in him.

The night was quickly fading into a steady stream of headlights and taillights. Ian turned the radio up until the distortion from the speakers became offensive to his ears. He switched from rock and roll to country, and back, looking for anything with a rousing beat. It was drizzling steadily. The rain seemed to absorb the light from his headlights, leaving little to illuminate the road. Patches of thick fog appeared at irregular intervals and without warning. Visibility was poor and steadily deteriorating. At least the police were not bothering to run speed traps. No one in their right mind would speed on a night like this. Ian was flying low, twenty to thirty miles per hour over the legal limit at all times.

Several hours later, he came upon a small city straddling the interstate. A river glistened in the reflected lights of downtown. Steep dark hills rose to frame the town. By the paucity of lights, Ian surmised there were not many buildings on the mountainsides. He imagined that they were deep green in summer, though surely still in shades of gray and brown this early in the spring.

Finally, the weight of the fatigue inflicted by the day's events was bearing down on him. Realizing that he was probably already on his second or third wind, he found a motel room and unpacked. Sleep, however, eluded him. It was well after midnight when he gave up, got out of bed, threw on a pair of his new blue jeans, and headed once again into the night. He walked several blocks before his urban paranoia began to kick in. Should he be walking alone after midnight in this neighborhood? The streets were deserted. He noticed a neon sign announcing "Debbie D's Cabaret" and under it, in neon script, "a gentlemen's club." Ian chuckled to himself. A titty bar. Cynthia had never allowed him to pursue such plebian entertainment. It was *so* consistent with midlife crisis, how could he pass it up?

The club was surprisingly busy for 2 AM on a weekday. The tables were all taken.

He took a seat at the central elevated stage runway next to a gracefully weathered gentleman who looked to be in his late fifties or early sixties. A woman clad only in the most inconsequential of g-strings stepped up in front of the old guy and began a slow, suggestive bump-and-grind. When it was over he placed a twenty dollar bill in her garter and she kissed his forehead and moved on. He noticed Ian watching so Ian felt the need to speak.

"That seems like a pretty generous tip," he observed.

"Yes, a dollar is more typical around here," the gentleman noted. "That particular young lady is supporting two young boys all by herself. And doing the best job she can of it." He raised an eyebrow slightly and whispered. "Their father used to beat her pretty badly but she never told *anyone*. She disappeared with the kids the night the house burned down. She'll do alright. She's a survivor. One of many around here."

"So you've known her for a long time?"

"I've known lots of people around here for a long time," he ventured, extending a large, weathered hand. "People call me Father."

Ian shook his hand. It was warm and strong. Strangely calming.

"Ian Gauley. Glad to meet you. So you're from around here?"

"Not too far from here. You might say it's a local call," he smiled.

"What brings you to this crossroads?"

"I had a very tough day today and I've been doing some driving and examining my options. Things seem a bit disjointed lately so I am just thinking about direction and hoping for perhaps a little divine intervention." Ian said it with a tinge of sarcasm in his voice, but the old man discounted the intonation.

"Not much likelihood of that. Each of us is just a speck of dust thrown into the wind. He can provide the wind, but each piece of dust will go where it will go. No intelligent design brought you to this bar, none will direct you when you leave."

"Thought maybe I'd head south and look for someplace where I could find some peace and quiet for a while."

The old guy swirled the ice in his empty glass. "Peace you will have to find within yourself, quiet I might be able to help you with."

Ian was all ears. "So you know the country around here?"

"I've spent a lot of time in the hills east of here. I might be able to make some suggestions"

So, the old man proceeded to give Ian directions. Ian wanted something to write them down but soon realized they were not the kind you could really follow with any accuracy anyway. They were very broad and ambiguous. The gentleman could not seem to remember route numbers or specific distances, only time and natural landmarks.

"Follow the river upstream for a couple of hours or until you feel like taking a less traveled road. Watch the hills. As they become taller and steeper, and the valleys more narrow, look for a small town. Stop if you want. Talk to the local people. You will find them to be very open, friendly, and helpful. They will direct you to what you are seeking." He went on for a few more minutes. Ian's bourbon and water became only ice and air. He lost track of what

49

the man was saying.

Ian found the old guy oddly fascinating. He was not your Average Joe. His physical presence seemed incongruent with his apparent age. Maybe the long flowing mane of stark white hair just made him appear older than he was. He was lean and, even in baggy work clothes, obviously well muscled. He projected a reassuring demeanor but did not use objective facts to that end, as people tend to do. Instead, he seemed to dwell in abstraction, although undeniably insightful abstraction.

The dancer came back around. She stood on the bar top in front of Ian, placed her hands behind her head, and did her grinding dance. He reached into his wallet and tucked a twenty in her garter. Pleasantly surprised, she stroked his cheek. "Thank you, Honey." The words flowed from her lips with a drawl as sugary and southern as night blooming jasmine. It startled him a little. He had not been driving long enough to have entered Dixie. He assumed she was not originally from around there either.

Ian set out early the next morning. The road tracked the broad river bottom upstream from the city. He was only a couple of hours out of town when he reached a fork in the road at a small town on the banks of the broad placid river. A more worn and narrow ribbon of blacktop turned left off the main road and ran past a few houses, a couple of small store-fronts and a gas station. He stopped at a little two-pump station for gas and a candy bar. A biker was filling his motorcycle at the other pump.

"What is the name of this town?" he asked.

"Laurel Ford," came the reply. "There used to be a place here where folks could drive wagons across the river in dry weather." They talked for a few minutes. Ian filled in a few of the blanks in the directions he had gotten from Father the night before. They shook hands and the biker introduced himself as Lucky. He directed Ian away from the more heavily traveled road and toward the far end of the tiny village. There the road turned to follow the steep, forested confines of the valley of a tributary river.

Ian paid for his gas and headed out of town. He forgot about the candy bar. A sign at a bridge crossing labeled this stream the Big Laurel Fork.

The stream flowed deep, bank full and fast. The trees were not yet drinking their share of the April rains, leaving the river to run in full springtime glory. Thousands of cubic feet of cold, clear grey-green mountain runoff poured past every second. Ian was slightly in awe of the nearly silent display of natural power. The little highway played tag with the stream for over twenty miles without the flow diminishing noticeably in size. Sections of new pavement marked where past high water had ripped away huge chunks of the road. Piles of boulders had been strategically placed by the Highway Department to prevent it from happening again. Ian imagined that failure to negotiate one of the many turns could easily result in a fatal plunge into the icy torrent. He gripped the wheel with both hands.

Eventually another town appeared. He could see that it was *not* a major bastion of modern civilization. With maybe a hundred yards of downtown, it still had all the necessary basic amenities including a grocery, gas station, sporting goods store and bait shop, feed and hardware store, small car lot, and most importantly, a coffee shop. Just in time, Ian's stomach had realized that there had been no breakfast today and was beginning to grumble. Suddenly very conscious of the Jaguar, he parked it at the far end of the lot and walked inside.

He slid quietly into a corner booth in an effort to go as unnoticed as possible. The very chipper waitress called from behind a small white Formica counter.

"Coffee?"

He nodded affirmatively.

She bounced over to his booth, altogether too perky for a woman probably in her mid-thirties, and proclaimed as she poured his coffee, "Nice Car."

Looking down at the menu, he managed a strained, "Thank you." He had no idea why, but never had the trappings of success made him so uncomfortable. After he ordered, he sat there trying to be inconspicuous and observe the goings-on in the restaurant, but felt as though he had been dipped in blaze orange paint.

The waitress didn't help him blend in. Maybe they didn't get many strangers here. Or maybe she just liked his car. Or perhaps she thought he could (would?) whisk her away from here. Whatever the reason, she seemed to take a liking to him. At one point, she was

51

sitting across from him in the booth pouring fresh coffee into his cup every time he took a drink.

Her name was Lori. Lori Thomas. She was not a local girl. Her story was much like Ian's in many ways, most of which he would not learn at this first meeting, if ever. She asked a lot of questions. Where was he from? How did he like the Jaguar? They talked about the road, the weather, the food.

The small talk, always a roadside diner staple, eventually came more easily for him. As they conversed, he mentioned that he was looking for some land and a place to live.

"You mean, like a hunting camp?" she asked. "That's what most city people come here looking for. Or vacation property." It was obvious to Ian that he was not going to pass for local.

"No, I'm looking for something more permanent. Something year-round," he assured her.

"Actually, it doesn't matter which you're looking for," she said with a bob of her head. "There's only one realtor in town, Charlie Jacob. You can't miss his office. Its fifty paces past your car. He's also the used car dealer, notary, and tax return preparer."

Outside after breakfast, Ian stood next to his car and looked up and down the main street. He could see most of the town from there. At the far end of town, against the base of the mountain, was a quarry and what looked to be a cement plant. Up the river he could see a sawmill, with hundreds of huge hardwood logs piled between it and the river, and another large sooty metal building which he would later learn was a factory that produced charcoal briquettes from sawmill scraps.

He shrugged and thought, "Wherever there is man there is industry. It is not always pretty, or even healthy, but it is our nature. Like the bees and beavers, our economic activity defines our species." Here industry seemed on a very tangible, personal scale. A man needn't be a number. Ian realized he probably couldn't be anonymous here even if he wanted to be.

Soon he found himself standing in Charlie Jacob's office. It was a twenty-year-old office trailer with scarred white plywood paneling and a naked one hundred watt light bulb sticking out of the middle of the ceiling. There was no shortage of light.

Charlie was a *character*, part Glenn Turner (of Dare To Be Great pyramid scheme fame) and part televangelist (can you say "be healed?"). A born again businessman by his own admission, his balding pate seemed to gleam with a certain entrepreneurial light. It was probably the glare from the bare light bulb.

Charlie, of course, had just the parcel Ian wanted. Looking at the Jag for longer than was necessary to draw the conclusion, he noted that it would never be able to negotiate the old dirt road to this wonderful piece of property. He insisted that they take his SUV. Charlie, bless his little capitalist heart, wasn't lying or mistaken. A rutted tank trap of a road split from the narrow one lane blacktop about a mile out of town. It wandered along a heavily forested and boulder studded mountainside for about five miles then forked. The left branch continued on out the ridge. "Where does that go?" asked Ian.

"It only goes about half a mile further, to another little farm, up the river valley," explained Charlie.

The right fork of the road dropped precipitously from the hillside into a broad grassy bottom. On the far end of the bottom land meadow the river flowed unseen, deep in its rocky channel. Ian swore he could faintly hear the sound of water coursing over boulders. A small tin-roofed frame farmhouse, ramshackle barn, and burned-out chicken coop guarded the meadow.

"The guy who lived here found that it was just too isolated for him. He listed it with me then left town. He went back to Washington DC."

Charlie continued, "There are a couple little parcels like this in the upper end of the Big Laurel. They are all too small to be self-sustaining commercial farmlands, but can provide a nice lifestyle if you have other means of support. If you look real hard through those trees," he said, pointing up the valley to a stand of bare poplars, "you can see another small white farmhouse. That is your nearest neighbor. Your property line runs along that fence about halfway between his house and yours."

Ian stood in awe and listened to the soft rain hitting the tin porch roof. He mutely stared at the tall hillsides surrounding the farm. In an ancient walnut tree on the far side of the drive, a large red tail hawk sat motionless on a high but relatively sheltered limb. Its feathers were fluffed for warmth and its head pulled down tightly, but its gaze seemed intent. Ian's own gaze returned several times to that same spot but the hawk never moved. Ian felt like the bird was watching him.

Charlie knew he had Ian right where he wanted him. He had sold this same farm twice in the past. Each time to a shell-shocked urban refugee. Each owner fixed the house up a little more, fenced a little more of the bottom, made the road a little more passable, and generally increased the chances that the next owner might stay longer. On the way back to town, they talked money. Charlie had already looked up the book value of Ian's Jag.

"The owner would probably even take your car as part of the purchase price," he suggested. Ian was well aware that the Jag would never get down that road to the farm. Charlie continued. "And I have just the vehicle for you."

By the end of the day Ian was sitting in the farmhouse, in an old wicker chair left by the previous owner, unwrapping a sleeping bag that he had picked up at the sporting goods and bait shop. A well-used F-250 Ford pickup sat parked in the yard outside.

Charlie had thoroughly exercised his dealmaker persona to get Ian into that truck. He proclaimed that real country living required a *truck*. Even an SUV would not cut it. He explained that, while a prior owner had rigged the house with electric baseboard heat, it was really only for emergencies. The real heat was provided by a long black cast iron log-burning woodstove in the living room. If you heat with wood, you need a truck. And his nephew who worked part time down at the hardware store could get Ian a good chainsaw. At a very reasonable price, of course.

Ian had called the power company from Charlie's office. He would consider staying warm tonight an emergency and go looking for the woodpile, if the prior owner had left him one, tomorrow. Outside in the darkness the cold drizzle, his companion for two days, quietly turned to snow.

CHAPTER FIVE

"Healing is a matter of time, but it is sometimes also a matter

of opportunity." Hippocrates

"Observe the opportunity." Ecclesiasticus iv. 20.

Silas McGraw tried very hard to lead a normal life after his wife's death. He never missed a day of work, even during the dog days of summer when the heat in the foundry would sweat half a dozen pounds from his frame in a shift. Those had been the days that he and Linda would steal away to the lakeshore. It was easier to work than to reminisce. Almost every free moment was spent with the brothers of the club. They talked, drank, got a little high, worked on their bikes, and

rode. He would never be able to express the visceral feeling of joy evoked by blasting down the open road on a big old American bike, engulfed in the unmuffled roar of a v-twin motor as colors, scents, light, sounds, and a relentless cleansing torrent of air flooded over him. He lived for it.

Silas hoped those feelings would heal his scars. Their power overwhelmed and strangled even the dark images of Linda's last day. The wind had always helped him with memories like those. Memories from Southeast Asia. Even memories of friends and acquaintances maimed or killed by lapses of judgment, careless cage drivers, or just bad luck while chasing those same windborne feelings. Undeniably, at some subconscious level, death rode as a silent companion every time he fired up his bike. The airbrushed laughing skull on the bike's gas tank was a reminder. Life, however, rode shotgun at a much more vivid and palpable level. Silas knew letting death or even fear of death guide his existence was to be half-dead already.

The times he spent in the saddle were the only times he seemed to be able to outrun the pain of losing Linda. Even then, she would creep into his head. Cruising at seventy on a country road, he would suddenly realize that he could feel her arms around his chest and her breasts pressed against his back. He could hear her voice in the wind taunting him to go faster. When the bike would squirm

55

ever so slightly in a tight turn, he swore that he could feel her shifting her weight just enough to mess with his composure, reminding him that she was there behind him.

And so he rode. Silas went with his club brothers to the big rallies at Daytona, Laconia, Sturgis, and dozens of smaller ones. They roared together through the pine forests of the Black Hills and across the South Dakota Badlands. They raced bar-to-bar over the beachside blacktop of Daytona, where they held a contest to see who could amass the most warning citations from the local police without getting a real ticket.

The winner scored eight warnings then got a real ticket that cost him over five hundred dollars. As his prize, the club took up a collection to pay his fine. At Laconia, they rode serpentine highland roads in cold rain for five days. No one acknowledged any discomfort. They were busy having too much fun.

There were other, more serious, rides. There was the annual Ride To The Wall in Washington D.C. to honor those who fought in Vietnam, and those who never came back. Silas joined the other middle-aged men in black leather standing frozen before a mute wall of polished black granite, weeping silently for their brothers and comrades who they would never see again. He was able to find the names of several who had gone with him into that jungle. Summer brought memorial rides to raise money for medical bills or funeral expenses of fallen brothers and sisters. There were also rides to fund worthy causes like legal defense of those snared by the authorities.

Silas's favorite road trip was the club's annual Labor Day pilgrimage to a small Ohio town for a big motorcycle rodeo. Bikers from all over the country gathered at an old county fairgrounds to compete in motorcycle rodeo events like the trike pull, the slow race and the barrel race. This meeting was the high point of a rodeo circuit that took the faithful from coast to coast over the course of the summer. However, only a handful of those in attendance were actually there to compete, most just came to party.

The memory of the first time that Silas went to the rodeo was still etched in his mind. He was rolling south with the band of brethren on a clear summer afternoon. The old pan head was running sweet and strong, loaded down with clothes, camping gear, food, wine, contraband, and anything else Silas felt would be helpful for a three-day stay in the Biker Kingdom. A hot, dry wind blew across the farmlands. It helped the sun etch the miles into their faces. Smiley led the way on his black FL shovelhead. Dee sat behind him, her long hair streaming. The bike carried no gear because they had sent it ahead with Critter and Doc. They had taken Critter's pickup truck and left two days earlier. Critter had wanted to get there early to nail down a prime campsite. The truck pulled two bikes on a trailer so that, once they set up camp, they could run the country roads or just go into town and hit the local bars for a few days before the crowds got there.

Behind Smiley and Dee rode the "Lata" sisters, Jane and Charlie. Several years back, at the club meeting when they were up for admission to the group, Smiley had moved for their admission with an attempt at a stirring speech on life and lifestyles.

He told the assembled bikers, "Today I want to introduce to you two sisters who already share much of the experience that defines us. They have chosen a lifestyle just a little out of the mainstream. Like the rest of us. They may make some of the citizenry out there a little nervous. Just like us. Some people may worry about what they do when no one else is around. Just like us. Regardless of some people's attitudes, they are proud of who they are and why they are different. Just like us. How can we not embrace them and their differences as they have embraced ours?"

A voice came from the dusky corner of the room. It belonged to Doc, who was as tenured and respected as anyone in the club. "Christ Smiley, get on with it. We all know they're lesbians and that's alright."

The room erupted in laughter. Of course, everyone knew. They were welcomed to the club by unanimous vote that night but the "lesbians, and that's alright" stuck. The sisters rode semi-matching rigid-frame, evo-motored customs. They were both red, with ape-hanger handlebars and ostrich hide seats.

Tiny had shut down the bar for "renovation," and was motoring along with the group. His girth dwarfed even his old Super Glide. He looked like a dancing bear on a bicycle.

The pack also included Red Ed, whose newish girlfriend, Surely, "I'm not just calling you Shirley" Shirley, insisted on referring to him as Mr. Ed. She smiled suggestively when asked why. Stragglers included Big John, Fetus and half a dozen other unnamed co-conspirators.

The last leg of the trip got fuzzy from regular stops at roadside watering holes, but a five-mile full throttle blast down a four-lane highway then a sudden exit onto a two lane country road, shocked everyone back into focus. A short distance down the road they passed a massive grey prison ringed in razor wire. Hundreds of inmates crowded the high wire mesh fences, hands held high in closed fist salutes. No doubt, many were downed brothers captured for various infractions which, while minor in their impact on society, had been enough of an insult to the Powers That Be to justify their removal from polite society for a portion of their time here on earth.

A second prison, or another section of the original one, appeared on the other side of the road. Crowds of inmates also pressed against its wire to salute the free riders outside. Dee and Shirley lifted their tops and flashed their breasts at the cheering prisoners. Silas could easily hear their response over the roar of the bikes. The group was soon engulfed in the serenity of sun-baked corn-fields, then the fairgrounds appeared. Clouds of dust drifted from behind the distant grandstand. The far-off roar of v-twin motors filtered through the summer air. Silas could hear it even over the sounds of his own bike. His heart rate picked up just a little.

The fairgrounds stood large above the expanse of corn and hayfields. Behind it, a stand of tall trees flanked a broad slow-moving muddy river. Silas thought to himself that this was an interesting place for a motorcycle rally. They were miles from the nearest citizenry that might be offended by noise, dust, alcohol, public nudity, foul language, poor personal hygiene, political incorrectness, or just plain ugliness.

At the main gate stood a uniformed policeman. He looked uncomfortable and out of place. Next to him was a sign that said "No Firearms, No Attitudes, No Dogs." Dee leaned over and asked Silas why he thought the cop was there. She said that she had never seen one at this rodeo before.

Silas responded. "Probably just to keep respectable people out." The cop overheard him, smiled a broad smile, and slowly shook his head in the affirmative. He waived them into the fairgrounds. Actually, it seemed like a pretty good idea. Take a large, socially unacceptable group and set aside an area for them to play in, far from everyone else. A fairgrounds perhaps, in the middle of open farmland, between a river and a big prison. A place where they could scream and rev and race to their hearts' content. And make smoke and noise and love in public, if they so choose, without bothering anyone but their own kind. New arrivals could feed the party and an occasional ambulance could remove the ones who had too much fun or could not adequately meter their poisons.

To hear Critter describe it, this rodeo was a biker paradise. Silas suspected that putting tens of thousands of motorcyclists, many of whom were assholes to begin with, in such an unstructured environment, might just as easily be a little taste of Hell.

The group rode outside the area set aside for rodeo games, to the back of the grandstand area where fair vendors would normally set up. This was the designated camping area, commonly referred to by rodeo regulars as "The Jungle."

Critter and Doc had taken a roll of yellow plastic tape emblazoned with the repeating phrase "crime scene-do not cross," and cordoned off about a quarter of an acre for the club campsite. The battered F-150 pickup sat in the middle of the site. A yellow plastic tarp lined the bed of the truck. Many lengths of green vinyl garden hose snaked out of camp and across the road toward the public restrooms. Critter and Doc sat naked in eighteen inches of water in the back of the truck, drinking beer under the warm late afternoon sun.

"What took you guys so long?" Critter chided. "We saved you the best camp in the place. This road here is just up-wind of Burnout Alley. We picked some good neighbors," he pointed across the narrow asphalt strip that wound through the campground. "They're building a two story scaffold with flood lights and claim to have a killer PA system. They've got twenty strippers from Columbus who will be dancing there over the next three nights." He waived his beer and stood up.

"Jesus, Critter," screamed Jane, thrusting out her hand as if to ward off an evil spirit. "Put some damn clothes on. I just ate." Critter mooned her and jumped down to get his jeans out of the truck.

New arrivals began the serious business of setting up camp. Silas was traveling self-contained, so he untied his duffle and began to spread his stuff out on the ground. He purposefully chose the spot the furthest from the road to minimize interruptions to his sleep. At three-thirty the next morning a drunken partier would lose control of his bike while doing a burnout and run over Doc's foot as he slept in his tent, a full ten feet from the road. Doc, who had been a medic in Vietnam, ran the sucker down on two broken toes. He then administered a therapeutic beating to the dumb SOB, which the recipient was probably too anesthetized by alcohol to truly appreciate. Doc then hobbled back to camp to set and wrap his toes.

Doc spent the next day in the pickup truck wading pool. He soaked his purple foot in the cool water to keep the swelling down. He did not attempt to ride his motorcycle for the rest of the weekend.

By nightfall the tents were all pitched. A keg of beer sat in a washtub full of ice, and a dozen lawn chairs were lined up next to the road, so the group could relax and enjoy the night's festivities. Already the camping area roared with the sound of unmufflered Harleys doing smoky burnouts and reckless wheelies. The smoke of spinning tires mingled with the sooty haze of dozens of campfires. An oily fog cast an otherworldly pall over the area. This cloud was penetrated by intense and wildly pulsing beams of light cast by bobbing and weaving motorcycle headlights. Piles of hot coals from early evening bonfires glowed eerily among the campsites.

Critter had painted a sign that said, in letters six inches tall, "SHOW US YOUR TITS." He stretched the banner from the truck to the dining canopy. Silas was amazed by how many apparently sober women, upon seeing the banner, complied with its directive. He reclined in a folding lawn chair, closing his eyes often to give them a break from the dust and smoke. On at least one occasion, he opened them to see a woman in front of him with her t-shirt hiked up. He was mildly startled, but remembered the sign behind him, and gave her a big "thumbs-up."

Sometime well after dark strippers appeared on-stage across the road from camp. A large crowd gathered to cheer them on and occasionally stuff dollar bills wherever they would stick. The dancer who caught Silas's attention was a muscular blond who danced with a ten-foot-long live golden python draped over her nude body. The snake was as big around as her arms, maybe bigger. It must have weighed forty or fifty pounds, yet she still danced gracefully, suggestively. He could still see her even when he closed his eyes. Hey biker boy…want an apple?

An unending river of motorcycles flowed past camp. They were mostly Harleys, but there were some old British bikes and even a rice burner or two. Silas was fascinated by the spectacle. It was part motorcycle show, part strip show, part street riot. An even seedier Mardi Gras, it had noise, alcohol, brute force, lust, and a little danger. It burned the eyes, nose, and eventually, the brain.

Suddenly a strange contraption, probably the motor and frame skeleton of an old pickup truck, rolled past. Three long-bearded bikers lounged on the remains of its bench seat. Sprayed in glowing lime-green paint, it pulled a pink hay wagon. On the wagon was a long cylindrical steel propane canister, also painted bright pink. It was garnished with two inflated pink beach balls to emphasize the obvious phallic allusion.

Astride the propane tank were three nude women waiving their cowboy hats in the air. Critter noticed the rig and howled in appreciation. Silas made the observation that one man's obscenity is another man's art. It was about what you would expect at the Fat Tuesday parade if they ever let Critter build a float.

One of the women blew Silas a kiss.

Somewhere in the darkness a loudspeaker blared Axel Rose screaming the Guns N Roses sone, "The Jungle."

"Welcome to the jungle, it gets worse here everyday. Ya learn to live like an animal in the jungle where we play."

Someone behind him passed Silas a joint. He took a long deep hit and passed it back. He let the smoke escape slowly from his lips into the dirty night air, then took a deep drink of his rapidly warming beer, and settled back into the chair. Sleep overtook him just as he began thinking about Linda.

Silas awoke to the subdued light of pre-dawn. Big John, another of his bro's, was walking toward him wearing nothing but a pair of soaking wet white cotton boxer shorts and black boots. He was rolling a motorcycle wheel with a limp tire flopping around on it. They were covered in thick brown road dust that had turned to mud wherever water mixed with it. In the grey vestigial light, he looked like a Viking warrior returning from battle. John's description of his night was consistent with his physical appearance. "Baddog and I went into town shortly after dark to drink at the clubhouse of a local bike club. It always opens its doors to out-of-towners on rodeo weekend. When we got there, it was packed solid. We drank a bunch of beers with some guys from Detroit, then followed them to a pizza joint about midnight. We were there until the place closed and the Detroit crew left. Baddog, sleaze-ball charmer that he is, talked two of the waitresses into going for a motorcycle ride. We all ended up in the hot tub at their house. While I was soaking with the ladies in the hot tub, Baddog decided to hide my shirt and jeans. Then, in true drunk asshole style, he claimed that he forgot where he hid them. At that point, the motorcycles got involved. We both fired up and chased each other around the yard a few times. Baddog had gotten about half-dressed while we were arguing, but I had nothing on but my wet shorts and boots.

Then Asshole decides to run like a scalded dog. We blew through town at speeds three times the legal limit until I finally caught him out past the prison. In the course of trying to kick his sorry ass at high speed, I managed to run into Baddog's rear brake lever with the front tire of my bike. The pedal bent, but Baddog was able to bend it back. My tire, naturally, was shredded. It was all I could do to wrestle the bike down into the ditch without crashing. Asshole checked to see that I was alright, and headed back into town.

I left the bike leaning up against a tree, unbolted the front wheel, and walked back across the fields and into the fairgrounds."

John rolled the ruptured wheel slowly ahead of him. Later in the morning he would be able to get a new tire from one of the many parts vendors at the rodeo. Baddog was MIA for the rest of the day. Everyone assumed that he was back in the hot tub, which John could not find again, trying to bob for waitresses.

It was not long after John's return that Critter fired up his bike and barrel raced between the tents in the campsite. The roar of his drag pipes brought most of the club members in residence to the doors of their tents barking obscenities. The Lata sisters in particular took turns threatening him with physical violence and violation. Amazing considering the early hour, people began to dress and come outside. They set about preparing a large communal breakfast. Dee assumed the role of executive chef and everyone pitched in, even Critter, once he figured that it was safe to get off his bike. Jane put a big pot of coffee on the fire and three camp stoves were called into action. Soon there was food everywhere. Pancakes, French toast, breakfast steaks, bacon, sausage, eggs, even Dutchoven biscuits. More than a dozen people, some still drunk from the night before, ringed the campfire to take on fuel and caffeine for the day ahead.

While the others were still cleaning up after breakfast, Jane noticed Critter slipping off toward his tent. She allowed him enough time to drift off to a peaceful sleep, then backed her bike through the door of the tent and lit it up.

The big pipes roared. A huge pulse of exhaust, ripe with the products of combustion, billowed the sides of the tent.

Shirley yelled, "Goddammit Jane, just teach him a lesson in manners, don't f'n *kill* him!"

As Jane's bike pulled forward out of the tent, Critter appeared at the entrance. He looked a little dazed, but then again he always looked a little dazed in the morning. He crawled like a reptile on his belly until his head was outside of the tent in the dew soaked grass. His lungs sucked up the cool, clear air. It was thirty minutes before he moved again.

By the end of the weekend, constant partying had taken its toll. Baddog survived the trip to town, but got his left hand bloodied and bandaged from a rough spill taken Saturday night while doing burnouts in the campground. He got traction unexpectedly and the bike wheelied out from under him. Never letting go of the handlebars, he jumped back on it, feet flailing in search of anything solid, and rode the screaming machine right down to the cold pavement. Luckily, the crowd managed to dodge the out-of-control bike and no one was injured, except Baddog.

Sunday morning Smiley had to organize a search party for Critter's motorcycle. He claimed it had been stolen while he was partying at another campsite somewhere in the bowels of the jungle. It was found leaning, unmolested, against the fence on the far side of the campground. This was the spot where, coincidentally, Critter remembered meeting a "hot almost-naked babe with a bottle of Jack Daniels®." It was assumed by the rest of the party that Critter had been having alcohol-induced hallucinations.

Silas was one of the last of the group to leave the fairgrounds. He stayed behind to help load and secure Big John's bike in the bed of Critter's pickup. Red Ed, Shirley, and Silas provided Doc, Critter, and John with an escort home. John's bike added probably six hundred and eighty pounds to the old Ford's burden. They were not sure the old truck was still capable of handling the added weight. John himself added enough load to cock the truck slightly to the passenger side.

On the way home, mile after tedious mile, Silas' head throbbed in rhythm with the highway expansion joints. He attributed it to noise, dust, and lack of sleep because he had only had ten beers and a couple shots of Jim Beam over the entire weekend. Thankfully, everyone made it back in one piece. Silas needed to go back to work so that he could unwind.

CHAPTER SIX

"One generation passeth away, and another generation cometh." Ecclesiastes v. 4.

"We're leaving Babylon
We're going to our Father's land." Bob Marley

After Linda's death, Dee had given Silas the name of a lawyer, Gregory Wesley, who had helped the family of a friend killed by a drunken cager. Mr. Wesley seemed a tad slippery for Silas's tastes. The man wore dark grey or navy pinstripe tailored Italian suits with red satin lining and an American flag lapel pin. Regardless, he went after the insurance companies of the hospital, anesthesiologist, ventilator manufacturer, and gynecologist like a rabid pit bull. For over a year, even as his attorney was preparing for trial, the insurance people and their lawyers refused to admit that anyone had done anything wrong. Silas occasionally questioned whether his perception of the events was somehow unrealistic, but he always came back to what seemed so obvious. Linda had been so innocent and what had been done to her so violent and horrible. Many times he had wondered whether he should somehow take matters into his own hands. Fortunately, he had enough common sense to know that no good could possibly come of that.
The day of the trial he sat at a table in the front of the courtroom with his lawyer. Another long table to his right was crowded with at least half a dozen lawyers representing various insurance companies. They all wore expensive looking dark blue or grey business suits. The new suit that he bought for the occasion felt foreign and uncomfortable. The lawyers argued all morning over arcane preliminary legal points. Then they battled over the selection of the jury members. By noon they had finished asking questions of prospective jurors, and striking the people they did not like. Silas was comfortable with the folks left sitting in the jury box. It was filled with plain people like him. An unemployed autoworker, a retired bus driver, two housewives married to union steelworkers, a guy from the State Road. They were people who did not know someone who could get them out of jury duty. They looked like people who knew pain and injustice when they saw it. He imagined

them familiar with the slights and indignities routinely meted out to those who could not buy themselves an option.

These were not folks who would need theatrics, which Silas could never bring himself to provide, to realize that he missed Linda, and that she had been through Hell the morning of her death. Silas wondered if the lawyers could see the same thing.

Whatever their impressions, they spent the rest of the day going about their professional business of making opening arguments to the jury. Silas sat mutely stoic through Gary's impassioned plea for justice. He knew his eyes had to be blood red because he fought the tears the entire time. Only the anger that had become a steady low grade constant in his life and psyche kept him from breaking down. He tried not to listen to the other lawyers. He knew it would only make him angrier. It was obvious, however, that the heart of the case for many of them was to blame one or more of the other defendants for the tragedy. The judge adjourned the trial at the close of the presentations, admonished the jurors not to speak with others about the case, and sent everyone home for the day.

In the morning, it looked like Mr. Wesley's case would get off to a rocky start. He was forced to call one of his most valued witnesses out of order. The witness, Ethan C. Reynolds, State Medical Examiner, had been strategically scheduled for late in his case presentation. Dr. Reynolds showed up early, explaining that he was going to Europe that evening and would not be back for nearly two weeks. Silas' attorney would be forced to put him on the stand before the stage was set for his testimony. He had performed the autopsy on Linda. His findings were critical to the case. The jury was hungry to know what had happened, but Gary Wesley had hoped to provide them with some background information first and to set the stage for the medical testimony. He wanted the Doctor's words fresh in their minds when they went to the jury room to deliberate.

The M.E. was a distinguished, if somewhat tired appearing, gentleman in his early sixties. A physician and dentist both, he had dedicated his life to the often thankless and not terribly lucrative, tax-supported practice of forensic pathology. Often his job became to find a voice on behalf of the violent crime victims whose remains were so ungraciously laid on the stainless steel tables of his morgue. His unique combination of skills had proven very useful over the years in piecing together forensic evidence for local prosecutors. Perhaps he had been too useful because his steadily increasing workload was taking a toll on his health.

Greg began his questioning with routine inquiries regarding his qualifications and experience. Dr. Reynolds soon began to show subtle signs of impatience with the questioning. He was not a man comfortable with wasting time. It had been years since he had that luxury. The lawyer sensed the witness's frustration. He realized the usual methodical exchange might not be the best approach to take with this witness. Best to cut right to the heart of the matter.

"Dr. Reynolds, I'm going to show you a document, which will be marked Plaintiff's Exhibit One. Do you recognize this document?"

"Yes, I do. It is an autopsy report"

"Did you prepare that report?"

"Yes, with the help of my clerical staff, of course."

"Could you read the report to the jury?"

A chorus of objections arose from the various lawyers at the defense counsel tables. Their basic premise was that such a report was not probative of either the damage, as Linda was clearly and obviously dead, or the liability question of how she died.

The judge asked all counsel to approach the bench. There, out of hearing range of the jury, he let them all know that as far as he could tell, this was relevant testimony and that he would not tolerate grandstanding in his courtroom. When they returned to their chairs, he made his ruling for the record.

"Overruled. Mr. Wesley, please continue."

"The whole report?" asked the Dr.

"Please. At least until I ask you to stop."

Dr. Reynolds reached into his pocket for his reading glasses.

"Case number OH-92-947. External examination. The body is that of a nude white female appearing the reported age of twenty-six years, well developed and well nourished with a body length of sixty-four inches and a weight of one hundred and twenty-one pounds. An identifying hospital toe tag is noted on the left. There is marked rigor mortis throughout and pink liver is noted posteriorly except in areas of pressure in this refrigerated body."

Silas turned away from the jury, his vision suddenly blurred. He could feel warm redness spread over his face.

"This body shows no external evidence of injury other than the therapeutic procedures as listed below. The scalp hair is of the usual female style, about fifteen inches in length and blond. The ears, external auditory canals, and nasal skeleton are without note. The face shows diffuse moderate swelling inclusive of the upper and lower eyelids, presenting a "moon face" appearance, with slight subcutaneous emphysema elicited in the left cheek area."

Dr. Reynolds's professional detachment aside, Linda had been a strikingly beautiful woman in life.

"The lips show no injury. The neck and anterior chest inclusive of the breasts also suggest slight air distention with crepitation elicited in the left pectoral region. The breasts are well developed and without masses. The upper extremities are unremarkable and show numerous intravenous lines. The pubic hair has been shaven due to therapeutic procedures. There is slight edema of the labia."

The attorney for the ventilator company jumped to his feet.

"Objection, Your Honor, this area of questioning is clearly irrelevant and prejudicial."

The judge turned toward Greg. "Mr. Wesley, we are getting off track here. Where are you going with this testimony?"

"Your Honor, the autopsy results clearly establish that something was very wrong in that operating room the morning that Linda McGraw was killed. I will try to focus on the most important portions of this report."

"Proceed."

"Dr. Reynolds, let's proceed to the portion of your report entitled Evidence of Medical Therapy."

The doctor dutifully flipped to the next page of the report.

"Please read your findings to the jury."

"A small bore catheter is inserted within the right frontoparietal scalp penetrating through a one-eighth inch burr hole in the underlying calvarium, and terminating within the white matter of the right frontoparietal region. This catheter does not enter the right lateral ventricle and shows no evidence of perforation into the ventricle. Rather, it terminates within the adjacent white matter and is surrounded by a 2.5 centimeter in diameter recent hematoma of white matter."

"Doctor, could you stop for a moment and explain to the jury what that passage meant?"

Doctor Reynolds grinned in recognition of the fact that the medical jargon probably hadn't been very helpful to the jurors.

"A small tube had been placed through a hole drilled in her skull to relieve pressure caused by brain swelling due to the intense trauma that she had sustained sometime before she died." He continued.

"An endotrachial tube is present within the mouth and terminates in the distal trachea."

He and Greg exchanged knowing glances. Turning toward the jury, he noted, "at the time of death she was breathing through a plastic tube anchored in her throat."

"A fourteen-inch anterior thoracic midline vertical sutured incision extends from the xiphoid process of the sternum to the jugular notch area. A median sternotomy has been performed and a large bore thoracotomy tube drains the anterior mediastinum underlying this incision with this tube exiting from the body in the epigastrium through a separate small incision. A sutured and stapled left thoracotomy incision involves the approximate left fifth intercostal space extending from the lateral margin of the sternum to the approximate anterior axillary line. It is approximately nine inches in length. There is underlying surgical separation of the approximate fifth intercostal musculature. The pericardial sac has been opened."

"Doctor, does all of that mean that Linda McGraw had several huge incisions down her chest? That she had been cut open like a fish?"

"Objection."

"Sustained. Counsel will please refrain from inflammatory characterizations of the evidence. Doctor, you may answer the question."

"Yes, she had several large incisions. She had received open heart massage, probably in an effort to resuscitate her after cardiac arrest."

"Let's proceed to your examination of her internal injuries. What were your findings with regard to her lungs?" The lawyer backed away from the witness stand and turned to face the jury.

"Moderate diffuse atelectasis of the left lung. Left hemothorax of 250 cc serosanguinous fluid."

"In layman's term?" Mr. Wesley was looking straight into the jury

69

box.

"Her lung was blown out, collapsed, and the space it had occupied filled with fluid."

"What about her brain?"

"It had moderate edema and marked compression of the lateral ventricles due to edema. It had swollen as a result of insult to her body immediately prior to her death. The swelling had caused it to be injured from pressing against the inside of her skull. She might have sustained brain damage.

"This would have been a serious concern if she had lived"

Greg noticed a juror starting to fall asleep. It scared the piss out of him that Dr. Reynolds's testimony might be going over the jury's head. He thought that he had better cut to the chase.

"Doctor, what was your final diagnosis?"

"My principal diagnosis was coma, subsequent to pneumothorax and cardiac arrest arising out of the administration of endotracheal general anesthesia. I made over a dozen secondary diagnoses including microscopic myocardial infarction from systemic hypoxia, cerebral edema from hypoxia, congestion of the lung, liver and kidneys, et cetera."

"And your professional opinion?"

"This young woman died as a direct effect of systemic hypoxia with complicating cardiac arrythmia due to pneumothorax, resulting from the administration of endotrachial general anesthesia for laparoscopy. This death falls within the category of therapeutic misadventure."

"What is a therapeutic misadventure?" Greg Wesley's voice was deep and calm. This was the essence of his case. He cast a focused and lingering gaze toward the jury. He needed to be sure they were listening.

Dr. Reynolds looked puzzled for a moment.

"It is when a medical procedure does not go as planned or anticipated."

"When someone screws up?" came the rhetorical question from counsel.

"Objection to the characterization of the witness's testimony." The objection was delivered by a shrill and theatrically angry voice.

Now all of the lawyers on the entire defense side of the courtroom were on their feet.

The judge cast a stern look toward Greg.

"I withdraw the question Your Honor."

The judge looked at his watch, gave a few brief words of warning to the jurors not to discuss the case or evidence among themselves or with others, and recessed the proceedings for lunch.

The Defense Team looked worried. Instead of leaving the courthouse for lunch, they huddled among themselves, then with Silas's lawyer. Two hours later it was all over. Even after Greg took forty percent, plus his expenses from the settlement for his efforts, Silas was left a working class millionaire.

Silas never wanted the money, and felt it a pathetic compensation for a beautiful life ended so young. But he knew, as inconsequential as it might be, that taking their money and perhaps blemishing a few otherwise pristine reputations was as close to avenging Linda's death as he could ever get without making himself a criminal. So he took the money and shouldered the guilt. Financial independence under these circumstances would always leave a bitter taste in his mouth.

He tried not to think about it. He kept going to work and running with his club brothers. Life goes on. He never mentioned the money to anyone. No one ever asked. Silas assumed people had their own lives to worry about. The newspapers did not run a story. Perhaps it just was not newsworthy. Maybe, he thought, this sort of thing happens every day.

The only person to comment on the settlement, except for his attorney as he separated his fee from the rest of the check, was the old long-haired maintenance guy at Greg's office.

Everyone knew him as "Dad" and he had unlimited access to every room in that building. He had obviously overheard Greg discuss the case with someone, probably his secretary.

Silas was in the firm conference room. Greg had gone to his office to get release documents. The old man laid his tool belt on the conference table and sat for a moment in the chair next to Silas. He extended a large weathered paw and gave Silas a slow but powerful handshake. His gaze was focused and penetrating. He offered congratulations in a deep solemn tone, but soon became more reflective.

71

"Lots of folks never get the justice they deserve, good or bad. Life events like what you have been through sometimes present far larger implications than you can visualize right now." The comments came now in hushed tones. "For now you may not have the immediate responsibilities and routines most people struggle with, like finding enough hours to work and pay bills and still keep a family together. Even though yours is not a freedom we would wish on anyone, it nevertheless comes with a certain responsibility born of opportunity. It comes with the obligation to use this life to accomplish something beyond what could be achieved by those with all the usual daily duties and distractions. You have a special burden to make the world a better place."

Silas was not sure how to take the old man's comments. At first he considered being angry. Was this bullshit some kind of cosmic guilt trip? But the old guy had a wisdom about him that seemed incongruous with his role in Greg's office. Silas felt strangely grateful and thanked him for the advice.

Later, he asked Greg to deposit the money in the bank for him. He did not quit his job. Silas was so used to spending his days in the foundry that he was not sure what else he could do with himself. Several years had passed since Linda's death when he got the news of his father's passing. Years of hard work and the strain of black lung had finally sapped the strength of the old mountain man. Unable to get out of bed one morning, he had called an ambulance.

They took his father to the hospital. The diagnosis was congestive heart failure and chronic obstructive pulmonary disease. Tired and worked out. The old man gave the hospital staff all the usual information on relatives and who to call in the event of an emergency. Silas was all he had of either. After his father closed his eyes and found his peace, Silas got the call from the hospital.

Shortly after Silas hung up the telephone, he heard a bike pull into the driveway. It was Smiley. He shouted up to the kitchen window where he could see Silas walking toward the back door.

"Ya wanna go for a putt?"

By now Silas was standing on the cement stoop outside the door.

"Swap meet up at Riverview. I need a few things. Thought I'd check and see if you wanted to ride along."

At that moment Silas didn't really need any bike parts that he could think of, but clearly needed a ride to clear his head. Smiley was a good guy to ride with. Their riding styles were compatible. Steady, deliberate, fast, but not crazy fast.

Silas grabbed his leather jacket and gloves. There was a damp chill in the air that very nearly matched the one in his heart. It would eventually work its way into his bones if he did not overdress a little. The old scooter fired on the first kick. They headed across town toward the open road. Riverview was about thirty miles to the northeast. Twenty of those miles were nice cruising road.

When they turned onto Highway 20, two lanes of rolling blacktop splitting miles of green fields of corn and soybeans, Smiley opened his bike up. He did this sort of thing occasionally "just to blow the carbon out of it."

Silas twisted his throttle. The machine jumped forward eagerly. The revs surged toward the red line. Vibration levitated Silas slightly above the seat. A flick of his left hand on the clutch lever, a light lift of his left foot, the rpm dropped. The vibration buzz stopped, replaced by a deep heavy throbbing. Second gear.

Silas had put a great deal of time into his motorcycle. Its motor was "warmed-over just a bit." It had been bored and stroked a bit, to 93 cubic inches. He had ported the heads a bit, polished them up, increased the compression, and put a big-lobed camshaft in the old iron monster to help it breathe.

As Silas reached for third gear, the wind pounding at his chest was beginning to try to lift him out of the saddle. The hissing shriek of the fresh air being violently sucked through the big S&S carburetor almost overpowered the machine gun note of the wide-open straight pipes. Combined with the increasing roar of the wind, Silas was enjoying an internal combustion symphony roughly mimicking the howl of an F4 tornado bearing down on a trailer park.

He was closing in on Smiley fast as he reached for fourth gear. Slowing down had been a consideration, but had been discarded in preference of a ton-plus flyby. Silas was hanging onto the thrashing mass of native steel like the crew hangs onto a brakeless freight train on a long downhill grade. Soon he was a small speck on the gray line between the farms.

Suddenly a large buck deer appeared at full run from out of the high green corn. Sure that it was the fastest creature on God's earth, it intended to cross the road ahead of that loud, predatory sounding beast out there on the blacktop. Silas forced himself to not look at the deer. To do so would have synchronized their courses toward a rendezvous that would surely be fatal to them both.

In a small fragment of a second it was over. Silas could swear that he felt that buck's breath as he passed in front of its nose. A mile down the road he stopped the bike and did a little dance by the side of the road to burn off some of the adrenaline. Smiley stopped and asked if he was alright.

"You went past me like I was chained to a post. You had enough distance on me that I couldn't tell whether you hit that deer or not. I guess when you went by it the damn thing was trying to stop so hard that it slipped and fell. It spun around and, by the time I got there, was flailing its hooves trying to get some traction, and heading back toward the corn." Smiley was laughing from the relief of not being required to scrape the intermingled remains of his friend and the buck from the highway.

They rolled on, more slowly now, toward the old Riverview flea market grounds.

As they walked around at the swap meet looking at the long tables of used motorcycle parts, Silas and Smiley talked about riding, the club, their lives, their jobs, and their women. Not necessarily in that order. Smiley sensed something seriously wrong with Silas.

"You still shook from that deer?" He knew Silas well enough to know he was more unflappable than that. Try again.

"You still bummin' 'bout your old lady, man?" he asked in his usual unpolished, but solidly compassionate, style. It had been several years, but he knew it would take several more before Silas would let her go.

"No, " Silas answered quietly. "When you rolled up, I had just hung up the phone. It was a nurse at the hospital back home calling to tell me that my father just died." Silas shook his head. "I never even knew he was sick."

Smiley winced. "Shit, I'm really sorry, man."

"Nothing for you to be sorry about. I appreciate you showing up when you did. It was a good time for a ride." Then Silas was quiet,

CHAPTER SEVEN
"I never found the companion that was so companionable

as solitude." H.D. Thoreau

"Many waters cannot quench love, neither can the floods drown
it." The Song of Solomon viii. 7.

The Appalachian Mountains rise green and cool from Maine to
Georgia. They are old and weathered, heir to natural and human
history steeped in power, passion, mystery, and treachery. Wet
mountains, they strain the water from air masses originating in the
Great Northland and carrying the moisture of the Great Lakes.
The rains make these highlands what they are; pulsing with the
natural energy of abundant life. The mountain colors are those of
water. They are the pale greens and blues reflected in the streams
and the dense vegetation that spring from the earth at the first sign
of warmth that comes with the passing of winter. They are also
the brilliant white of the deep highland snows and the pale ghostly
consuming white of the thick mountain fog.

The hollows of Appalachia often spawn dense, disorienting fogs.
Sometimes they linger for days at a time. Fog's quiet power lies in
its ability to deprive even the savvy and logical of their confidence
and senses. Many a trapper, settler, hunter and hiker has felt the
faint but undeniable twinge of fear caused by losing their bearings
in a deep mist-shrouded highland forest as smoky daylight fades
into bone chilling mountain night.

Silas stood at dawn on the weathered wooden porch of the old
home place watching fog lift from the river valley. Wet mists clung
in wispy sheets to the steep dark hills. He could swear that he felt
the presence of invisible forces, perhaps spirits.

He knew these mountains harbored spirits. The same forces that
inspired stories of vampires and werewolves in the dark Old World
Alps of Transylvania live in these hills to this day. The ridges and
hollows are very old, very still, very damp. They have a primordial
fecundity unparalleled anywhere else in the New World.

Silas could feel the hairs on the back of his neck begin to rise.

"If there are any spooks around here, they're kin." he mused. With Silas's family history, that was not terribly comforting.

The area of the Big Laurel River had been a veritable no-man's-land for a thousand years. Once early native inhabitants quit hunting and gathering to the point that agriculture became important to them, they moved to larger river valleys where the soil would better reward their efforts. From the broad bottom-lands they would send occasional hunting parties into the unaccommodating canyons and deep forest of the Big Laurel drainage. Later the watershed would serve as a largely unpopulated buffer zone between tribal groups linked to the Iroquois to the north and tribes affiliated with the Cherokee nation to the south.

The McGraw's had come to this country before the Civil War. Jeremiah McGraw was a hard working, hard drinking long-shoreman on the docks of Baltimore. Then one night he left a ten-inch knife in the chest of a Canadian sailor at a harbor-side bar. Knowing that his reputation probably negated any chance of an effective self-defense plea, Jeremiah headed west, then south into the mountains. The further he got into the highlands the safer he felt from society's need for order, stability, justice, and his hide. Many of the crusty mountaineers that he met there had histories of their own. They were now just trying to scratch out a living and be left alone. The wilderness had always been a good place for a second chance. Outsiders who tried to interfere sometimes disappeared into the forest, never to be seen again. Jeremiah fit right in. Jeremiah's descendants were often credited with keeping the lands of the Big Laurel uncharted and remote. Old maps show the entire watershed as "Wilderness" or merely as "McGraw's." The whole area remained as wild and foreboding as anything east of the Mississippi River. Even outlaws and poachers kept a low profile. It was generally accepted that it was better to be discovered by the police or game authorities than by the McGraws.

Industrial interference in the headwaters of the Big Laurel had been very limited. The land was logged, with permission of Silas's great grandfather, shortly after the turn of the 20th century. Coal companies stole the mineral rights back in the 1920's but Silas's grandfather, who worked part time in the coal company land office, stole them back.

When he was not altering records at the coal company or the courthouse, Pappaw McGraw was trapping or making whiskey along the river. No one in his right mind wanted to stumble upon his trap lines or his still, both of which he guarded very jealously. Generations grew up, and old, avoiding trespass on the lands of the upper Big Laurel.

Silas's father gladly accepted the legacy from Silas's grandfather. Silas could remember him walking out to the road to greet strange vehicles, shotgun hanging loosely from his right hand. He never had to point it at anyone that Silas could remember. Its mere presence was message enough.

After his mother's death, Silas led what probably appeared to be a very lonely childhood. Actually, he was a happy child. The woods and river provided him with all the entertainment he needed. The farm chores could have easily filled his waking hours, but his father, to his credit, appreciated the need for play in a young boy's life. He knew that a healthy love of the outdoors was his son's best defense against the distractions and temptations that life would throw at him as he matured.

Silas's seemingly inborn independence made him a natural for the isolation of mountain life. His father once told him that even as a toddler he was happiest stumbling and crawling around the yard without adult interference. As soon as he could walk, he headed for the woods, and to his mother's consternation, the river. She was sure she would find him drowned at an early age. Silas always loved the freedom and majesty of the wild.

Not that he did not fit in at school. Quite to the contrary, he had loads of friends and was a popular fixture on the baseball and football fields in his early years. Until he was old enough to get a driver's license and a sawmill job, so he could buy an old Ford® pickup, he remained relatively isolated from the small town social scene. The farm was too far out of town for most of his friends to visit very often. His father was almost always working the farm when he was not in the mines. The family seldom got into town more often than once every week or two.

Every now and then his father would grab his old Ted Williams fishing tackle and walk down to where the Big Laurel Fork tumbled out of its upstream canyon. There, in the first deep pool, they would catch bass, walleye, and an occasional trout. His father would gut them on the riverbank and take them home to fry. If they caught fish, they would eat fish. Silas's dad would not refrigerate fresh caught fish.

"If you can't eat them now, throw them back and catch them when you *can* eat them," he'd say. Occasionally he would make an exception and keep a few to hang in the smokehouse. Smoked trout was a rare and special breakfast delicacy.

His father was careful, however, never to kill more than they intended to eat. He had no problem with storing vegetables like potatoes or turnips but was more conservative even with the bacon and ham from the smokehouse.

"It ain't right to hoard food when that food is God's creatures." he'd caution.

So much had happened since those days, Silas had gotten away from the rhythm of the seasons and the moods of the sky and river. He had become embroiled in the petty disputes that people indulge in when there are no more pressing matters at hand. Matters like survival.

Standing once again on the porch of the old home place, he could feel the power of the hills and the forest. It was one of the things that had been missing in his life for many years. There were other things. He knew now that he would find them eventually.

But first he would treat himself to breakfast at the diner. The old Harley® soon traced its way into town. It had been that way before. On arrival, he threw the kickstand down, found himself a booth inside, and ordered biscuits and gravy. The seat was not yet warm when Billy Caldwell sat down on the other side of the booth.

"I heard tell that you had come back," Billy noted without even offering a handshake. Silas knew Billy since grade school, but they were hardly ever what either would consider friends.

"My father passed away a few weeks ago. I came back to look after the farm."

"Fixing it up to sell?"

Silas wondered how long it would take Billy to get around to that...he had coveted that land since he was old enough to appreciate that it was the key to development of the upper Laurel Fork valley.

"No, I think I'll just work it."

Billy frowned reflexively, then quickly changed his expression. "I thought you had a life up north? Why would you want to move back up a hollow and become a poor dirt farmer?"

"Things change, Billy. Somehow dirt farmer seems like a good job to me right now."

"I could pay good money for that crappy ground. You would have a nice start on a new life."

"And what would you do with that crappy ground if you had it?" Billy hesitated a moment. He knew how the McGraw's were about that valley.

"I'd manage it responsibly so it doesn't get ruined."

"What have you done with all the other land you own around here, Billy?"

"What do you mean by that?" Billy responded only slightly defensively.

"Well, how about that big parcel down by the river? The one your father dug the stone quarry on. You know, where you put up the cement plant. Or maybe, that piece downstream that you logged and turned into the mobile home park? What about that mountainside you bought over at Buzzard Rocks. I hear that you are starting another limestone quarry over there."

"And what's wrong with using your own land to its maximum potential?" Billy bristled.

"If you think a mountain's maximum potential is to be turned inside out for crushed gravel or that river bottom land is best used for trailer sites then I wouldn't want you *responsibly managing* my family farm. Are you really sure that land's value is in what it can do for your wallet?" Silas stared into his coffee cup then looked straight at Billy.

"You are just a stubborn hillbilly. You're worse than your old man," Billy snorted, flinching visibly at Silas's gaze. "You act like there's something wrong with me for supporting progress and this community!"

"You're a greed-head Billy." Silas said it softly. He was just stating a fact. "You think life is all about money. You always have. You and your Chamber of Commerce friends sit around at your monthly

79

meetings and reassure each other that you all have the vision of the Better World. In that world I would just bet that the whole bunch of you have more cash than anyone else."

"So what *is* life all about then?" Billy taunted. "I suppose you know? I suppose you can show me how I am so wrong?"

"How the Hell would I know?" Silas said it coolly, looking again straight into Billy's eyes. "I ain't no prophet and I ain't your fucking shrink. I surely can't help you with your problems. All I can tell you for sure is that you will never own my farm." Silas drained the last of his coffee from the cup.

"That's alright, Silas. I was offering to do you a favor. The place won't be worth a shit after the new dam dries the river up anyway." Billy rolled his eyes dismissively, gave a last smirky smile and waltzed out of the diner, shaking his head in disgust. He climbed into his dual wheeled diesel pickup truck and headed toward the cement plant. His tires threw gravel against Silas' motorcycle as he exited the lot.

Silas was puzzled by Billy's last comment and it showed on his face. The waitress, who had been eavesdropping on the entire conversation, explained it to him. She told him about the dam and water project and told him, "to pay no attention to Billy Caldwell, you are doing the right thing."

"I still sorta regret not kicking his ass thirty years ago." Silas noted, holding out his coffee cup.

Silas came back upon the land late in the summer of the year. His father had not yet made the first cut of hay. Half of his small herd of cattle had found holes in the old wire fence lines and were wandering through the surrounding woods and along the river. One by one he tracked them down and herded them back inside the fenced pastures. He cut locust posts and strung new wire, closing the broad gaps in the fence.

Turning his attention to the hayfields, he coaxed his father's antique tractor to life and began the task of cutting the season's first overdue crop of hay. Silas was amazed at how much his muscles ached every morning as he baled, hauled, and stacked the hay in the weathered grey barn. Even years in the foundry manhandling iron castings had not prepared him for this. He had forgotten the quiet unforgiving power of the midday sun. It blistered his skin and reddened his eyes after only a few hours. The memories of working the farm as a child had either dimmed with time or he had been in better shape back then. The pains marked the passage of too many years as well as, perhaps, too many beers.

Once the hay was in, Silas climbed up on the barn roof with tin and tar to be sure that the hay would stay clean and dry. After a few weeks the work began to feel right. The redness of his skin changed to tanned brown. It finally stopped peeling. His body quit aching, at least most of the time. Despite the long hiatus, the country life still appealed to him.

Silas realized that not many people could afford the privilege of struggling like this on a subsistence farm. It amused him that he, bearded, tattooed, sun baked and sweating on this hardscrabble piece of real estate, was a "gentleman" farmer. But as he settled into a routine, the loneliness began to wear on him. It was undeniable that he had always been something of a loner, and was quite comfortable with his own company, but in the city he had the club's brothers and sisters. Here he had only the farm and its ghosts.

A few days after he finished putting up the hay, he decided to try to trim up the edges of the main hayfield. It stretched from the barn down across the bottom for about a quarter of a mile to the banks of the river. The forest had started to reclaim the field. Its first soldiers, the sumac, sassafras and locust, were growing a hundred feet out into what had once been tilled land. Down by the river, paw-paw, sycamore and scrub willow were marching into the bottom from the riverbanks. It would not be long until only a chainsaw and a bulldozer could reclaim the pasture.

Silas sharpened the blade on his father's bent and dented old brush hog. Might as well give it a try. If it did not cut that stuff he would go looking for the chainsaw. He waded right into the thickest of the brush.

The machine growled and roared. Shredded sumac flew out from under the rusty steel deck along with sassafras and poison ivy. Then came a swarm of very angry yellow jackets. Silas kicked the tractor into neutral and let it coast to a stop. Once he got back on the tractor, after outrunning most of the bees, he motored along the edge of the woods toward the river.

Turning to parallel the river, Silas drew a bead on the far side of the meadow. Nevertheless, he could not resist taking a sweeping view up and down the Big Laurel. From the high vantage point of his tractor he could soak in a little of the valley's quiet green majesty and maybe spot some wildlife. It was common to see deer drinking at the water's edge, or turkeys looking for food along the tree line.

Today there was more wildlife than he had anticipated. Not far upstream of his fence, but well below him on a large streamside boulder, a young woman lay sunbathing. Nude. His glance lingered just a moment. A change in the tone of his brush hog's growl made him spin around to see why. It spit out a pair of shredded blue jeans and a few other bits of brightly colored rags.

"Oh shit" he muttered, but could not resist a smile. He continued on his way.

It was his fourth pass around the field before he was confronted by a pretty and very pissed-off young woman dressed in tattered rags and holding a pair of tennis shoes with their toes cut off. Her red hair reflected glimpses of fire in the bright sunlight. It also reflected her temperament.

"Okay asshole, I suppose you think this is funny!" was her greeting. Silas's first impulse was to meet aggression with aggression. "Price of admission," he shouted, leaning down from his seat.

"Are you saying that I am trespassing?" she challenged. A relatively petite woman, she stood tall on her toes, chest thrust out defiantly like an angry rooster.

He looked at her shredded Reeboks®. "If the shoe fits…" He stopped in mid sentence.

She looked boldly and starkly sexy, all pumped-up like that. Half his size, she was ready to go toe-to-toe with him. She would have punched him in the mouth if he was not so high out of reach. He started laughing. Aware that it was probably not the right thing to do under the circumstances, he immediately regretted the response, but it was a done deed. Silas had never been good at fighting with women. He shrugged his shoulders sheepishly.

"I'm sorry ma'am, I didn't see your clothes laying in the grass until it was too late."

"Well, you should Goddamn watch where you're going," she

insisted, still indignant.

"I got distracted," Silas offered in explanation. He looked away briefly, grinning.

"Yeah, right. By *what?*" she demanded reflexively. She too had to look away, breaking into a tight smile of her own. That answered one question. He *had* noticed her sunbathing.

Silas introduced himself. Her name was Kathleen Joseph. Her family owned the hardware store in town. She was its manager, at least when she was not feuding with her father over how to run it. She was clearly an adult, had probably seen thirty come and go, but still had the air of a cocky tomboy.

"So you're the big bad biker boy from up north? Your daddy used to talk about you all the time. Said you worked in a steel mill. And he said that you were a fighter, like all the McGraw's." She smiled and swayed a set of firm, well-sculpted hips slightly as she spoke.

"Well," Silas began, slightly embarrassed, "I suppose that could be me, but I'm a farmer now."

"No one can make a living off of this farm," she challenged him again.

"*I* will," he stated with calm conviction.

"Your daddy always let me swim here," she pointed out. She wanted to get that out onto the table.

"He's not around to say otherwise," Silas observed.

"You calling me a liar?" Her hands were back on her hips. Her chest thrust out again. Swatches of silky tanned flesh shown through her shredded sweatshirt. She still stood on her toes, stretched as tall as she could be in bare feet.

He looked down at her feet, then at what was left of her shoes. Best just to pretend he did not hear her over the sound of the tractor.

"Do you want a ride to your car?" He shouted over the now throttled-up tractor motor.

"Not really," came the reply, not entirely convincingly. She remained a bit difficult, but was warming. She tried a few tentative steps in the field stubble and chopped blackberry canes.

"Damn stickers," she thought, and it showed on her face. Silas reached down. They locked hands and he hauled her up onto the tractor's fender in one smooth motion. By the time the old tractor got to her car in the woods along the old dirt road, they had agreed to meet at the town diner that evening.

On her drive home Kathleen could not get that son-of–a-bitch out of her head. She had a weak fluttery feeling deep in her abdomen. Hopefully, it was just indigestion. She had a nagging suspicion that she was in big trouble. Later, the two of them lingered over their dinner and coffee and talked. Kathleen's best friend, Lori, who was a waitress at the diner, finally ushered them out the door so she could lockup.

From that day forward Kathleen and Silas saw each other on an almost daily basis. It was a good thing for both of them, although not the kind of relationship that Silas had with Linda. Both he and Kathleen were far too stridently independent for a traditional sort of pairing, at least not so soon.

Kathleen had always been a handful. Her parents raised two sons to adulthood. They were amazed at how much easier it was to raise her two brothers than it was to raise her. Things the boys took in stride would send her into a screaming rage or, worse yet, a three-day pout. In grade school she was the most regular female visitor to the principal's office. In high school her parents knew not to expect her home until the conclusion of after-school detention.

It wasn't that she was a bad kid. There was not a malicious bone in her body. She just would not keep her thoughts and opinions to herself. Nor did she particularly like authority. Her father could tell at the year's first parent-teacher meeting whether it would be a good year or a bad year. If the teacher was easygoing and willing to work *with* her, things would be just fine. An authoritarian or controlling teacher virtually ensured a year-long test of wills.

Her disciplinary problems kept her out of the cheerleading/prom queen circuit or she would have most certainly been a contender. The boys loved her bad girl image, but most were too intimidated by her combination of beauty and attitude to actually approach her. She was a mediocre student who invariably left her more perceptive teachers with the suspicion that she maintained an incredible vault of native intelligence. If they could only figure out how to unlock it. Their suspicions were confirmed when, in her senior year of high school, she scored the highest scores ever obtained by a student at that school on the college admission exams. Kathleen laughed when they gave her the news. She was going to whatever college was cheapest. It would almost certainly be a state school, and virtually any score would have been high enough to get her in. Her years in college were not terribly memorable, either. She made a number of personal discoveries including Black Russians, tequila, and Panama Red. While she certainly did not discover them in her college curriculum, she also perfected her technique with boys. Kathleen could make an otherwise worldly and poised college man cry, beg, or walk on his hands and knees through broken glass for a kiss, or even a lingering glance. That was certainly no surprise. By the time she graduated, she was probably the most physically stunning woman in her high school. She was petite but athletically built, with hypnotizing green eyes like an enchanted forest pool of her ancestral Irish homeland. Her red hair cascaded in long flowing curls over the creamy fair skin of her neck. In her senior year, the quarterback of the school football team offered to run naked through an automatic car wash for a date with her. He did, so she went out with him, but ended up kneeing him in the groin when he made it obvious that he expected more than a kiss for his efforts. Kathleen never *needed* a man, like some of her friends did, to feel complete. Men could be fairly annoying. She found them generally shallow, self-absorbed, whiney, and obsessed with getting into her pants.

On campus, Kathleen stood apart from the crowd, but did not go unnoticed. One day she was approached by a man who identified himself as a photographer for a well known "men's" magazine. He handed Kathleen his card and inquired as to whether she had ever considered modeling. Being an honest and straightforward woman, she said that she had, but had never pursued the idea. He, of course, suggested that appearing in his magazine would be a great way to jump-start a modeling career.

While such a proposal appealed to her rule-breaking side, Kathleen could smell exploitation from a mile away. She politely thanked the gentleman and turned to walk away. He placed a hand on her shoulder and began a sales pitch, the gist of which was that she might be able to turn this into a lot of money. Unfortunately, he grossly underestimated her distaste for being pressured and her ability to make up her own mind and stick to her decisions.

She turned back in his direction and fixed her eyes solidly on his. "At first," she began, "I was flattered by your offer. And I will admit that the money is tempting. But I come from a tiny little country town where everybody knows everybody else's business. This sort of thing could haunt me for life. It is just not worth it to me."

The photographer opened his mouth as if to begin to speak, but she cut him off. As she spoke, she became more agitated.

"Don't try to argue with me. It won't work. If you think that I want my picture out there so that my brothers' creepy friends can stare at me while they whack off, you have the wrong damn girl." She began poking him in the chest with her index finger as she spoke.

He instinctively backed away from her and fell head over heels down the marble front steps of the student union, necessitating campus police response. A picture in the student newspaper showed him sprawled across the sidewalk with Kathleen standing over him, not looking particularly remorseful, above the caption "Student comes to the aid of magazine photographer."

A generally competent student in college, Kathleen took several semesters to get around to selecting a major. She eventually let her advisor convince her to concentrate on accounting. This was based on Kathleen's stated interest in returning home and getting involved in the family business.

She did well, if not spectacularly, and finished her junior year in acceptably good stead.

When she was home that summer, she began to try to apply some of the things she had learned, to the running of the family hardware, car wash, and coin laundry businesses. Her father made the mistake of trying to herd her back to school. She, true to form, pushed back harder and refused to return to campus in the fall. She had realized she did not want to be an accountant. To her, school was a dry and pointless exercise. At some level she realized that if she got the degree there would be too much temptation to use it, to go out and get a 9 to 5 job counting other people's beans. That would be a pitiful, mind numbing waste of a perfectly good life. Besides, she would be the first to admit that she did not have the attention span for accounting. It bored the piss out of her.

So, she learned everything she could about the family businesses. Since her older brothers had gone away to school, it was just she and her father. They were two hard-headed people with very different ideas about how to run a small business. Needless to say it was not a serene and blissful coexistence.

Her brothers did exactly what she had been afraid she would do. They earned degrees, one in engineering and the other in education, and moved to cities where they could earn twice what they would ever make at home. At every visit home they would talk about how much they missed their little home town, but how they could never find appropriate jobs locally. Their nests in the city were built. They would have to live in them.

Sadly, Kathleen had written off the men she grew up with even before she left for the university. Upon her return, her social life was meager at best. She dated a few local guys, but always ended up disappointed and regretting having gone out with them. She had an undeniable taste for outlaws, but the local renegade types were basically losers. She didn't mind that she could not find Rhett Butler, but she was a little concerned that in the course of sorting through the Billy Bobs she might stumble onto Ted Bundy.

Silas, oddly enough, was almost exactly what she had in mind. His outlaw credentials were impeccable, but he was smart and fairly articulate. He seemed self supporting, though she was not sure how. Frankly, that little bit of mystery was strangely attractive. He was obviously physically strong and appeared to hold his beliefs just as strongly. More importantly, he did not seem to want anything from anyone else. Most importantly, she was beginning to trust him.

One day a few months after they met, she told him that she had been approached by both Billy Caldwell, prominent local businessman, and Cletus Hansen, deputy sheriff, within days of each other. They both purported to do her a favor by warning her that Silas McGraw was a dangerous man who would eventually show his violent side.

They also noted, "He would never amount to anything." Billy said that he had known Silas since childhood and that he had always been an unpredictable, undisciplined loner. Cletus said he was basically a criminal personality.

Silas just smiled and rolled his eyes when she told him.

"Those guys haven't changed since high school."

Later, he felt compelled to elaborate.

"I have no regrets about whatever I am or even what I have done with my life up to this point. If I have any regret it's that I haven't done more for the other folks in my life. What Billy and Cletus are trying to say is that I am a threat to them and whatever it is they stand for because I am my own man. They and their cronies can't figure out a way to get a handle on me. They would like to see me sour on keeping that old farm, sell it to Billy, and leave town," He sighed in resignation.

"Of course, they know that is less likely if I meet a woman I really care about."

Then he added, "But I am sure they will keep trying. Their lack of control over what I might do scares them, but I doubt they could even express what it is they are afraid I might do. Billy was always envious that I had peoples' respect. For all his money, he never had even the respect of his own father. I will never have the authority that Cletus has, but I wouldn't want it. It is illusory. People like Billy give him only the authority necessary to carry out their bidding. I have all the authority I need already."

At first her father was none too pleased when he heard that Kathleen had taken up with the legendary bad boy of Big Laurel Fork. Within a few months he accepted Silas, probably figuring that he might be the only man in the county that could handle his wild, green-eyed daughter. Her brothers joked that the sound of the two of them making love probably caused the cattle to cower in the farthest corner of the fields.

CHAPTER EIGHT

"There are truths which are not for all men, nor for all times."

Voltaire

"I have been a stranger in a strange land." Exodus ii. 22.

Ian was more than a little surprised to see the meadow blanketed in white when he rolled out of his sleeping bag at dawn. It worried him to see snow this far south in April. Mother Nature was just messing with him. The snow was gone by noon. There would be no more for over six months.

Ian spent the morning making lists of things he needed. He was still the compulsive but methodical, anal-retentive lawyer. One list was for the grocery store. Another was for the hardware store. A third was for the sporting goods store. Perhaps he should have a gun and some ammunition. The remoteness of his farm was starting to make an impression on him, but he resisted the urge to do the full emergency-generator-and-bottled-water thing. After all, he still had the truck. If it got real bad he could leave. The generator could wait at least until fall.

Sometime around noon he realized that he was hungry and had no food in the house. Time to head into town. He got in and out of the little town market fairly quickly, but the hardware store was another matter. The very attractive saleswoman who was helping him find tools and other stuff had a million questions. He was new around there, wasn't he? Where was he from? Why'd he decide to come here, of all places? He'd bought the old Handley place, hadn't he? That was the first Ian heard it called that.

She did, however, save him a trip to the sporting goods shop by selling him a stainless steel .38 caliber revolver with a six-inch barrel. She swore up and down that it was a good "snake gun." "And if you need any help learning how to shoot that," she offered, "Silas McGraw, my boyfriend, has the next farm up from yours. He's real good with a gun."

Ian was not completely comforted by the offer, but thanked her and headed for the door and the coffee shop down the street. Easing into the same corner booth that he had taken the day before, Ian heard the same cheerful call.

"Coffee?"

He nodded yes and looked up to see Lori already halfway across the floor.

"I knew you would." She was almost beaming. "Charlie said you bought the old Handley farm yesterday and Eddie from the bait and tackle said you got a sleeping bag. A night in that old farmhouse without heat, I figured you'd need a good breakfast."

"I had heat. I called the power company." Ian held out the coffee cup that had been on the table. He made a conscious effort not to roll his eyes. Welcome to small town living. "I'm surprised you didn't know that. I made that call from Charlie's office." He said it with a smile, more amused than annoyed.

For a moment Lori was unsure how to read him, but then discounted any misgivings. She turned in his order and plopped down in the booth. "So what are you doing for Easter? Do you have family near here?" She held the coffee pot at ready.

"No, I don't have any family around here. At least I don't think so."

"What do you mean you don't *think* so?" she asked. "You should know the answer to a question like that."

"Well," Ian began, "my mother, who I haven't seen in years, lives on Little Elk Creek. I have no idea where that is but I don't think that it is too far."

"Its about sixty miles," came the instantaneous reply, "but it's not the best road in the world. Probably take you a couple of hours to drive it." She felt fairly authoritative for a relative newcomer to the area. She only knew of that particular hollow because last autumn she had helped the restaurant owner take a turkey dinner to an elderly couple there, as a Thanksgiving surprise.

"Can you tell me how to get there?" Ian inquired.

She thought for a moment. Shaking her head, she began to speak slowly.

"No, but I could probably show you the way." It was merely a factual statement, not intended as an attempt to invite herself along on a road trip. At least not until the words left her mouth. Once she had verbalized them, the idea sounded pretty good to her.

Ian looked slightly quizzical. Nice offer, but he did not really know

90

her. It could be a long, strange day if she turned out to be a nutcase.

Lori caught the hesitation but forged ahead.

"The owner's daughter is home from college. She'll work Good Friday and Saturday if I work Easter Sunday. I'd be glad to try to find it with you."

"What about your family?" Ian asked.

"None within driving distance," came the reply.

He nodded. "Ok, tomorrow we look for Little Elk Creek." He smiled, still a little unsure that he would not regret the proposal. That settled that. It looked like Ian might meet his mother tomorrow. His throat tightened just a little.

He picked up Lori at the coffee shop not long after dawn the next morning. When he offered breakfast, she suggested another restaurant thirty miles down the road.

"I spend too much time here already," she observed.

They set off down the *other* road out of town, the one Ian had never taken. It wound its way up the side of Middle Mountain, often without the benefit of guardrails or even reasonably wide shoulders. The views were fantastic. On a few of the more exposed turns, Ian felt like an eagle banking on a thermal and gliding up the face of the mountain. Squealing tires reminded him that the big truck was not an eagle, or even a Jaguar®, and should not be expected to corner like one.

Lori could not resist asking about the Jag. Ian responded, distracted by yet another switchback in the road.

"Couldn't get it down the old dirt road into the farm. It was really my wife's car anyway." Even as the words crossed his lips he felt the urge to cringe. A lengthy explanation would, unavoidably, be forthcoming.

Naturally, Lori could not sit there passively and let the wife reference sail by. Passivity would be in dereliction of her responsibilities to the Sisterhood. A simple response seemed adequate.

"*Wife?*" was all she said. That was good enough. It was a very succinct demand for explanation.

So Ian started into the story of his unusual workweek. He wondered to himself even as he was doing so, why he was telling this to a waitress whose relationship to him consisted of bringing him breakfast twice. What the hell. Guys have told deeper, darker things to bartenders, although that could typically be blamed, at least in part, on alcohol.

She cut to the chase, "So you're still married." She was obviously disappointed.

"Yes, but I left her. I just got a post office box. Yesterday I sent letters to her, to my friends, and to my business associates telling them what I have done. I should hear from her attorney within days."

"Do you think you'll reconcile?"

"Not a chance. For the last ten years I was only married because it was the path of least resistance. It was comfortable and allowed me to devote myself to my job. She was absorbed by her social and charitable activities. We had long since lost everything else that makes two people a couple. It really wasn't much of a marriage. But it's not just the marriage, I'm not going back to that entire life."

"But you are a *lawyer*," she observed. "You will never be able to maintain the kind of lifestyle you would have working in a big city law firm, around here."

Ian shrugged, never taking his gaze from the road or his hands from the wheel.

"That lifestyle, whatever it is, has no appeal to me anymore. As far as being a lawyer, I can be a lawyer anywhere. Monday I will call the state bar to get an application for admission. Lord knows that little town could use a lawyer. And I never wanted a high profile lifestyle in the first place. I want a garden. I want to learn to fish. I've been to enough cocktail parties to last a lifetime."

"You will starve to death. People around here will have you taking chickens in payment," she smiled. If he would actually accept chickens as payment, she would be all the more impressed with him.

A brief lull gave him the opportunity to turn the tables.

"Ok, that's my story. What about you?"

"Me?"

"Yes, you. Are you from around here? Have you always been a waitress?" He was really just trying to get the focus off of himself.

"Well, no, I'm not from around here," she began. "My family is from Philadelphia. I've only been a waitress since early last fall."

"What did you do before?" Ian insisted, though he was only making conversation.

"I was the Chief Operating Officer of a chain of restaurants in Philly."

Interesting. Ian was stung by how badly he had underestimated her. He felt a little embarrassed by his own presumptuous arrogance, but did not show it.

"How'd you get into that line of work?" He tried to sound matter-of-fact, like he was just making conversation, so as not to show his sudden interest.

"I was wrapping up a business degree at the University of Pennsylvania and working as a cocktail waitress. One of my regulars ran this chain of steakhouses. Over the course of about six months, he found out that I wanted to go into business and offered me a job in his organization. Within half a dozen years I was running the day-to-day operations of all ten restaurants from Allentown down to Dover, Delaware."

"So what happened? It's a long way from there to here." Ian prompted.

Lori squirmed a little. "Well, the gentleman who owned the restaurants got weird over time. At first, he was all business. His judgments seemed to make good business sense or at least seemed consistent with what I had been taught in business school. I learned a lot from him in the early years. He was an elderly man even when we first met. As he got older, the restaurants became more and more of a sort of crazy hobby-obsession. Every day, no matter how early I got to work, he'd be in his office chain smoking cigarettes, and pouring over financial reports. The problem was that he had no other life or family to distract him or help make him less one-dimensional. If an employee took time off, even for legitimate health or family reasons, he'd complain that they were stealing from the business.

"At some point, I don't know what precipitated it, he became cruelly manipulative and began playing his people off against one another. For example, if he was going to give a raise to one person, he made sure that anyone who that person even vaguely competed with, was aware of the raise. Perhaps he thought that would motivate people. What it did was destroy any real chance for meaningful teamwork. All the managers within the organization hated each other. The environment within the business got weird, almost sick.

"Maybe he was having difficulty dealing with getting old. A lot of his actions could have been to show others that he was still a force to be reckoned with. Every business lull was responded to with cold savagery. We terminated people who had been loyal employees for twenty–five years without advance notice or severance. He closed one restaurant ostensibly because it had a marginal return. I think the real reason was that its staff was very loyal to its manager and the manager didn't pay him appropriate deference.

"On top of all the rest, he had a son who was very covetous of my position. He spread the rumor in the industry that I was his father's girlfriend. Frankly the old man and son had both hit on me over the years. I dodged them, and rather diplomatically, I think. They were both control freaks and I had seen that coming for a long time. Eventually, however, I realized I would never be appropriately respected in the business. Staying too long would probably lose me whatever respect I had within the rest of the industry, at least in the Philadelphia area.

"The final straw came when he asked me to lay off about half the staff of one of the restaurants that had been lagging in sales. His logic was that they were getting too independent and complacent. Halving the staff would force the remaining people to work harder and would give them less time to interact, or in his eyes, conspire, with each other. It would also send a message to the other restaurants that he was still the boss.

"I laid in bed that night thinking of all the lessons from business school about building high-performing organizations. My whole concept of teamwork was in shambles. My real life experience was at odds with what I had been taught was right. I had become a key actor in an egocentric organization based on medieval management techniques whose primary purpose was to stroke the boss's ego. It wasn't just at odds with my college training. I knew in my heart that what was happening to our employees was just wrong. I quit in the morning. A few days later I came down here."

Ian was still wondering how he had underestimated her, at least her professional accomplishments, so badly. He liked to think that he was more perceptive than that.

"How did you choose this area?" he asked.

"My father used to bring me down here on long weekends. He was a devoted fly fisherman. He drowned fly fishing for arctic char in the Brooks Range of Alaska three years ago. This place reminds me a lot of him." She looked down at her folded hands and smiled sadly. For a moment, Ian quit thinking about himself.

"These mountains seem like a good place to heal," Ian observed. As they drove he thought about his professional achievements. Had his years of effort, the Saturdays and holidays, made the world a better place to live? Probably not, although very likely, a little more stable and orderly. Was that a good thing? His efforts resulted in a strengthening of the stranglehold of those already in control. Maybe he would try to be an agent of real change in his next twenty years of practice. If his clients had to pay with chickens, maybe he should take chickens.

The road traced down the other side of the mountain to a tiny crossroads hamlet where Lori and he got some breakfast. He looked at her differently now, a fact that continued to give him a small but nagging twinge of guilt. He liked what he saw. She was classically attractive, with high cheekbones and a distinguished chin. Her dark, straight hair framed her face softly. Her large deep brown eyes hinted of intellectual depth and, just maybe, of carefully guarded secrets. She was on the tall side, some might say statuesque. Very feminine, undeniably womanly. Her waitress uniform played down her curves. The jeans and sweater that she now wore did not.

On the road again, they followed a slow moving log truck. It was hauling a heavy load of massive oak logs along a sparkling stream far into the shaded recesses of a steep hollow. Occasionally they would pass a house trailer perched on a narrow bench bulldozed into the wooded hillside. Carelessly parked pickup trucks required constant attention and careful maneuvering to avoid collision. The log truck driver's skill, or nonchalance, impressed Ian.

"Turn here." Lori blurted the words out without warning. She was pointing to a gravel road that turned right at ninety degrees from the road they were on. It crossed the stream on a well-weathered low water bridge, and headed up a tiny side hollow. Ian locked up the brakes. The truck slid into the turn and almost missed the bridge. For a moment, Ian pictured the drop to the creek bed below.

"Sorry, that road surprised me. It came up so fast," she apologized, "This is Little Elk Hollow. It winds at least six or eight miles, all the way up onto the mountain. There are probably twenty houses out this road. Do you know which is your mother's?"

"I have her address from a card she sent on my birthday. Box 47."

They began watching for numbers on the roadside mailboxes. Before long, they pulled up in front of a pale yellow doublewide with brown trim. It was immaculately cared for. Daffodils were already in bloom in a sunny spot in the yard. Chickens pecked in a fenced area next to a rough lumber chicken coop.

"This must be the place," Ian announced, thankful that his voice did not crack. His throat was very tight. "Do you want to go in?" He looked at Lori.

"How long has it been?"

"Twenty years."

"You go in. I'll wait out here. You can come out and get me if everything is ok," she suggested.

Ian found himself standing at the little house, knocking mechanically at the cold metal door. Suddenly, it was opened by a tall, soft-featured mountain woman. Her dark hair was salted with gray and pulled back into a tight bun.

"Yes?" was all she said.

Ian choked momentarily, then ventured "Mrs. Gauley?" It stuck in his throat. He tried again, "Mom?"

"Oh, my God, Ian, come in." Her face glowed as she swung the door out of the way and hugged him. She did not let go until she began to worry that she might be making him uncomfortable. Tears filled both their eyes.

He went inside. The house was as spotless as the yard. There were pictures of Cynthia and himself displayed in the living room. And one of his father. He did not have any idea of how to begin a conversation. He did not have to.

"I've been praying for twenty years that you'd stop by one day. What took you so long?" She was not really looking for an answer. She waved one away with a flick of her hand. She turned away,

96

slightly embarrassed by the tears that still ran down her cheeks.
"That's ok, our family wasn't the closest. I'm sorry about the way I left. After you went away to college, things got overwhelmingly cold and lonely. I had to get out of there." Her eyes were bright but misty.

"Coffee?" She headed toward the coffeemaker. It reminded Ian that Lori was in the car.

"Sure Mom. I have someone I'd like you to meet."

"Cynthia?" came the reply.

"Well, no, Cynthia and I have called it quits. This is Lori. She's just a friend who helped me find you."

"I'm sorry I never met Cynthia." She smiled sadly, seemed to think for a moment, then added, "your father didn't tell me much about her. He told me that she had high aspirations for you. To him that sounded like a good thing but I wasn't quite so sure. It wasn't my place to interfere."

"She was a good friend and companion for many years, but we developed serious differences." He looked away. The serious differences still hurt enough that he was afraid that it might show in his eyes.

"I understand," she assured Ian. "I will always love your father but I had to leave, too. Sometimes things just work out that way."

Ian looked at her. He could not think of a thing to say. After an uncomfortable moment of silence, she continued.

"I just couldn't spend my life with a man who saw me as a burden. I was just a distraction from his business. As distant and detached as he could be at times, he would never have made me leave. He had far too much of a sense of responsibility for that. I had to take that step myself. It was very hard leaving you. I knew that he would probably do everything he could to keep me out of your life, but I just couldn't bear to live a financially secure but emotionally empty existence anymore.

"As remote as this hollow is, I am much less lonely here than I was living in your father's house in the city. I only regret that I lost contact with you. That was your father's way of punishing me for leaving. He helped me financially at first on the condition that I not contact you. He wouldn't give me your address or keep me posted on your achievements. I didn't learn of your marriage until over a month after the wedding."

"That's not surprising. Dad was always very evasive when I asked about your whereabouts," Ian acknowledged.

"I finally got your address from an internet lawyer directory on the computer in the library in Coalton," she smiled. "Even old hillbilly ladies can learn new tricks."

"The return address was all I needed to find you. At least once I moved down here."

"Down here?" She looked up at him, almost spilling the coffee she was bringing back to the kitchen table.

"I bought a little farm on the Big Laurel Fork about five miles out of Elton. I'm going to try being a small town lawyer for a while." He had never voiced that sentiment before, but it had a nice ring to it.

She looked a little apprehensive. "Dear, that's a big step. I wish you the best of luck, but this is a tough place to make a living. I drove an hour each way for fifteen years to my job. I worked in the county clerk's office filing deeds and liens. There's just no money in these parts."

She seemed to reflect for a moment. "But I love it here. It is very peaceful. And, in time, you will meet real friends who you can trust and count on. Maybe you already have." She motioned toward the outside.

Ian went back outside and got Lori. When he introduced her, he said "Lori, this is my mother. Mom, this is my friend, Lori."

His mother, who seemed to take an immediate liking to Lori, added, "my name is Alma, Alma Kessler." She turned to Ian and offered in explanation. "My maiden name, I took it back."

They all sat at the kitchen table, drank coffee, and talked until dusk. Ian could not have imagined a more comfortable reunion. It was decided that they would have a big Easter dinner at Ian's house after Lori got off work on Sunday.

They had the warm Easter family dinner that Ian had imagined but never expected to actually experience. After they cleaned up and made little Tupperware packages for Alma to take home, Ian and Lori collapsed on the old leather sofa Lori had found at a local auction. They watched Alma's faded Chevy® sedan climb the dirt grade away from the farm.

Ian thought to himself that Lori was a wonderful woman, gentle, smart, kind, and sexy. She was tired from a day of cooking and trying not to be self-conscious. For just a moment, she fell asleep with her head on Ian's shoulder. When she awoke, she caught him looking at her with a far away mist in his eyes.

"You should probably be heading back to your house and going to bed," he noted in a whisper.

"You're right," she agreed, "except for the going back to my house part."

It was probably about a week after Easter when Ian got the call. Not that he had not been expecting it. Still, it was enough to make him wonder why in the hell he had felt compelled to get a telephone installed so soon. Lori said that many local folks, including his nearest neighbor, seemed to be perfectly content without one. Not having a phone just made *other* people, the ones who were trying to sell you something, crazy. Unfortunately, after a lifetime of urban living, Ian could not bear to be that isolated.

So he brought the call upon himself. The caller was H. Robert "Bob" Hawthorne, old money industrialist and philanthropist. His father and grandfather had amassed a fortune cutting and selling the forests of a significant portion of the upper Midwest. His daughter was in the process of suing Ian for divorce.

His voice was gruff and stern, his tone more than slightly condescending.

"Ian my boy," he began, "what's this I hear about you leaving my Cindy (only Bob dared to call Cynthia, "Cindy") and running off to the sticks? What would make a grown man do something like that?"

It was a rhetorical question, he expected no answer, nor did he give Ian any opportunity to proffer one.

"My Cindy deserves better than that. You can't just wash your hands of your responsibility to her like you owe her nothing. My God, boy, she's your wife. I never would have let her marry you if I thought that someday you'd pull a stunt like this. Lots of people have midlife crisis without leaving their families high and dry. Perhaps you'd like to explain yourself for me."

Ian did not like being patronized. He was extremely comfortable with the fact that he was a middle-aged man, and that he might well be having a midlife crisis. Nevertheless, he did not feel like he had to tolerate that kind of treatment.

"Bob," he began, "this is a matter strictly between Cynthia and me."

He did not get any further before Bob cut him off.

"That girl is not prepared to be on her own. She has devoted her life to taking care of you. Then you took off and left her with nothing. Do you think you'd be where you are in your career without her, and my, help?"

As he thought that last question through, the answer he kept coming up with was "yes." He was already at the firm when he met Cynthia. Her father had always refused to move his company's legal work from a competing firm where one of the partners was an old school chum of his. She never got involved in his career. She just was not interested. She did not even want to hear about it. Cynthia never had any interest in having a career of her own, either. She did not even do laundry, clean house, or any of those domestic engineering things. For dinner, the only thing she could make was reservations. This frankly did not particularly bother Ian because very early in their relationship she had actually tried to cook a couple of times. Not only was the food unpalatable to the point of being a public health hazard, but she became so frustrated that he had to devote the rest of the evening to consoling her.

Ian was beginning to get angry. "That's right, Bob, I left her with nothing," he began. "No debt, no responsibilities, no mortgage, no car payment, but she does have a pretty nice paid-for condominium and a new paid-for Toyota. And a daddy who could find her a job in his company in less than a heartbeat. Or don't you want her on *your* payroll?"

Bob ignored his challenge.

"Son, I've retained Walter Greystone to represent her in this divorce. He'll take you for everything you have," the old man threatened.

Ian laughed. "Tell Walter that I have nothing to take except a little hardscrabble land and a run down shack in the middle of nowhere. If he were to seek equitable distribution of the marital property in this case, I would have to come back for some of Cynthia's assets. And tell him that if he pushes it. I will."

Ian drew a deep breath. "And you should sit down with both Cynthia and Celia and ask them about their relationship with Celia's husband, Jim. That would be a much better way to learn about your family's extramarital recreational pursuits than in the local newspaper."

"Don't try to intimidate me with made-up bullshit." Bob warned.

"My imagination could never approach the perversity of your family's reality," Ian responded. "I am willing to walk away with a no-fault divorce and closed lips, thanking God that there are no children involved, but I am also willing to put up a big ugly public fight if Walter and you think that is what you want."

"I can see that there is no point in trying to talk sense into you," came Bob's reply. "You realize, of course, that you will never practice law in this town again."

"Bob, I think that is a safe bet"

"You will be hearing from Walter within a few days."

With that, he hung up. Ian felt relieved. He had expected that call for some time. It really was not as bad as he thought it might be. Sure enough, later that week he received a package with a summons and a proposed property settlement agreement. Strictly status quo on the property, and a strictly no-fault divorce.

CHAPTER NINE

"Angling may be said to be so like the mathematics that

it can never be fully learnt." Isaac Walton, The Complete Angler

"Let thy words be few." Ecclesiastes v. 2.

Springtime falls on the central Appalachians like the divine blessing that it is. Flowers appear where days before there were only damp leaves, rock and black earth. The trees erupt in intense yet delicate green lace. White dogwood, wild cherry, and pink-purple redbud trees add color to the forest tapestry. On the ground, trillium blooms in white, and occasionally pink, profusion. Fresh fern fiddleheads begin to unroll and open into soft and intricate green leaves that blanket acres of the forest floor. Wildlife awakens and begins to shake off the drab cloak of winter. Turkeys strut through the forest calling for a mate. This year's bear cubs follow mom into the daylight to learn to fend for themselves. Newborn fawns in white-spotted coats walk on wobbly legs looking for tender spring grass.

In the streams, as days lengthen and the waters begin to warm, trout shed their winter sluggishness and start to feed. The same warmth stirs dormant insects that soon begin racing through their short cycle of life, hatching from the water into the spring air. They fly in delicate clouds above the tumbling creeks and rivers. This exquisite ballet of nature in turn brings the fly fishermen out of their winter dormancy.

One sunny morning in early May found Ian at the diner. Lori sat across from him, coffee pot in hand. She seemed to feel comfortable sitting with him while she was working so long as she was holding coffee at the ready.

"This is the kind of day that my father used to wait all year for," she mused. "The streams are running perfectly. I am sure there are mayflies hatching. He would be out there standing hip deep in cold water from dawn to dusk. In the morning before he left, I'd put a sandwich in his vest and hang a thermos of coffee from his belt. "Sometimes I'd fish with him for a few hours, but I couldn't keep it up all day like he could. I enjoyed it, but he was in love with it. Fly fishing tweaked some nerve, or maybe it was indexed to some receptor, that was very central to his brain. He talked of getting in the 'zone' like runners prattle about their runners' highs.

All I ever got running was tired, but I *have* had days when, for no apparent reason, I would slow down and become extremely relaxed and focused and catch fish after fish after fish. That must have been what he was talking about."

Ian listened intently. Was she angling to go fishing?

"Does this mean you want to go fishing?" he asked earnestly. "I would be more than glad to take you but I need to warn you I have never fished a day in my life. I would probably make you crazy. You would have to teach me, but I'd love to learn."

"If you really want to learn, I can teach you to fly fish in twenty minutes." She intended it as an offer but it sounded like a challenge to Ian. "Eddie Hedrick down at the bait and tackle can get you all of the gear you need. Tell him I sent you and you don't want any cheap shit. Eddie knew my father. He'll fix you up right. Tonight, after I get off work, we can walk down to the river and I'll show you some basic stuff. Tomorrow we'll go to one of the streams my father used to take me to as a child. I caught my first trout there."

"It's a deal. I'm off to buy new toys." Ian stood up and started toward the cash register.

"Oh, and don't forget to get a fishing license."

"You need a license just to fish?" Ian turned to face her. He meant the question seriously.

Lori rolled her eyes, cocked her head slightly, and replied. "Yes."

Maybe she should have adjusted the twenty-minute projection upwards slightly.

The evening lesson, all misgivings aside, went well. Ian showed up at Lori's house about two hours before sundown. It was an incredible spring evening. Mayflies were rising from the Big Laurel in gossamer waves. Tiny, delicate creatures, their only purposes as adults being to mate and feed fish. A weaving of intentional and unintentional destiny.

Lori had not expected to be teaching Ian under actual battlefield conditions, but was very pleasantly surprised by the ease with which he learned. Ian felt a bit odd at first, walking clumsily through town in hip-high rubber boots, but the fishing rod was adequate explanation in these parts for such behavior.

The twenty minutes lasted nearly two hours. Ian felt hopelessly uncoordinated and awkward as he flogged the water with his first casts and drowned the flies he knew were supposed to be fished "dry." Lori patiently explained each step in the casting and drifting process, and provided demonstration as necessary to keep him on track.

His self-consciousness began to fade as he hooked his first fish, a small bass, from the riverbank right in the middle of town. Lori applauded as he tried to unhook it without falling face first into the water. He was unsteady in his new boots on the slippery rocks. It reminded Lori of the tentative first steps of a new foal.

The next morning they were sitting in Ian's truck, climbing the grade out of town. They were bound for one of the small, cold rocky tributaries of the Big Laurel Fork. Lori said it was a classic Appalachian Mountain trout stream, with an abundance of the things trout need to be happy. Things like clear, icy water full of dissolved oxygen and a vast selection of randomly sized boulders to hide under and behind. It had the requisite vigorous and healthy benthic ecosystem and was loaded with lots of prehistoric looking bugs. Trout food.

Lori directed Ian though multiple forks of long dirt roads that snaked in and out of deep shaded hollows and across the flanks of spur ridges. At each intersection the road became progressively less maintained. In the last few miles, it bordered on impassible. Deep water-filled mud-holes alternated with slippery bare limestone ledges. Twice Ian had to stop and move trees that had fallen across the road. Luckily they were small trees, since he had no winch, chain, chainsaw, or other tree moving equipment. Lori saw the downed trees as a good sign, since that meant no one else had driven this road lately. Her father had taught her to be conscious of the effects of fishing pressure on a stream.

Finally, the road gave out at a forest clearing barely big enough to pull in and turn the truck around. Ian faced the truck outward, so no one could block him in. Lori appreciated the irony of his compulsive adherence to urban habits in a parking lot that probably had not seen a vehicle for months.

The stream they were seeking was identified on topographic maps as Hell Roaring Branch. Full color plastic laminated picture-placemats have been made of far less beautiful streams. The crystalline water cascaded over limestone stair steps running into deep rock-lined pools. Mountain laurel, dogwood, and rhododendron intertwined with huge boulders and hemlock boughs to discourage access to the water, except by slow and careful wading along the streambed. The idyllic atmosphere on this warm spring day likely belied the roar of this stream during heavy rain or fast snowmelt. Whoever named it had probably tried to cross in the high water of early spring.

Ian struggled and strained. He got ice water over the top of his hip boots at least three times, each acknowledged with a clenched-jaw gasp. It was slightly embarrassing to witness the grace with which Lori negotiated the slippery rocks and strong currents. Her casts were smooth and accurate. The fly touched down delicately. It drifted like a living insect spent after its life's work of passing its genetic code to the next generation. The trout took the fly smoothly, without hesitation. The stream-bred native trout glistened with a rainbow of colors. They were as dazzling as the most precious tropical aquarium fish.

"Patience and presentation is the key," she counseled Ian, delicately lifting the fly from the water with hardly a riffle to its glassy surface. Ian was not listening. He was too busy trying to untangle his leader and fly from the branches of an overhanging hemlock tree.

Ian caught several fish as well. His fish seemed more impetuous, as if his less refined presentation only attracted the more aggressive, less sophisticated, and smaller trout. They would grab his fly with a splash as soon as it landed and before his unpolished technique became apparent. That was fine with him. He was ecstatic at the thought that he was now a fly fisherman. It was a fraternity he had always relegated to the likes of doctors, old money industrialists, and new-world royalty.

With fly rod in hand, gracefully laying a cast upon the water, Lori took on the air of the Queen Mother waving to the adoring masses. Yet, even in thigh-high rubber boots and a khaki vest

106

adorned with insect-like tufts of feather, she appeared even more strikingly feminine and graceful than usual. Sexy. Orvis®-meets-Victoria's Secret®.

On the way back to the truck, in a fern carpeted glen, on a deep bed of moss-covered hemlock needles, they made love in hip boots (well, Lori in one hip boot), and vests covered with feather bugs. Ian was awed by the soft silky paleness of her skin in the evergreen-filtered sunlight. He could almost picture her glowing as a luminous forest fairy, hovering above him on translucent wings, surrounded by an ethereal halo of white light.

CHAPTER TEN

"Nothing happens to anybody which he is not fitted by nature to bear." Marcus Aurelius

"We will now discuss in a little more detail the Struggle for Existence." Charles Darwin

Ian realized that he could not sit back and feel sorry for himself. Eventually the money would run out and he would be forced to scratch out a living like everybody else. He had not yet heard from the state bar regarding his application to practice law, but wanted to be ready when he got word. Today he would shop for an office. He drove into town looking for Charlie Jacob.

Charlie, as Ian predicted, had just the space for him. It belonged to Billy Caldwell, the owner of the cement plant and quarry at the far end of town. Billy used to have offices in the middle of town near the river.

His business had picked up in the last few years to the point that Billy had to move his office to the main cement plant complex so that he could better monitor that operation. Ian could rent one of his old offices. The rent seemed reasonable to Ian. In reality, it was quite high by local standards, but Ian could have predicted that. Ian and Charlie shook hands on the deal.

His next stop was the diner where he told Lori what he had done. She seemed more excited than he was. "You'll need a sign. I'll make one for you," she offered. Ian must have looked skeptical, because she quickly added, "I once worked for a sign painter. I know what I'm doing."

Once she concluded that he believed her, she added, "it will say 'Ian Gauley' in bold script. Under that, in smaller letters it will say 'Honest Lawyer.'"

Ian smiled. "That would be very nice. I'd like that."

Ian left, promising to return to get Lori at closing time.

Shortly after he left, a rough and road-worn looking couple walked into the diner. With them was a bouncing three or four month-old German Shepherd puppy.

"Sorry," advised Lori, "no dogs in the restaurant. Health Department rules."

They told her that it was not their dog, that they had found it picking through some roadside garbage up on the mountain. It was probably abandoned by someone who no longer wanted the responsibility of a hungry dog to feed. When the couple left the diner, they did not take the dog. He sat outside the restaurant for the rest of the afternoon.

Occasionally, when a customer opened the door, he would try to slip inside. Cletus Hansen, county deputy-sheriff, was the only person he was actually able to get around. Cletus chased him down, grabbed him by the scruff of the neck, and dragged him back into the parking lot.

With only Lori watching through the restaurant windows as a witness, the pup marched over to Cletus's patrol car and relieved himself on the driver's side front tire. He then returned to his vigil at the door. Lori giggled to herself but did not say a word to Cletus, who would have taken the dog to the county pound.

The pup was still there when Ian came back at closing time. The pup followed her closely when Lori came outside to his truck.

"Did you get a puppy?" asked Ian. "Good looking dog."

"Well, no," began Lori, "he's a str...I got him for you. His name is Cletus."

Ian opened the passenger side truck door for Lori. Cletus sat looking up at Lori until Ian lifted him up into the truck.

They soon discovered he was incredibly headstrong for so young a pup. Ian never owned a dog before, so he was an easy mark. Cletus took full advantage of Ian's naïveté. The entire farm became his personal turf. He ate constantly, quickly growing into a formidable beast. He would be well over one hundred pounds by the end of his first summer. They soon began to suspect he was no purebred Shepherd. There was something wilder and more restless in him. Possibly coyote but probably wolf.

It showed in the way he approached strangers. Quietly, with his head low. Watching intently, he would circle them slowly and look to Ian for clues as to their status. It was obvious that he could smell the most vestigial traces of fear. Even as a puppy, he could be quietly and frankly intimidating. He became devoted to, and protective of, Ian and Lori. Perhaps he realized that they had rescued him from the short hard life of a stray. Maybe he knew how much he, in turn, had come to mean to them.

One day, when the trees were still in their bright green spring colors and the fields were already a deep lush green, Ian heard Cletus's low puppy-growl. He was in a quandary because the water in the house had suddenly just stopped for no apparent reason. He knew that the house had a well somewhere. That, and where to find the fuse for the pump, was all he knew about his water supply. Now the water was "off," the fuse was not blown, and he was clueless.

There was a hard knock on the screen door. Outside stood a large, long-haired, bearded man. His exposed forearms were covered with tattoos of knives, demons, and spider webs. "G'mornin'," he said in a deep resonant voice. "My name's Silas McGraw. I'm your neighbor up the valley."

Cletus sat between him and the door. He growled quietly, then stopped altogether and just stared up at the man. Silas ignored him at first ,then gently moved him aside with his foot as Ian introduced himself through the screen and invited Silas in.

"Dog too?" came the question. Ian nodded affirmatively. "Com'on pup," was all Silas said to him. It was obvious to Cletus that the guy was not intimidated. He followed Silas in.

Ian's first impression of Silas was that he was colorful, artistically and figuratively, and rough-hewn, but not overtly threatening or dangerous.

Silas thought Ian looked a little soft, but figured he might have a fighting chance to survive the mountain lifestyle, if his pain threshold was high enough. He was probably better equipped than the last two jokers who had lived in the house. Maybe with some rural re-education and a little work-hardening, he could make it through a winter. At least he would have six or seven months to prepare.

Ian apologized that there was no coffee, and explained his predicament. Silas mentioned that he had done a lot of work on the house for the former owner, including the plumbing.

"Up until about five years ago," he explained, "the place was owned by an old man who had always worked as a logger. He didn't believe in indoor plumbing. 'A man shouldn't shit in his house,' the old guy would say. His wife had been dead for twenty years so there was no one around to convince him otherwise. Back then the plumbing consisted of an outhouse and a hand-dug, rock-lined well."

Silas continued. "When he died at 97, his kids bickered over the farm until they finally sold it to a trust-funded Zen-airhead. He meditated and worked on his karma here, until one day when he stepped barefoot on a timber rattlesnake that had been living under the porch. After his release from the hospital, he moved back to wherever it was that he came from and never set his bare feet upon the farm again."

Silas walked toward the kitchen as he talked.

"The next owner was a burnt-out political expert of some kind from Washington D.C. I never quite figured out what it was that he did for his money, but then I have that problem with all politicians. He wanted to civilize the place. He hired me to completely rewire the house. I also plumbed it, brought in a backhoe and installed a septic system, and put an electric pump on the well. The old well didn't have enough flow, so I hired a driller who hit lots of water at about sixty feet.

This close to the river you don't have to go real deep," Silas assured Ian.

He opened the lower door of a cabinet near the kitchen sink. Inside was a large blue steel tank. Ian had noticed it before. Ian had even guessed that it was part of the water system, but did not know what it did.

"This is your pressure tank," Silas began. "It holds a certain amount of water. When the level in this tank gets too low this little gizmo here," he pointed to a small box on top of the tank, "tells the pump, which sits submerged at the bottom of the well, to pump up some more water. That way the pump isn't always running. It would burn itself up. Sometimes, however, a power surge or clog in the line, or low water in the well will cause the little switch in that box to just shut-off. When that happens," he reached for a small metal lever on the side of the switchbox, "you have to reset the switch by lifting this lever."

He lifted it. Ian could hear water gushing into the tank.

"If the problem is a dry well, the switch will kick out again. Most of the time there is no apparent reason why the switch kicked. You reset it and it will be fine."

Ian thanked him for getting the water back on.

"No problem," assured Silas. "Actually, I came over to ask you a favor. You have a pretty good-sized pasture down towards the river. I'd like to rent it from you to graze my cattle." Then he added, "I'll maintain the fences."

The proposal sounded good to Ian. Money for nothing as far as he was concerned. Every little bit helped while he worked on getting licensed to practice law.

Cletus had curled up in a sunny spot on the kitchen floor, ignoring them both.

As Silas worked his way back toward the door he commented, "my girlfriend, Kathleen Joseph, she works at the hardware store in town, tells me you're a lawyer."

"Well, by training, but not right now, at least not here. I do hope to get licensed here real soon, but I'm not licensed yet." Ian responded, once again vaguely embarrassed by his social and occupational history.

"We may be the last town in America without one. I suspect you'll find enough work to keep you busy," Silas commented as he walked back out the door. "Good luck with it."

Cletus opened his eyes to watch him go but didn't move.

That night, Ian told Lori about meeting his neighbor. "I know. Kathleen told me that you two had met," she responded. "He says you seem ok. At least that's what Kathleen said."

"Do you know Kathleen? She works in the hardware store, right?"

"Hell yes I know Kathleen, she was one of the first people I met when I moved to this town. And I know Silas. In fact, he's done work for me. He fixed my shower. Something was leaking inside the wall. He had to tear the whole wall apart. I like them both." She propped her chin on one hand and smiled.

"This guy seems to fix a lot of plumbing." Ian mused, "I sense I should assume that everyone in this town knows each other and will know everything that happens to me a fraction of a second after I do."

"Honey, it's a small town. You're the new guy. Everyone will **lose** interest after you've been here a while." She looked contemplative for a few moments. "But, I *would* be careful what you say about people. It *does* get back around." She cast an exaggerated shifty-eyed glance around the room.

"Since we aren't in public, what did you think of Silas?'

"He seems ok," Ian had not given his impressions much more thought.

"Guy answer. Tells me nothing except that you two are not blood enemies, at least not yet." Lori teased. "He'd make a bad blood enemy. Kathleen tells me that he used to be a pretty tough guy. He was in the Special Forces, then he belonged to a motorcycle gang. She said he's just a big teddy bear now."

"I saw the biker tattoos. I suspect that the teddy bear still has some Grizz in him," Ian responded. "Cletus likes him though. They say dogs are good judges of character."

Ian also had the canine seal of approval. As the days lengthened and grew warmer, Ian ranged further and further from his house and his farm. Cletus was never more than fifty yards from his side. They explored upstream on the riverbank until the canyon sides became so steep and rocky that walking turned into a gymnastic routine. He climbed over huge rocks and struggling through tangled laurel. Cletus would sit at the base of the boulder piles and howl until Ian returned. The river here ran swift and loud as it surged and crashed between car-sized boulders in a noisy mael-strom of foam and motion.

Downstream, where the gorge widened into the broad bottomland of Silas's and his farms, the river ran through deep quiet pools separated by swift runs over cobblestone bottom. Car-sized boulders still littered the riverbed but now there was space to move between them. They were perfect sunbathing decks. A few begged to become diving platforms.

Spring faded into the dog days of summer. The river relaxed from its springtime torrent into a warmer, calmer summertime mode. Silas, Kathleen, Ian, Lori, and Cletus found its call irresistible.

The women, and geographical proximity, brought Silas and Ian, neither very social animals, closer. Silas had never associated with lawyers or other white-collar types before, nor Ian with laborers or bikers. They each found the other surprisingly interesting, both for the differences in their perspectives and for their unanticipated similarities.

The four of them became the best of friends. Lori and Kathleen were excited to do things as couples. It was one way to get the guys off the farm and into town. Occasionally, the guys would refuse to come out of the hollow. On those days, the women would drive out to Silas's farm. There they would all prepare a meal over a hot charcoal fire, eat, then go for long walks along the Big Laurel.

One hot and muggy day in midsummer, they decided to go swimming in the low, clear river. They met where the paths from the two farmhouses converged in the bottom near the spot where Silas had first run over Kathleen's clothes. The four of them spread towels on the rocks and lingered in the cool water. Cletus demanded to play his version of "fetch." He would chase down a tossed stick then chew it to pieces. Or he would bring it back to the thrower, but refuse to allow them to remove it from his mouth. This naturally turned into a dog vs. human tug of war replete with feigned aggression and playful growling and cussing by both sides.

A few hundred yards downstream, the river narrowed and accelerated into another gorge-like stretch that continued nearly to town. The flow became deep but still very fast. Directly under a steep rock bank, conflicting currents spawned an ongoing series of whirlpools. Once formed, they spun off downriver, eventually dissipating in deep fast water.

Silas had discovered as a teenager that he could dive from the boulders high above the water, directly into the vortex of a whirlpool. It would propel him right to the river bottom where the downstream current swept him along the riverbed at what seemed like fantastic speed. He would surface fifty yards downstream, grinning. He would then swim toward shore as if a great white shark was chasing him. He also learned as a youngster that the rapids just downstream from this play spot could administer a serious rocky beating. Collecting bruises in that manner transcended even a country boy's idea of manly recreation. Silas demonstrated the whirlpool trick several times for the others.

Ian decided to give the submarine ploy a try. He dove where Silas instructed him, dropping vertically into the bucket-sized vortex of water. It did not spin him as he had expected, but instead drove

115

him deep. He rocketed right to the bottom, deep enough that the pressure hurt his ears. It was strangely silent. The light shining through the clear water painted everything in deep emerald green. He was whisked along, as if by a giant unseen hand, toward distant seas.

Suddenly a large round boulder appeared before him. He was instantly plastered, spread eagle, on its upstream face. The impact nearly knocked the breath out of him, but he fought to keep control of his vital air. For what seemed like forever, but was probably only seconds, he was pinned by the force of the current. Unable to lift his head, his heart raced. When a pulse of current peeled him off the boulder and sent him downstream, he stroked for the surface like a dolphin on approach to a high leap. As he surfaced, he could see that he had plenty of time before the rapids began, but swam like a mullet in a school of bluefish for shore anyway. He had plenty of adrenaline to burn.

As he stood wet and slightly trembling on the safe, dry rocks of the riverbank, Kathleen observed that, "for as long as you were down there, you sure didn't go very far."

Ian smiled weakly. "I spent most of the time stuck on a rock on the bottom. The current was holding me and I couldn't move. It scared the hell out of me." His heart was still thumping in his chest, his blood pressure throbbing in his ears.

The group did not dwell on Ian's dance with the river gods, but no one else ventured whirlpool-diving that afternoon. His experience was a gentle reminder from the river that it needed to be taken seriously.

After the sun went down, Ian and Lori drove the truck into town. Silas and Kathleen led on the old pan-head, picking their way around the rocks and potholes that littered the rough dirt road. The sweet rumble of the scooter filtered back into the cab of the truck. Even Ian, who had never been around motorcycles much, found something innately satisfying in the sound.

He first heard it one quiet spring evening. Silas was weaving his way up the dirt road. As he passed near Ian's farm, he tapped the horn to say hello. Ian was out on the porch. The distant but strong mechanical heartbeat floated, serenely powerful, in the still air. They were headed for The Stand, the primary, the only, 'nightspot' in town. The Stand had gotten its name by first opening many years before as a roadside market and fruit stand. Business had been disappointing to its owners, who soon remodeled it into a tavern. As a bar, it did much better.

The Stand was not an upscale establishment, but it had all the necessary accoutrements. These included a long oak bar, a couple of relatively flat and true pool tables, cold beer, and a cook that knew his way around a vat of boiling fat. Because it was the only bar in town and couldn't be picky about the clientele it chose to cater to, everyone was welcome. Like so many small town establishments, it was almost a second home for many of its patrons. There were also many less frequent regulars who stopped in for a beer or game of pool every now and then.

It did not matter. Bernie, the owner and bartender, knew them all by name. He knew which of the town's citizens drank too much and would eventually need cut off, who were the happy drunks, and who got mean. A master politician, he generally kept things as under control as humanly possible.

They got a table in the back, a round of beers, and put in an order for some good greasy bar food. Lori held up her beer, "to a day in the sun and to Ian not drowning." It seemed a reasonable enough toast.

"And to the river. Not many wild ones like it left. For a few more months at least," Silas added. He spoke with a hint of sorrow in his voice.

"What are you talking about?" asked Ian.

"You don't know about the dam?" Kathleen chimed in.

"Dam?"

Silas looked up from his beer. He took a deep breath. "I hate to be the one to tell you this, but the river may not be like it is now for much longer. About seven miles upstream from our farms they have been building a huge earthen dam. It will back up a lake for fifteen miles into the river's headwaters. Most of the river will be diverted into giant tubes run through the mountain to a spot just below town. They say that there will be a small amount of water released into the old riverbed, which includes the stretch of river through our farms, to keep a few fish alive. It'll be a pitiful reminder of the wild river we have now."

"How long has this project been going on?" Ian queried. "And why are they doing it."

"For years, I'm told, but I heard about it when I moved back. Its official purpose seems to shift between flood control and electric power generation, depending on when and who you ask. I'm sure, as with most government projects, its real reason for existing is money. That, and providing our politicians with something to show as justification for their sorry-ass existences. This state has always been a resource colony of the eastern cities."

"Tell me more," demanded Ian, leaning forward and placing his forearms squarely on the table.

Lori spoke this time. "My father first told me about the project probably fifteen years ago. The power company was trying to sell it as an economic development ploy. Local politicians from the town to the state level were pushing it like it would be the eighth wonder of the modern world. The Governor at the time claimed that it "would deliver this county from the shackles of deep, dark depression into the bright light of economic prosperity." Blah, blah, blah." She gestured toward her open mouth with the index finger of her right hand, as if to induce vomiting. It was an uncharacteristically rude gesture. "Gag me with a chain saw."

She continued. "The power company wanted special tax breaks and other preferential treatment from the state. That proposal got kicked around the state legislature for several years until the United Mine Workers came out against the project as anti-coal and anti-miner. Labor had enough political clout in this state that it killed the project. For a while.

Unfortunately, there was too much money involved for this thing to just go away. It reappeared two years later as an Army Corps of Engineers flood control project. Never mind that, for a tenth of the money that it would take to construct and maintain the dam, all of the flood prone land in this entire watershed could be purchased and set aside as parkland. It was at that point that my father became involved. He loved the Big Laurel and was a board member of a group that supported responsible stream and fish management. Sort of like Ducks Unlimited, only for fish.

"One of those 'save the animals so *we* can kill them' groups," ad-libbed Kathleen. Lori knew that she was just exercising her cynical sense of humor, but stuck her tongue out at her anyway. Lori continued to explain.

"They began to work to stop the dam, by showing that it didn't make any sense, economically or environmentally. Other groups, including the local chapter of the Sierra Club, other fishing groups, even canoeists and whitewater rafters, got involved. And the UMWA still didn't like the project because they figured that even if it were built only for flood control it would be retrofitted eventually for electric generation. Of course, they were right.

"But government is very predictable. Money talks and altruism doesn't pay campaign bills. All of the opponents were painted as meddling, tree hugging out-of-staters. The dam proponents, especially the politicians, implied repeatedly that the local people were unanimously in favor of the dam."

Silas interjected, "My grandfather would spin in his grave at *that* suggestion. Or rise up and haunt some politician's ass. My father threatened to run the surveyors and landmen out of the valley, but he was too tired and weak to actually do much more than pull a few survey stakes and take down a few survey ribbons by the time this thing became general public knowledge. He *did* go to the state capitol and testify against the project, but I think he was ignored because he was old and had no political connections. He saw the whole project as an affront to God and nature. As far as he could tell it was just another way for government to steal land."

"And God knows he was funny about land," Kathleen chimed in. Silas felt the need to explain her comment to Lori and Ian.

"My father and his father before him were real land-conscious. You couldn't suggest to them that land was a commodity to buy and sell any more than you could have sold the concept to Tecumseh, Crazy Horse, or Geronimo.

Tecumseh, Chief of the Shawnees, said 'These lands are ours. No one has a right to remove us. The Great Spirit above has appointed this place for us, on which to light our fires, and here we will remain. We are determined to defend them, and if it is His will, our bones shall whiten on them, but we will never give them up.' My father could have said that with the same conviction. The fact that his ancestors stole it from the Indians didn't change the way he felt in the least. I guess he figured that they stole it fair and square."

119

A gleam came to his eyes as he spoke. Silas was starting on a roll. "He believed that having land defined a person more than anything else. As a child, he would tell me that the world has two kinds of people, those who have land and everybody else. If you have land, you are possessed of purpose, something to live and die for, a solemn responsibility to succeeding generations and to the earth. It hurt him very deeply when I left to work in the city. I know he rationalized that I had to go work out the demons that I had acquired during the war. But he never doubted that I would be back. I just wish that he had lived to see it happen."

Silas realized he had digressed.

"Anyway, he was always very suspicious of urban people. They have no roots to the earth and live opportunistically, like scavenging packs of jackals. They are always prowling for a buck, ready to attack where they see weakness. Politicians are their agents, willing to use the power of government to distribute the spoils to their friends or wherever the most votes lay. The most votes, of course, have always been in the cities.

I remember him saying that the Civil War was really based on the urban-rural struggle. He claimed that slavery was only the superficial justification for Union aggression. It was an easy point to rally around because the institution of slavery was undeniably ugly. But, few southerners, he was quick to point out, actually had slaves. This was certainly true in the ranks of the soldiers who did the fighting and dying. They weren't fighting to enslave black people, they were white trash country boys fighting to keep from being enslaved by urban business people from up north.

What the rebels were really fighting against was control of their homeland by the Union. The more industrialized North needed to exploit the agrarian South to maintain its standard of living. The government in Washington acted on the belief that, if the southern states were able to secede, the price of agricultural commodities and raw materials would be out of its control."

Silas realized that the other three were staring at him.

"Ok, ok, so my old man was a little radical for a coal miner. He read a lot of political literature. He even had some of Mao's writings. The point is that nobody was going to separate him from his land. And no one did. I buried him myself up on the hillside behind the barn. On a sunny, south-facing knoll. Next to my mother

." Silas looked at the others, who were quiet. "On his land."

Lori brought the conversation back to the dam.

"This project slid in under the wire. The cost-benefit studies, both for the original power project and the flood control plan, are so marginal that this thing could never pass muster to receive the necessary funding today. The project only survives because it started under the previous political administration and has gotten too far along to kill now."

Silas added. "It is supposed to be completed by next spring."

Ian agreed. "It's a damn shame. Bad pun intended. There aren't many rivers like the Big Laurel left, especially in the East." He was beginning to get serious. "Why would anyone in their right mind want to destroy something that unique and magnificent? There are lots of dams. There seem to be lakes everywhere but, personally, I don't know of any other rivers like that one."

Silas gave him a mock incredulous stare. "Like I said before. Money. The business people in this entire corner of the state were led to believe that they would make a ton of money off of this dam. Right here in town, they had Charlie Jacob convinced that he would get rich selling vacation homes around the lake. Of course, no one pointed out that a flood control lake is surrounded by mudflats much of the year because it has to be drawn down to have the capacity to catch floodwaters. Besides, the Corps won't usually let you construct residential developments around their projects.

Billy Caldwell was flat-out *told* that his quarry and cement plant would provide all the concrete for the project without the necessity of competitive bidding. Of course, they didn't underscore that it would be an earth fill dam, just a giant rock pile. Billy has, I believe, already make a good bit of money on the project. He may be the only one.

Your boss," Silas looked up at Lori, "I know she's still waiting for the extra business she was led to believe she'd get, first from the construction crews and later from the tourists. The construction site is too far out of town to generate much business. Most of the workers stay down in Marysville and drive over an hour to work every day. The bulk of the big contracts went to out-of-state contractors because no one around here was big enough to handle them.

Basically, we didn't get much compared to what we lost. Politicians got a monument. Contractors got a temporary job. A few other miscellaneous entrepreneurs got a check or two. And the people who actually live here, as well as the wildlife, the river, and the land, get a screwin'."

Then he seemed to have second thoughts. "Don't get me wrong. The whole business community, both in town and around the state, is squarely behind this dam. Don't go badmouthing it and expecting much sympathy. If you don't like it, just keep it to yourself, especially as a new person in town. You will need to do business with these people."

It was now Lori's turn to speak again. "Most people have no concept of the beauty or importance of a wild river. It is fearsome to them. People think a river without a dam is a river that can dish-up killer floods. They imagine torrents of muddy water carrying their homes away. They don't look past the irrational fears. They are taught young that fast currents drown people. And, admittedly, you can't run a motorboat or water ski on a river like the Big Laurel. It is too untamed for most people to appreciate. It is, in fact, an affront to the need many people have to control nature. They have no understanding of the delicate and complex ecosystems that exist in a river like this one. Or for the need some of us have to know that there are still wild and powerful things in nature, like that river out there."

Ian was a little surprised by the strength of Lori's feelings. Her father had been an avid devotee of wild rivers. He had obviously passed that torch to her.

It was very quiet for a few moments then Ian spoke up. "I want to see the dam."

"Not much to see," responded Silas. "A big pile of rock and clay, lots of trucks and earth-moving equipment, huge piles of burned trees."

"I'd still like to see it." Ian persisted.

"Tomorrow," Silas volunteered. "We'll take a little walk."

CHAPTER ELEVEN

"By nature, men are nearly alike, by practice, they
   get to be wide apart." Confucius

"Civilization largely consists of hiding human nature."
   Mark Twain

The bar talk had Silas thinking about his childhood. He realized the
local people who were behind the dam project were his generation,
people he had grown up with. Charlie Jacob the notary, accountant,
car dealer. Billy Caldwell, cement and gravel mogul. Cletus Hansen,
deputy sheriff and keeper of the peace. Even Bernie Warren,
proprietor of The Stand. They were all within a few years of each
other in high school. For Silas, his familiarity with all of them and
their personal circumstances had bred some contempt.
Charlie had always been the kid that everyone picked on in gym
class. Silas could still remember quite vividly when he had pissed
his pants in second grade. The teacher was going to paddle his butt
for repeatedly talking in class but ended up sending him home to
change his clothes instead. Cletus was always the chubby kid,
though he later became large enough, and moved well enough, to
be a lineman on the high school football team. Billy was the scholar
and politician, always running for class office or getting some
achievement award. Bernie used to sell whatever stuff his mother
packed for lunch that Bernie did not immediately decide to eat.
Silas mostly tried to keep his head down, although he did quarterback the football team for most of his junior and senior years.
It struck Silas as interesting how little they all had changed over the
course of their lives. As a child, he saw adults as very different
from kids. Back then, his father seemed possessed of patience,
wisdom, and restraint far beyond the grasp or even appreciation of
Silas or his peers. But after all these years, he marveled at how little
difference there really was between children and adults. They had
many of the same needs, wants, and even thought processes.
Discipline seemed the main distinction.
Education apparently did not change either Charlie or Billy, both
of whom completed four years (Charlie in six) of college. They

123

still approached life much as they always had. Billy went into the family business and was, although firmly entrenched in middle age, still trying to prove to his father that he was worthy of running it. Charlie was doing alright. At least he was self sufficient and seemed to have perfected his bladder control. Bernie opted to skip school and go right into business, but had achieved a stature around town not appreciably distinguishable from that of the other two. Then there was Cletus. Silas, quite frankly, had always had a bit of a problem with Cletus. Cletus was the kid, every class has one, who could not, no matter how he tried, mind his own business. He was hopelessly nosy and an unsurpassed tattletale. Once, when Silas was in third grade, Cletus snitched on Silas for scribbling some long-forgotten graffiti on the blackboard while the teacher was out of the room. Silas had gotten three swats with the principal's wooden paddle, and a healthy enduring suspicion of authority and its sympathizers. At home that evening his father dutifully asked him if he had learned his lesson. Silas assured him that he had. Then he asked his father what it was that made Cletus tell the teacher. Silas just did not understand what would motivate a classmate to do that.

His father was a man who wore his independence like a suit of armor. He was probably one of the last of that very rare breed of individual who genuinely did not give a rat's ass what other people did or thought, considered the question for a long moment. Finally, he looked across the supper table at Silas and said, "That is a hard question, Son. People may have different reasons at different times. Generally, though, it is because they know deep inside that they can't compete with you head to head. By cooperating with those in authority, they get to use the power of that authority to get an advantage over you. Any time you give another person a secret about something that you did, but were not supposed to do, you give them power over you. A very, very few of your true friends may not use that power, but most of the people you meet over the course of your lifetime will. Of course, there are also some people who just can't stand to see anyone get away with anything. They feel that they would never be able to do it, so something makes them deeply resent others doing it. It's a form of envy, although they would like you to believe that it's just their sense of fairness.

Whatever it is son, do not overly concern yourself with what others are doing. It will only frustrate you and take your focus off your own work. Mind your own business and avoid people who won't mind theirs."

The words still echoed in Silas's ears a few years latter as he sat in the back of the sheriff's cruiser. One night, just after his graduation from high school, he had gone to a party down by the river and gotten more than his fill of warm beer. On the way home he noticed a logging truck idling in the yard of the sawmill. No one was around so he jumped in and took it for a spin around town, picking up several girls from the party as he went.

Before he could return the truck to the mill, he saw the bubblegum-machine lights of the sheriff's car in his mirror. He ignored them, driving back to where he got the truck and parking it before getting out of the cab. The sheriff was waiting outside the truck. He immediately knocked him to the ground. The girls screamed. His first urge had been to jump up and fight back. Luckily, he was not that drunk or stupid so he kept calm. The girls and he were taken to the sheriff's office at the county seat, a forty-minute drive away. Parents were summoned. Everyone except Silas, was released to their parents.

Silas learned another important lesson that night. If it used to be that enemies were obvious, fearsome and evil, like the medieval fire-breathing dragons of childhood fairy tales, those enemies are long gone. Danger in the modern world comes from people just doing their jobs, perhaps fueled a tad by envy, who wait patiently for their victims to make a minor mistake of judgment. They then swoop down to self righteously remove the hapless piece from life's game board and position themselves one move closer to their perceived victory.

Years later Silas would remain acutely conscious that Cletus, Billy Caldwell, even Charlie Jacob would gladly see him captured and caged for life if it meant they would have greater access to the imagined wealth that could be extracted from the lands of the upper Big Laurel.

In the morning, Silas and his father met with the prosecuting attorney. Silas was a week shy of his eighteenth birthday. The prosecutor explained that Cletus Hansen had seen Silas climb up into that log truck. He said they had Silas cold for underage drinking and joyriding. There was also the matter of the girls. He did not even bother to elaborate on that. What he *did* say was that he had already spoken with the judge who had agreed that the whole thing could be forgotten if Silas simply enlisted in the military. America had more pressing needs than wasting money prosecuting joyriding kids. A week later Silas was on his way to becoming a soldier. What the hell, he had considered enlisting anyway. He needed a change of scenery. In a few months, he was in Southeast Asia.

CHAPTER TWELVE

"Remove not the ancient landmark." Proverbs xxii. 28; xxiii. 10.
"Speak to the earth and it will teach thee." Job xii. 8.

The morning after their night at the Stand, Ian and Silas walked the old logging road that began behind Silas's barn. It ran high on the gorge side, several hundred feet above the river and continued upstream all the way to the dam site. A new sun rose to begin a brilliant summer day. Hot sunshine filtered through the dense canopy of white oak, beech, poplar, and hickory. Below them the river roared through a boulder strewn, hemlock-lined defile. They could only occasionally catch a glimpse of sunlight on water, but the distant sound of cascading water was with them most of the trip.

Silas commented, "The Indians believed that, if you know how to listen, you can hear the voices of your ancestors in the sounds of the river. I often catch myself thinking I hear voices when I know that there is no one else around. As far as I can tell, it's just the water pouring over the rocks. Maybe I haven't learned how to listen yet."

"My ancestors are in Europe and Chicago," came Ian's bemused reply.

"Looks like you'll just have to listen to mine."

Silas told Ian about his childhood of exploring these canyons. He had fished every pool and trapped mink and beaver in the main river and up every side hollow. Once, while setting a trap at the water's edge, he looked up to see a five-foot long muskellunge watching him from the pool. He spent most of the rest of the summer trying to catch that monster. He used everything from frogs to small trout and even live mice as bait. Once, fishing a foot-long creek chub minnow at dusk, Silas was able to hook the fish. It turned and dove like a silent torpedo to the bottom of a huge mid-river rock pile. His line parted with a singing snap and threw a pitiful limp loop back over Silas's shoulder. The memory of his heart pounding wildly in his chest was still vivid.

"It was one of the great experiences of my childhood to have even hooked that bastard. I was, after all, playing on his turf, and he didn't get that big and old by being stupid," Silas observed.

As they drew nearer to where the dam was being built, Silas's focus shifted to it.

"Dams like this one are just a symptom of a much greater evil. They are a symbol of disrespect. Disrespect for nature and disrespect for those of us who live where they are built." Silas was also still on a multi-day binge of being uncharacteristically reflective.

"They are a reminder that we, as rural people, are colonists. The cities are our mother country. They can and will tax us for all we are worth. They take our raw materials, our labor, even our children, and pay us just enough to keep us from revolting. What urbanites do best is consume. From where I stand it seems that lots of resources are poured into the cities, but very little of use comes out.

"The value of this river to the generations of people who grew up here and lived by her rhythms is irrelevant to a city dweller who thinks his electric power bill is too high. Rural political leaders come from the business class whose main concern is generating money for themselves and their friends by selling our resources to the urban purchasers. They don't care, or even realize, what they are giving away. They can't, or won't, see the future impact of their deeds. Every deal leaves us with a little less to call our own."

Not far from here was a place where the canyon walls closed in tight on the Big Laurel. The whole river poured between sheer rock walls over a massive fifteen-foot high shelf of sandstone, and piled into house-sized boulders at its base. If the river was running high, you could feel the ground shake with the surging of the water. From upstream, all you would see was a broad horizon line and a huge cloud of mist. On cool summer mornings, fog and vapor would fill the narrow gorge for hundreds of yards in both directions.

I used to fight my way along the sharp rocks to a spot below the falls where I would set my traps. The old timers called the spot Mink Shoals. I never got many pelts, but that wasn't the reason I worked so hard to get there. I went for the power. The place roared and pulsed with raw natural power."

"I'd love to see it," Ian remarked.

"It doesn't exist any more," Silas noted sadly. "Because of the way the cliffs crowded the river there, it was also a very good spot to build a dam."

Soon they stood at the edge of the forest. Ahead of them for hundreds of yards, the trees had been leveled by enormous bulldozers. Extensive sections of the gorge side had been scraped to bare rock and dynamited for building material. This was piled over a hundred feet high across the river's eons-old course. At the base of the rock-pile, the Big Laurel poured from a concrete pipe back into its original riverbed. Upstream of the rock pile, the mountainsides were being denuded of trees and other vegetation up to what would be the future shoreline of the lake. Dozers, huge loaders, and rock trucks scrambled around the construction site. They cruised over hundreds of acres, like ants on an anthill.

Ian stood in awe of the sheer magnitude of the destruction. He started out onto the open ground. "Don't go out there," warned Silas. "That is a construction site and public access is prohibited. This is not our countryside anymore." Silas looked at the dam and pointed. "Mink Shoals is buried right there, under a million tons of shattered sandstone."

Ian could not help but notice Silas's demeanor as he gazed out across the expanse of raw rock, earth and crushed vegetation. He was not just looking. He was *reconnoitering*. There was no resignation in his eyes. Even as the giant machines were scurrying in and out of the gorge, he methodically scanned every corner of the site like a fighter sizing up his opponent. He was assessing strengths and weaknesses. Clearly, he had not yet accepted this project as a done deal.

On the way home Silas was more somber.

"For generations country people have felt that the route to our own prosperity is to cater to the needs of the cities. We have sold them anything we have that they would pay us for. We have sold our forests. We have even sold the minerals under our feet and destroyed our own land to dig them up and ship them away. Now we have sold our river and our river bottom farmlands, the only land in these parts suitable for anything resembling sustainable agriculture. If we are poor, it is because we have sold our future." It was an obvious and painful truth.

129

CHAPTER THIRTEEN

"The more corrupt the state, the more numerous the laws."
Tacitus (55-117 AD)

"Here I stand; I can do no otherwise. God help me. Amen!"
Martin Luther King

"There is no peace, Sayeth the Lord, unto the wicked." Isaiah
xlviii. 22.

Silas told Ian about the people that used to live on the land that
was soon to be lakebed. "Down below town, in an area called
Tannery Bottom because there used to be an old tannery down
there, are three little single-wide trailers. In them live three tired old
men."

He pointed upriver. "Above here the canyons open up into several
nice pieces of bottom land. There were three small high-country
farms up there. Each farm was little more than a few good
hayfields, room for a big vegetable garden and a little feed corn,
and some pastureland for a couple dozen cattle. Yet each had
supported a family for generations.

"When the Feds came in and condemned land for the water
project they drove those three families off the land. One clan
scattered to the winds. Only the patriarch remained. He was too
old to start again somewhere else. His wife had died years ago. On
another farm lived a couple who moved reluctantly to the trailer in
Tannery Bottom. The old woman died shortly thereafter. Her
husband said her heart and spirit were broken by being forced to
leave her home.

"The third farm was tended by a gentleman who is a veteran of
three foreign wars. He still cannot understand how, after he put his
life on the line for his country countless times, it would turn
around and take the one thing he had left which meant anything to
him. He fishes the river behind his trailer almost every day. If you
talk to him for long he will tell you that he doesn't think this dam
will ever really be built. Or that if it is built, somehow the river will
take it back. I'm glad he isn't here to see this mess. It 'd kill him."

131

Silas looked away but continued to speak. "On the other hand, he's lived on this river for over eighty years. If anyone knows what the Big Laurel is capable of, it's him. The river has destroyed the entire town twice, once in the twenties and once in the fifties." Silas liked the thought that the river might win in the end. He appreciated, however, that it might not be in his lifetime.

"Is that the reason for the dam? Flood control?" Ian asked, mostly to avoid uncomfortable silence.

"That's one of the *stated* reasons for the dam. It's one of the *excuses* for the dam. That whole flood control thing just gives the people downstream a false sense of security. They really think that engineers can guarantee them safety from nature itself."

"Could a dam like that one ever actually wash out?" Ian asked. Such an event seemed incredibly unlikely. Even the partially completed structure so dwarfed the river pouring from a pipe at its base that its demise seemed inconceivable to Ian.

Silas grinned, "I don't know. Years ago a big earth fill dam in Colorado let go in a summer storm. It killed a lot of people in a campground downstream of the dam. The river in that case was smaller than the Big Laurel.

"Never underestimate the power of running water, especially in the mountains. Plain water weighs eight pounds to the gallon. A good rain can send millions of gallons spilling gravity-driven down every little ravine and hollow. Every drop on every mountaintop must eventually head toward the sea. I can remember floods as a kid that shook the ground and took the first row of houses in town, lifted them up, crumpled them and floated them away, never to be seen again. If lightning is God's terrible swift sword, floodwater is his shovel and broom. Upstream of the farm are several boulders as big as railroad cars that washed into their present locations during spring floods when I was a boy. Unless you have witnessed a mountain river in full flood, you cannot fully comprehend its power to change a landscape.

"You realize, of course, that we live downstream from that dam." Silas shrugged. "Our houses sit on fairly high ground. Before water ever reached our homes the whole town downstream would be gone." It was just speculation, but he realized there is no safety in numbers when it comes to natural disasters.

132

Ian's conversation with Silas had been a good heads-up. The very next day, while he was still painting and nailing down trim molding, his first client walked into his office. He was a sturdy looking gentleman, probably in his early seventies. He obviously had put in a life's worth of hard work already, but probably still had plenty left in him. His name was Junior Harper and he was one of the three old men Silas had told him about.

"I hear tell you're a lawyer," he began.

Ian smiled broadly. He had been admitted to the Bar less than a week before, after several months of paperwork, background checks, and other bureaucratic exercises. Small towns have very efficient grapevines. He did not even have a sign outside his office.

"Yes, I am. Can I help you?"

The man extended a leathery calloused hand. His handshake was powerful, deliberate, and steady. "The government took my farm." Right to the point. Junior was not a man for subtlety or politics. "Sure, they paid me for it, but I never had a choice or a chance to stop them. They told me they had the right. Then they told me what it was worth. I didn't feel I had an alternative. My family has left the area to find work. My sons are in Charlotte. My daughter went to Richmond. Lately, I've been thinking that I don't have much left to lose. I've decided that I want to fight the bastards. My neighbors lost their farms, too. They want to fight, too."

He paused very briefly. He looked Ian straight in the eye. He was clearly without reservations or second thoughts.

"Can you help me?" He raised one eyebrow. "I certainly hope so." Ian shuddered a little to himself. There are few things worse than a deserving client who has already signed his rights away.

"I don't know," came Ian's frank reply. "It may be too late to do anything for you legally. Why don't we sit down and talk about exactly what happened."

He talked of a life on the land. Of cows and hayfields. Of cutting huge oak timber and floating the logs on the Big Laurel. Of the seasons and the moods of the river. The deep snows of 1977. The big flood of 1958. And the one after the hurricane in 1985.

Junior was the epitome of a solid old mountain man. His face had been beaten by the sun and the wind to the texture of weathered oak. He was determined to keep pushing against the things that he

133

thought needed pushed against. When he spoke of the lands of the Big Laurel, and of mountain life, it was obvious that he belonged there as much as fish belong in water and birds in the sky. He told a tale of life along the Big Laurel years ago. Roads better than temporary logging skid tracks did not penetrate the watershed until almost the Second World War. The first rock-based road came up the river from town. It only went as far as the McGraw farm, which was a good ten miles downriver from his place. Old man McGraw made certain that it would go no further.

"Just after I got back from the South Pacific," he began, "where I collected a little Japanese shrapnel in my leg, my brothers and I, using only a farm tractor with a bucket on the front and a bunch of dynamite, which was easy to come by in those days, dressed up an old logging trail into the upper end of the drainage. It climbed the flank of Stone Coal Mountain and switch-backed its way down the other side to a small piece of bottom land at the confluence of the river and the Jeremiah Fork." Silas had also mentioned the Jeremiah Fork in conversation. It was named after one of his ancestors and remained to this day a wild, steep, and laurel-shrouded tributary of the Big Laurel.

"Cutting the road took a little over a year, but my father had given me the deed to a couple of hundred acres *his* father had won in a poker game some fifty years before. I was bound and determined to get to that land and start a small farm there. No one in our family had ever even seen the land. My father figured it to be useless for anything besides hunting.

Once there, we set about clearing woods to enlarge the existing meadow into a field big enough for a few cows and a tiny rough log cabin. We built the cabin out of the tall straight yellow poplars that filled the bottom near the river. By the fall of the second year, the house was weather tight and the bottom had been fenced. I bought a couple of skinny Holsteins and led them over the mountain to the farm.

The first winter was horrible. I had trouble getting enough hay for the cattle. They pawed at the snow and ate the remnants of grass and vegetation beneath it. They looked like giant black and white deer browsing for whatever might keep them alive. To their credit, they survived. I was lucky that there was no ASPCA back in those days, because those cows got so skinny that I would have been accused of animal abuse. I didn't fare much better myself. The heavy work of clearing land, hunting food, cutting firewood, hauling water, building fences, and whatever else needed doing, burned at least thirty pounds from my already lean frame.

My old truck didn't make it to spring. It sat through most of February in the corner of the field. Sharp stones had deflated three of its tires and water found its way into the fuel system. The aging battery had finally given up while I was trying to get it started on a snowy, sub-zero morning.

By early April, the worst was over. I patched up the truck tires, but missed getting over the mountain to have Easter dinner with the family because a rockslide had blocked the road. I spent the next several days with a pick and shovel making it passable again. Two weeks later, probably more than a little concerned for my physical well being, my parents made the trek into the valley to pay me a visit.

Spring was in the air and on the mountainsides. The redbud and wild cherry were starting to bloom. The grass was greening up so the cattle finally had plenty to eat. The fish in the river were beginning to actively feed. I was able to add fish to the bland diet of canned goods, potatoes, dried beans, and cornbread I had been living on.

When my parents got there my mother gave me a big hug and told me how great it was to see me again. Her very next comment was a mild cursing about eating ramps, which I had been doing for several weeks by then. I must have reeked pretty bad, but couldn't smell it myself."

"Ramps?" Ian quizzed laconically. Junior was only too glad to explain. The wild leeks of Appalachia are a fairly highly regarded traditional delicacy, albeit one subject to differences in opinion. Junior began. "After a long mountain winter, especially for folks living off canned and dried goods, your body craves fresh greens. Ramps are sort of a cross between wild onions and garlic. They sprout right after the snow disappears, at least by late March or early April. So you pick a bunch of them and throw them in fried potatoes, or in your soup beans. With a little bacon grease, they make a hot green vegetable. Raw, mixed with dandelion leaves, they

135

make spring's first green salad. My father and I used to pick them in the spring and eat them in everything from soup to salad. Usually after a couple of weeks or so my mother would make us stop.

"The problem is that after a few days of eating ramps their odor permeates your entire body. It's on your breath. You sweat it out constantly. A burp will make your eyes water. And so on. The good news is that if you stay away from the plant for a few days the smell will blow off and you will be back to normal.

"My mother was a school teacher. She taught in a one-room mountain schoolhouse. The only heat was an iron pot-bellied coal stove. In early spring, when the ramps were the first greens to poke through last fall's brown blanket of fallen oak leaves, all the mothers sent their children to gather them for dinner. The result was a schoolhouse full of ramp-stinking children. The musky smell was intensified by the close quarters and the heat of the coal burning stove until it sometimes became more than anyone should have to endure for a teacher's salary. So, she was sensitive. But back to my story. When my folks came over the mountain they brought all sorts of treats including several big heavily smoked hams, canned green half-runner beans, corn, and sweet potatoes, and several bags of seed corn.

"My father warned me 'Don't plant this too early, because if a frost kills the sprouts I don't have enough to try again.' It was sweet corn from last year's crop, which had been the best they'd ever gotten. I gave them some homemade cheese and butter, which were the only things I had enough of at the farm to share. They said my brothers would be over in a few weeks to see how I'd weathered the winter.

"My father also told me that a coal company over in Jenkinsburg was hiring for a new mine at Deep Hollow. I knew that I could probably make enough money there to buy a new car or truck so I could get in and out of the farm. With a little bit of grading and culvert work, the road might possibly get to the point where I could cross the mountain in little more than an hour.

"A few weeks later I was a coal miner at the Deep Hollow #1 Mine. Work wasn't that difficult to find in those days, especially if you looked like you weren't afraid of working hard. That mine was also known as the 'Hightop' mine. The mine's nickname was just an ironic miners' joke. Deep Hollow Mine was what we call 'low coal.' The seam, while of high grade, was only 29 to 48 inches thick. It was encased between layers of glass-hard sandstone. Miners were forced to work all day on their knees, bent over with pick and shovel, sometimes in three or four inches of cold standing water. My bones ached each night as I drove that new pickup back over the mountain."

Junior realized even in those days that the secret to not being stuck underground for the rest of his life was to not alter his subsistence lifestyle. Most miners immediately started to spend their entire paychecks, living check to check. This was especially true for those with a family to support. Junior's one concession was his truck. After he made his payment on that, the rest of the money went into the bank. When the truck was paid off, he would quit the mine for good. Until then he would pray that none of the nightmares that plague miners, like mine gas, underground fires, roof falls, or the 'black damp' ever caught up with him.

His escape plan almost evaded him when he met Dorcas Givens. "She was as sweet and beautiful a blossom as these hills had ever produced." He gushed. "If she had wanted to live in town and raise her children there I would have gladly spent my life on my knees in some dark pit. Luckily, she was the daughter of a miner. She had seen one uncle crippled by falling rock and a young cousin killed in an underground gas explosion only weeks after following his father into the mines. She didn't want to have to spend the rest of her life wondering whether her babies' father was going to come home from work each day.

"When she saw the cabin she immediately fell in love with the place. I built a second room onto the side of the original cabin. It became her sewing room. She made beautiful quilts. She was legendary in the boutiques where she sent them to be sold to affluent city folk. I paid off the truck, married Dorcas, quit the mine, and became a full time farmer and 'wood hick' in June of my twenty-seventh year."

Life on the farm was not easy by any stretch. Every so often, as they saved a little money ahead of their bills, Junior would buy a little more land from the timber company that owned the thousands of acres of forest surrounding the farm. The land manager liked Junior and appreciated the fact that he was there to report fires and keep the road open. Once they established a price per acre, Junior had an ongoing understanding that he could buy as much land as he wanted at that price. The land agent, of course, realized that it would never be a large amount of land from a logging perspective. Junior would never have much money to spend.

Still, the farm grew steadily.

"I built a small sawmill and gradually logged the bottomland, which I turned into pasture, and selected trees, mostly red and white oaks, beech, and an occasional walnut, from the hillsides. I sold some of the lumber, but kept most for use around the farm. I built a large barn and added steadily onto the house.

"One day in springtime, Dorcas announced that she was pregnant. I was ecstatic and immediately set about building a room for the baby. Each child warranted another room. Then I constructed a classroom and library. We had four children, three sons and a daughter. Dorcas home schooled all of them until junior high. When they got to public school they were well ahead of their classmates in virtually every facet of their education and soon became honor students. All four went to the state university on scholarships, though the youngest boy's scholarship was for his football ability, not his academic performance. No family in this area had ever sent that many kids to the university." Junior was obviously very proud of his family.

"But my children hadn't been raised just by their mother and they weren't sheltered. Each one of them, including my daughter, could do any task or chore that farm life threw at them. They know how to cut, bale, and put up hay for the winter. If the tractor, rake, or bailer broke down, they could fix it laying on their backs in the middle of the furthest field in the pouring rain, if that was what it took to get the job done.

My daughter wanted to be a veterinarian. She showed an incredible talent with animals at an early age. The huge bull which she raised as a 4-H project would run her brothers out of the pasture at every opportunity, but would follow her around the farm like a puppy. When they tried their hand at raising sheep, she could help deliver breeched lambs from ewes that her brothers thought they would have to shoot to put out of their misery."

It was very saddening for Junior as they realized one by one that the farm could not support them all. They would have to go elsewhere and learn a new way of life. As they drifted away to college, the farm grew quiet. Dorcas and Junior would sit on the front porch of their now rambling but empty farmhouse and listen to the night sounds of the woods, fields, and river.

Occasionally they would hear a distant internal combustion engine and both simultaneously turn to look for headlights where the old dirt road came around the first switchback at the top of the ridge. They hoped it was one of their children, back from the city for an unannounced visit. Their door was always open. In fact, Junior had never installed a lock on any door at the farm. Usually, the sound was just a small aircraft flying over the hills, bound for points unknown.

Still, for all of them, and for all their lives, the farm was their anchor and roots. It was a safe place where they could always come when things got too crazy. It was a healing place and a place where hope and comfort and love lived.

Then the Government men came. They told Junior that soon the farm would be under twenty feet of water.

"Where are my kids to come home to now when their lives get too fast? They can't very well bring their families back to my little trailer sitting in a run-down trailer park. That's just not home. The dam is not even finished yet, but those bastards have already torn down my house and barn."

Ian promised, and meant it, that he would research all of the legal issues and precedent relating to government taking of private land. Overall, however, his initial appraisal was pessimistic. At *best* he *might*, if he could show improper conduct by the land agents, get the price paid for the land reexamined. Even that was a long shot. But that wasn't what Junior or the other old men from Tannery Bottom were after. They wanted their land, and not just any land. They wanted the lives that they had wrestled from the earth, that earth that flanked the Big Laurel Fork, back. Actually getting them their farms back was, as far as Ian could tell, impossible. Junior seemed to understand, but repeated that he had nothing to lose.

139

He shook Ian's hand slowly and firmly, and left.

The next day found Ian once again trying to get his office space shaped up for its eventual grand opening. He heard the front door open. It was Billy Caldwell, his landlord. With him was a heavyset man in a police uniform. Billy gave Ian a firm handshake, then introduced Cletus Hansen.

"How is the remodeling coming?" Billy asked, casting a quick and nervous glance around the room. It was obvious that interior design ideas were not what he was there for.

"Not too bad," came Ian's reply. "I'll probably have a handle on it before many clients see it. My client roster is still fairly limited." He gave Billy a modest grin.

"That's what we came to talk to you about," Billy continued. "The project manager at the Army Corps of Engineers up here above town asked me the other day if I knew of any local lawyers who could handle some ongoing property matters for them. You know, as civilian contractors on the project."

"Well," began Ian, a little hesitantly, "I obviously could use the work. Should I give him a call to see exactly what it is that he needs done, or does he want to call me? I should have a phone in here within a couple of days."

Billy grinned smugly. "We'll just have him call you directly in a few days. I don't think he has anything that he needs right away." He cast another nervous glance around the office, like he was looking for something. Maybe he had hoped for personal items that would give him some insight into Ian. There was nothing.

"Good luck with your practice. I have a feeling that you'll do real well around here." He and Cletus cast understated but stiff waives in Ian's direction as they pushed the door open to leave.

With that they were both gone. It was a short and not altogether comfortable meeting.

Outside, they began walking back toward the cement plant where Cletus's cruiser was parked. Cletus looked over toward Billy as they walked. "Do you really think that he'll be a problem?" he asked.

"There's only a few things that will bring a man who can afford a new Jaguar out here," Billy began. "More money is one of them. But this guy isn't here to open a coal mine, or drill for oil and gas, or even as a land man for a timber operation. He's not looking to

acquire an existing business like the sawmill or the charcoal plant.
"Some men move for a woman. He's seeing that good looking
waitress from down at the diner. She latched onto him as soon as
he hit town. But he didn't know her until he was already in town so
that's not why he's here. But, she's a dam-hater. Her daddy used to
come down here to fish. He was one of the most vocal opponents
of the whole flood control project.

"No, this guy had something big back in the city. He's come out
here to prove something, maybe just to himself. He probably wants
to be a one man Peace Corps. And he's been spending a lot of time
with that crazy Silas McGraw. No telling what crap Silas has put
into his head. If we give him a chance he's likely to try to save us
from ourselves."

Billy lifted his gaze from the dusty road to look Cletus in the face.
"And he's likely to go after that dam."

Cletus shook his head. "What can he do this late in the game? That
dam is almost complete. Do you really think he could stop the
project?"

"Not actually stop it," Billy replied, "but he could start throwing
up legal roadblocks. There's always a million government regula-
tions that no one notices until someone like him complains. Once
those issues get raised they can drag on in the courts for years. We
could both be in nursing homes eating oatmeal and stewed prunes
on social security and Medicare before that project got opera-
tional."

"So what are you thinking?" Cletus continued.

"Simple. The best way to neutralize a problem lawyer is to hire
him. We don't even have to fund it, now that the Army Corp
project manager has agreed to use him for little legal issues that
arise out of the project. He can't work for the project and against it
at the same time. Lawyers aren't allowed to do that. Even if they
were, he won't have that kind of time on his hands. We'll keep him
busy enough that he won't be a problem. Idle hands are the Devil's
workshop."

Billy was very pleased with himself.

CHAPTER FOURTEEN

"In that day a man shall cast his idols... to the moles and to the bats." Isaiah ii. 20.

"The answer, my friend, is blowing in the wind,

The answer is blowing in the wind." Bob Dylan

August was hot and dry this year. The cattle seldom strayed far from the shade of the trees and the cool water of the pond. The grass had quit growing and Silas was beginning to have his doubts about the second cut of hay that he had been hoping for. Probably no big deal unless it was a severe winter, but he would have liked a little cushion if he could get it.

Early one morning, before the heat of day melted the crispness out of the mountain air, he fired up the old Panhead and headed out of the valley. It was time for a road trip. Silas needed to get in the wind. The old hog had not been out for a putt in weeks. No big deal, it still fired on the second kick. The first kick was just to get its attention anyway. It wanted to run.

Silas threw some extra clothes in his saddlebags, grabbed some clear glasses in case he had to ride after dark, and headed into town. He stopped by the hardware store where he found Kathleen in heated debate with her father over the window display. It was virtually impossible to discern their relative positions on the matter, but it was clear that they both believed very strongly that their approach was the correct one. Silas stood in the doorway holding his helmet. Kathleen disappeared for a moment then reappeared with a helmet and her leather jacket.

"Do whatever you want Dad," she called behind as she headed out the door.

He and Silas exchanged raised eyebrows and knowing, resigned smiles. Silas swung the kick-start lever into position and gently brought a piston up to compression. With his hands on the handlebars, he rose up until he was fully extended above the sleeping hog, and came down with his whole weight on the lever. The big bike backfired and jumped to life. He climbed aboard, motioned for Kathleen to do the same. She did, and they were gone.

They headed for the high-road blacktop out of town. He had no particular destination in mind. The smells of town became the smells of the forest. The musky coolness of the deep hollows changed to the fresh breeziness of the ridge tops. They leaned in and out of sweeping curves and steep, sudden, kiss-your-ass switchbacks.

Forty-five minutes into the trip, Silas turned onto a steep dirt road. It climbed at a seemingly incredible gradient. Kathleen was sure that it was far too steep for a big old motorcycle like his to be attempting. It was all she could do to hang onto Silas, so she would not slide off the back. The bike steamed up the grade and into a high mountain meadow. The place was known locally as Bald Knob. It was one of several mountaintop "balds" in the area. Up there the constant wind and thin soil discouraged any vegetation bigger than grass, some wildflowers, and a few tortured shrubs from growing.

This particular bald hilltop was carpeted with a ten-acre meadow of blueberry bushes. Low and hardy, they were well adapted to withstand constant wind and thin soil. They were also heavy with fruit. Silas knew the berries would be ripe about now. Pulling a plastic quart jar out of his saddlebag, he and Kathleen filled it with sweet wild blueberries in a matter of minutes, even though every other handful that they picked went directly into their mouths. When they were done, they stood silent for a time marveling at the uninterrupted vista of green that stretched to the horizon. The afternoon haze was just beginning to obscure the most distant ridges, making the hills seem that much more expansive and untrammeled.

Silas produced bread, cheese and a bottle of Zinfandel wine. They picnicked in the sun.

"An old friend of mine first showed me this wine," explained Silas, certainly never the wine connoisseur. The friend, Smiley, was no connoisseur either, and did not care to be known as one. A beer drinker at heart, if he drank wine it was always the same kind.

"Smiley would explain that his mother was a big Polish woman, but that his father's people were tall mountain folk from the Dolomites in northern Italy. They were the descendants of barbarian Germanic invaders. He would lament that pussy yuppie suburbanites had slandered the name of this solid old wine by calling that wimpy pink shit ordered in bars by secretaries and stockbrokers, "Zinfandel." Smiley said his grandfather gave him his first glass at Thanksgiving dinner when he was five years old. It was deep dark red, heavy with flavor and a little bite. It was a no bullshit wine. It was the perfect wine for a live hard, ride hard guy like Smiley."

They toasted to Smiley, may he ride in peace. He was killed by a seventy year old woman with cataracts, who was talking to her daughter on the cell phone, when she made a left turn directly into the path of his motorcycle. That was over a year ago. Silas still thought of that son of a bitch almost every day.

"He'd have loved this place," Silas remarked to her as he gazed off into the distance.

"You can smell freedom in a place like this, real freedom, natural freedom, not just what politicians call freedom."

He told Kathleen the story of how he met Smiley and his "old lady," Dee, on a cold rainy night at Tiny's Bar. A night when all hell broke loose until the police came in with guns drawn.

Kathleen grimaced. "You mean to tell me that the first thing you did when you met him was knock him unconscious?"

"Yup, gave him a concussion." Silas looked into the wine bottle at the cork floating in circles.

"Brain damage must be a real male bonding thing," She rolled her eyes.

"Well, he grabbed me," Silas offered in his defense. "If I hadn't done something drastic his buddies would have kicked the living shit out of me. By the time we got out of the emergency room, Dee had straightened everything out."

"Figures that it took a women to straighten things out. I met my best friend, Lori, in the health and beauty aids section of the grocery store. We were both looking for the same brand of shampoo. We have been able to get to know each other pretty well without mortal combat." Kathleen was just inclined to mess with him.

Sensing an opportunity to move on to another subject, Silas stood up. "Time to ride." He turned and walked to the bike.

They cruised the back roads until dusk. Working their way back toward town, Silas turned onto another steep dirt road that ended in a high rocky field. He put down the kickstand and turned off the bike.

"This meadow was deep woods when I was very young. When I was in grade school there was an intense forest fire up here. You could see it from town. People said it was intentionally set to drive out snakes, but there never were many snakes up here. I think they were trying to drive away something else." He turned toward several huge chunks of almost-white limestone.

The first ledge was perhaps eight or ten feet high. Silas removed the leather saddlebags from his bike, shouldered them, and climbed up onto the rocks. Kathleen was only a few steps behind. At their backs, as they gazed out at yet another haunting vista of distant ridges and valleys, this one fading into the muted purples and grays of evening, was a three-story-high rock cliff. If they turned to face the cliff, their voices echoed back past them into the vastness. At the base of the cliff, almost unnoticeable to casual observers, was a dark hole roughly three feet in diameter. Silas knew from childhood that it was the door to a subterranean world that stretched, probably for miles, back into the limestone bowels of the mountain.

"When I was in high school, my friends and I used to come up here to watch the sun go down and test each other's courage. We would sit, as we're doing now, and wait for dusk."

"What happened at dusk?" Kathleen asked. This hadn't been part of *her* high school experience.

"You'll see. Just be patient."

Silas sat down in front of the opening. A cool breeze blew out of the earth. He could hear, or maybe feel, the awakening deep in the darkness. He had always wondered how they knew it was evening when, except in the first few feet of the cave, they were in eternal night.

As the sun set over the mountains, a palpable stirring began deep in the mountain. Thousands of eyes that had been closed in sleep, opened to total darkness. Thousands of tiny winged creatures, resting all day deep in the mountain, took flight at dusk in search of food. The deceptively small opening in the mountain became the muzzle of a living, breathing, pulsing bat gun. Sitting with their back to the winged onslaught, as hundreds of furry flying critters poured around their shoulders and into the night, was a unique test of teenage courage and composure. It was not much easier for adults.

An hour passed. Kathleen and Silas sat with their arms around each other and watched the last vestige of orange sun dip below the far horizon as thousands of little wing beats echoed in their ears. The immense power of mountain, and of the surreal moment that they had chosen to experience together, struck a chord in Silas's heart. Kathleen was no ordinary woman. She had the strength to be his partner. They kissed. She watched the mass of bats, which parted neatly to fly around them, come back together only a few yards from their faces before disappearing into the thickening darkness.

"Far fucking out," she whispered in his ear. She made a tiny, high-pitched bat-squeak and bit it gently.

CHAPTER FIFTEEN

"Whatsoever thy hand findest to do, do it with thy might."
Ecclesiastes ix. 10.

"The legitimate powers of government extend to such acts
only as are injurious to others." Thomas Jefferson

"They that give up essential liberty to obtain a little temporary
safety deserve neither liberty nor safety." Benjamin Franklin

The black bull had turned up at Ian's door again. It preferred the
grass right in front of his steps to anything in the entire river
bottom. Cletus eyed it from the safety of the porch. Could not
blame him, the damn thing was big as a truck. It was at times like
this that Ian wished Silas would break down and get a phone.
Luckily, the bull seemed unconcerned with Ian and Cletus. They
slipped past him and headed for Silas's to let him know that they
had The Beef in their yard. Of course, last time this had happened
Silas just smiled and noted that he would go back to the field with
the rest of the cattle as soon as he got horny. By the time Ian had
gotten home, the bull was back in the pasture chasing heifers.
The front door of Silas's farmhouse was ajar. Nothing unusual for
Silas. He could be anywhere. His bike was leaning on its kickstand
under the shed roof beside the barn. His rusted and dented Dodge
Power Wagon pickup sat where he last unloaded it, in front of the
barn. Ian stuck his head in the front door.
"Hey Silas. You home?"
He was obviously home. His stereo blared reggae music. Jimmy
Cliff sang, "As sure as the sun will shine, I'm going to get it, what's
mine. And then the harder they come the harder they fall, one and
all."
The voice drifted back from the dark basement stairwell.
"I'll be up in a minute."
Ian slipped through the screen door and pulled it behind him to
keep Cletus on the porch. He headed down the shaky wooden
stairs into the basement. It was just a single large dirty room with a
pile of stove coal in one corner. A long workbench of oil stained

two by sixes under a long fluorescent light sat against the longest wall.

On the bench were two plastic five gallon buckets which once held drywall joint compound. Spread out around them were multiple blue paper or plastic wrapped cylinders, little metal cans that were threaded as if to be screwed together, bits of wire and other electrical components. Silas stood with his back to Ian.

"I'll be right up, Ian," he said without any hint of irritation. He was silent for a moment then added, "You really don't need to see this."

"Maybe I didn't see it," Ian suggested. "What are you doing?" Silas just shrugged. He was not talking.

"Is this one of those 'if I tell you I'll have to kill you' things?" Ian challenged.

"No," Silas shrugged again, "but you *would* become an accessory before the fact. Right now you have no reason to think that there is anything illegal going on here." He glanced back over his shoulder.

"Explosives?" Ian offered tentatively. It was really only a guess.

"You already know that I am a third generation blaster. I have a rocky farm and multiple entirely legitimate reasons to be using explosives. Don't ask any more questions and you will never have to lie about what you saw." Silas still had his back to Ian.

Ian rolled his eyes. At least he now knew what he was looking at. "You know that it just isn't my nature to not ask questions. I need to *know* things."

"Tell you what," Silas turned to face him. "Sleep on this. If you still need to know more tomorrow, I'll answer any questions you have."

Ian grimaced and shook his head slowly. He turned away. "Your bull is grazing in my yard again," was all he said.

That night sleep did not come easy for Ian. Since moving to the farm and adopting the simple life (he was still sleeping in a sleeping bag six months after his move) he had finally stopped having his "treading water" dreams, including those bloody shark attack ones. Cynthia had advised him that their divorce was final. That probably helped. He was finally beginning to heal. Order was returning to his life.

He told Lori about the three men in the trailers. She assured him that there was nothing he could do. He mentioned the visit from

150

Junior to Silas. Silas had just shaken his head and remarked that the legal system is just another part of the same government that took the land in the first place.

He desperately wanted to know what Silas was up to, but deeply feared that it might destroy his tenuous hold on tranquility.

Silas, as much as Ian had come to like and respect him, had a strong undercurrent of revolution in his psyche. Not far beneath his quiet exterior, he harbored the stoic resolute heart of a holy warrior. Except that Ian knew Silas was not driven by the fever of fanaticism. Dogma, especially religious dogma, had no appeal to him. Nor did the petty jealousies of more secular causes. He harbored no envy for the worldly "success" of others. In fact, he firmly believed that his way of life was vastly superior to that of most unfortunate souls who had chosen to face rush hour twice a day, and was genuinely thankful for that fact. Silas was just a very strong soul who would never allow himself to be pushed too far. The fact that Silas was relentlessly logical but driven by immutable principle made him inherently dangerous. If plan "A" did not work, he naturally would move onward to plan "B," "C," and so on. If his alternatives crossed onto forbidden ground, Ian knew Silas would follow them to where ever he felt necessary.

Ian was sure he was up to something. Did he have financial problems? Was there some little local bank that was going to get its vault blasted? Ian knew he could not be making much money but that did not seem his style. Perhaps an age-old grudge or family legacy that needed responded to? A debt from the motorcycle club days?

The next morning, not long after dawn, Ian looked out his window and saw Silas stretching wire across the gaping hole in the fence line between their fields. The black bull grazed placidly less than thirty feet away from him. Ian pulled on his work boots, fumbled with the laces, and trotted across the river bottom.

"Good morning," he began. "I have to know what that was all about. That shit yesterday." He stopped well shy of Silas, suddenly cautious of crowding him or the bull.

Silas was twisting wire around a locust post. "It's not that easy to explain," he began. He looked up briefly, then back down at his work. He lifted a foot and kicked the bull, which was now crowd-

151

ing him from behind, solidly in the flank with the bottom of his boot. The bull nonchalantly moved half a dozen feet away. It never quit grazing.

"I used to have dreams. They began when I came back from Vietnam. In one, a bloody Vietnamese woman held up two dead infants. In another, a young boy with a crutch dragged his severed leg with his free hand. In each dream, they look at me not with anger, but with shock, surprise, and a sad, pleading expression. It was like they thought I could have prevented it.

"But I was just a soldier. I was as stuck in that war as they were. Helping them in any direct sense was, of course, not what I was there for. Once, in real life, I was surprised by a Viet Cong soldier who had been hiding just inside a tunnel opening as I walked past. Luckily I heard, or maybe *felt*, something that made me spin around. I shot him just as he was about to pull the trigger. He had that same look in his eyes as he died.

"Government does funny things. Thomas Paine said that even in its best state, it is only a necessary evil. In its worst state, it is an intolerable one. Government decides, generally without asking you, that something is good for us and goes ahead and does it. But its will is that of the majority, or worse yet, the powerful. The minority, and I'm not just talking so-called minority groups, get overlooked.

Did you know that over one half of all Americans now live in cities of over a million people? "How much voice does that leave country people in the halls of Congress? We built this country, but we are becoming nothing more than a comedic stereotype used to market patent medicines and corny family restaurants.

"As long as city-assholes want more electric appliances and toys, and keep erecting office buildings with windows that don't even open, and continue to insist on 70 degree air all year around, families will be run off their land and wild mountain rivers will be turned into dead still lakes or diverted through steel pipes.

"My father and grandfather lived off this land. Maybe they even exploited its resources a little bit. But they believed and taught me that we have a responsibility to the earth to treat it with respect. If we don't, we have no right to expect it to provide for us. They weren't churchgoers, but they felt that God was all around us in the natural things He created.

"Today we delude ourselves into thinking meddling with nature makes the world a better place to live. Our so-called leaders lead the way in proposing and funding this bullshit. They take credit for short-term economic activity, then move on before the long term natural effects become apparent.

"Are we expected, as rural people, to do what the Indians did? Are we supposed to get out of the way of progress? You *know* what resisting did for them." Silas looked up and moved to the next post. He kept twisting tie wires. They would have to hold the fence together against the almost certain test by the bull. For now the bull was quiet and apparently content.

"I've been having dreams again lately. In these dreams a well-dressed waiter brings me a silver tray with silver tea service. I'm wearing a black tux, and I've never worn a tux in my life. I'm holding a clear glass cup. The waiter pours me a full cup of blood." Silas's body language was becoming more agitated.

"Not many people know this, so keep it to yourself, but this farm doesn't have to support me. My wife was killed in a medical accident. I'm sure you understand how the legal system deals with that sort of thing. By the time the suing was done, I never had to work again. The dreams might just mean that I feel guilty about living off of her death. But death is part of the story of my life. It is part of all our lives, but people around me seem to have a harder time than most."

A strand of rusty barbed wire sprung loose from the staple holding it down. He snatched it in mid-flight and tacked it back to the locust post.

"Watch yourself," Silas looked up briefly. His face bore a look of resignation.

"I've been brought back here and allowed to get attached to this place and these people again for some reason well beyond my control, or even understanding. I've got to take that seriously." He looked up again.

"Do you really want to hear any more of this?"

Ian was not sure he cared for this. Silas was being far too intense. He preferred the relaxed, rough, basically stable, hillbilly-biker side of Silas. That Silas was scary enough. Unfortunately, he *did* want to know more. He nodded yes.

"Well, it's like *this*," Silas stood up and pointed up the valley. "That fucking dam up there is coming *down*." He spoke surprisingly coolly. His words were the product of reflection and conviction, not anger.

"I'm not exactly sure how, I'm not sure when, but I'm taking it out. It is an affront to nature and to the people of this valley. It is as much a form of political oppression as armed soldiers pointing rifles in our faces. It is a criminal act against the local way of life and a constant reminder that we are not important in the greater scheme of things."

Shock, perhaps fear, must have shown in Ian's eyes.

"You know what you're proposing is an act of terrorism," he blurted.

"Not by a long shot," exclaimed Silas, shaking his head in calm, muted frustration. Ian was clearly missing the point. "Terrorism is an attempt to control people by fear. It is an amoral gesture aimed at causing a governmental response by harming innocent people. I don't intend to hurt anyone.

"That is why I have to do something soon, before they fill that lake. Once there is water behind the dam I can't touch it because people *would* be hurt. I just want the project to go away. It is living on pure bureaucratic inertia. If I can damage it just enough that it requires another round of legislative appropriations, it may die of its own bloated pork-barrel wastefulness.

"At worst, what I am thinking about is vandalism. At best, it is an expression of an American tradition, resistance to the tyranny of those who exercise power without authorization from the people. Like a Boston Tea Party."

He eased back into story telling mode.

"My father taught me how to handle explosives at an early age. We used to go up on the hillside above the river. We would take a box of dynamite, some wire, and a car battery with us. He would select rocks of various sizes for me to move, split, or vaporize. He would tell me what he wanted done and I would have to decide how much explosive to use for what he wanted. If he just wanted a rock moved a few feet, but I shattered it, he would lecture me on calculating the charge and setting it to get the desired response. My favorite game was to try to loft rocks from the steep hillside into the river without shattering them. The hard sandstone on this farm will actually take quite a shock before it breaks.

"I know all the blasters for all the coal companies within fifty miles. My father knew their fathers. They were his fishing buddies. I also know where every one of them stores their stuff, their supplies. The cans of gel explosive you saw yesterday disappeared a little at a time from the powder houses of several different coal companies. Hopefully, they slipped under the law enforcement radar screen. I am not aware of anyone making any reports of missing explosives."

"Won't you need a lot more than what I saw?" Ian asked. "Do you have a plan?"

Silas did not answer him directly. He gazed at the distant mountainside, his eyes climbing to the ridge-top then following it to the horizon.

"These mountains have always been full of surprises. Especially for those who think they can do whatever they want because they have the force of governmental authority on their side." Ian could see that he was winding up for a major explanation.

"Lets look at a little Appalachian history," Silas began, drawing himself into a professorial stance.

"Once upon a time, up in Pennsylvania, where they refer to these hills as the Laurel Highlands, a Brit general by the name of Braddock, and thirteen hundred of King George's best armed and trained regular soldiers, were trounced by less than three hundred Indians, farmers, and French fur trappers. They opened up on the red-coated British from behind every rock and tree.

"The British were taught that the only way to fight a proper battle was to stand in formation in the open and fire upon the enemy. The woodsmen killed most of the soldiers and officers, and scattered the survivors. The General himself was severely wounded and died within a few days. George Washington, whose Virginia command was marching with Braddock, was one of the survivors. Four bullets passed through his coat in the course of the battle.

"Over a hundred years later, in the Civil War, or the War of Northern Aggression as my grandfather used to call it, the eastern slope of the Blue Ridge was defended by a band of irregular troops. They referred to themselves as Partisan Rangers, and were organized under a Confederate law allowing militia groups. They were led by a small wiry gentleman who had been a country lawyer before the war. His name was John Singleton Mosby. His specialty was fighting behind Union lines. He made swift night raids against whatever Union targets he felt would have the most impact. His men furnished their own guns, food, horses, and uniforms. They did not keep a common camp, but stayed wherever people would take them in. They would meet up for a mission, then disband and scatter once it was done.

"In 1863, with 29 men, he rode into Fairfax Court House, Virginia, and captured 100 Union soldiers, 58 horses, all their supplies, and Brigadier General Edwin H. Stoughton, who Mosby roused from his sleep with a slap on the butt. A year and a half later Major General Philip Sheridan sent a special unit of 100 elite soldiers armed with Spencer repeaters, the best weapons available at that time, to hunt down and destroy Mosby. All but two of that unit were killed or captured by Mosby's men.

"His men were declared outlaws by the Union and several were captured and hanged without trial. Mosby returned the gesture by capturing and hanging an equal number of Brigadier George Custer's cavalry soldiers. Then he sent Custer a letter explaining that Union soldiers captured in the future would, of course, be afforded the respect due prisoners of war unless the Union army insisted on committing further acts of barbarism.

"Grant later ordered the burning of an entire Virginia county and the arrest of all men under age fifty in a vain attempt to stop Mosby's guerillas. Mosby never surrendered, he just disbanded his group after the war ended. Surprise had been his greatest weapon and anonymity his shield.

The independence and obstinacy bred in these mountains didn't end with that war. It is still passed father to son in hills and hollows the length of these Appalachians.

The Civil War wasn't the last time the government turned its guns on us hillbillies.

"In 1921 a group of unemployed coal miners returned fire on a trainload of U.S. Army troops at a place called Blair Mountain. They were ready to take on Uncle Sam himself if he didn't quit siding with the coal barons and recognize their right to properly feed and house their families. Many of the miners had been living with their families in tents in the woods because they had been thrown out of coal company housing for trying to start a union. "You don't hear much about the Battle of Blair Mountain these days. It was an inconvenient piece of history. Even the United Mine Workers union doesn't focus on that part of its heritage." Silas was not done making his point. He just kept twisting wires and occasionally pounding another tack into the weathered locust posts.

"Life in these hills is about the long haul. Mountain people may scare occasionally but they don't run. You might fool them once, but they stay, and they remember. They will be there waiting for you if you ever come back around. And they will be prepared.

"These mountains make you hard headed. They teach you that you are responsible for your own life. They teach you not to fear pain, because pain is an inescapable part of life. If an outsider wants to take something important away from you, it's going to take more than the threat of a little pain or hardship. We are real comfortable with hardship. They had better be ready for a fight. When mountain people fight back, they fight back bitterly. When the land is the most important thing to a person, you can't beat him as long as he is still on the land. You can take everything else he has away from him and he'll still keep fighting you to his last breath.

"It was like that in Vietnam. The most powerful nation the world has ever known, with enough nuclear weaponry to shatter this planet, couldn't control the destiny of a country full of stone-age rice farmers. We couldn't blow them up. We couldn't burn them out. If we rounded them up and moved them to the city where we thought we could control them, they would sneak back into the countryside, no matter how hard we bombed it. Parts of that country aren't much different than the hills around here, just hotter." Silas looked up and smiled wryly. He shook his head. "We are not weak if we make a proper use of those means which the God of Nature has placed in our power...The battle, sir, is not to the strong alone, it is to the vigilant, the active, the brave." Silas smiled again, pleased that he remembered the quote.

"Patrick Henry said that. Remember, our revolutionary soldiers were fighting for their land, on their land, and were led by the same Virginian who saw what a bunch of untrained hill people could do to the King's professional soldiers back when he marched with General Braddock."

Silas reflected for a moment, then added, "What you saw wouldn't dent that dam." He also could see that he had Ian thinking.

"I need you to be patient." After an uncomfortably long silence, he asked, "Does this mean you're willing to help me?"

To suggest that Ian was uncomfortable would be a massive under-statement. He knew better than most people that only a few thousand years of civilization separated Silas from the most powerful of the killer apes. This primal aggression became pal-pable when Silas felt he had a calling that needed answering. Ian could easily picture Silas standing over some much physically larger prey he had just dispatched with a single well placed bite through its spinal cord. He also knew that Silas preferred to hunt alone.

Ian dodged the question. "I still haven't heard from you about your plan. Do you actually have one?"

Silas shrugged. "I guess I do, but it's not very complicated. It's actually pretty simple."

"No problem with that. If years of law practice have taught me anything, it's that the truth is usually simple. It's treachery that gets complicated."

Ian told Silas about his visit from Junior Harper. Then he remem-bered that he had already told Silas about the visit. He really just wanted to move on to a new subject. Silas played along.

"I knew he'd be around to see you. You're a lawyer. People come to you with legal problems. Like when the law is being used to steal from them. Around here the law has always been used to steal from people. Land, mineral or timber rights, whatever they had that was valuable."

"I don't think there is a legal solution to this one," Ian ventured, more to remind himself of that fact than to try to convince Silas of anything.

"That is because the *law* always protects the money, the political power brokers, the *status quo*. Not the man struggling to scratch a living out of a ragged mountain farm. There is something very wrong with the law. It is the fox in the henhouse." Silas was starting to get worked up again.

Then Ian figured, what the hell, he'd also tell Silas about the visit from Billy and Cletus. He was not surprised by Silas's reaction to that news.

"Those motherfuckers," he swore in a controlled, almost amused, way. "Those sons of bitches have got you pegged as a possible problem. They know that you associate with me. They know that Lori's father was active in trying to stop that dam. They probably even know that Junior approached you. That was their run at preempting and disarming you. If they can retain you to do legal work for the Corps, you can't work against the project because you would then have a conflict of interest."

Ian knew Silas was right. Once again Silas startled him with an unexpected degree of legal sophistication. That was, of course, exactly why they approached him and why he hadn't pushed for a more definite commitment out of Billy that day at the office. He needed time to think the situation through.

What Ian was faced with was basically a choice between making real money that would feed him and pay his bills for steady, easy and routine work versus taking on a questionably noble cause which he had no chance of winning and which would sour his relationship with the only potentially paying clientele in town. Why should *that* be such a tough decision?

Ian answered in the only way that he felt he could under the circumstances.

"I reserve the right to get the hell away from whatever crazy bullshit scheme you are hatching but, for now, *yes*, I will do whatever I can to help. And," Ian muttered through a contorted grin, "of course, I'll take whatever I know to the grave."

Damn. God help those who find a *cause*.

He could appreciate why revolutions are often fought by people who have little to lose. Comfort makes you cautious for fear of losing it. But Silas's quote of Patrick Henry reminded him that the American Revolution was precipitated by people who had a great deal to lose. Many of them lost everything including loved ones and personal wealth to see this country freed from the control of a foreign government. What if our own government is so out of touch with the needs of its people that it is no better to its citizenry than a foreign overlord? Is it then time to take up arms? Was that what Silas was suggesting? Ian knew how his actions would be interpreted. Sure, he was focused on property, not human lives or overthrow of the government, but the legal system would not recognize that distinction. His actions posed a terrible threat to the great societal need for order and stability. If he was caught, the police and prosecutors would willingly take up that banner and the jury would do the rest. Ian was still personally wrestling with the distinction between self help and eco-terrorism.

It really did not matter since the psycho SOB would probably get them both blown up anyway. This had all the allure of being asked to participate in a holy war. Just strap on the explosives and answer the call. Silas had proven himself to be a damn good recruiter. If Ian was not blown to bits, he might get the opportunity to become the subject of a major criminal investigation. There was the obvious possibility of jail time, lots of jail time. Quite possibly all of the rest of his God-allotted time.

He could almost picture himself in orange coveralls. At least in a holy war they guarantee you access to heaven if you are killed. And the promise of being met there by multiple virgins. No virgins in the federal penal system. Not for long.

He wandered back to the house where Cletus waited. The dog barked impatiently. It was time for his breakfast.

Silas realized that he had just given Ian the power to destroy him. He hoped he would not regret it.

About two hours flying time from Lisbon, Portugal there are nine small islands, the Azores. On one of the smaller islands, Graciosa, a small boy was playing in a vineyard. He looked out across the nearby sea and watched as rain clouds blew toward him from over the vestigial headwaters of the Gulf Stream.

"Another day with a taste of all the seasons," he thought, using a common expression in those islands. The rain began within minutes. Just in time, he ran to the shelter of the vineyard tool shed. It was a warm steady shower that refused to let up. Eventually he gave up waiting for it to pass and walked home in the rain.

CHAPTER SIXTEEN

"The noise of many waters."   Psalm xciii. 4.
"Are we having fun yet?" Zippy The Pinhead

The next week was dazzling in its normalcy. The heat of summer
had passed, replaced by the cool still nights of early autumn. The
sumac at the fringes of the meadow had already turned bright red-
orange in anticipation of coming changes. For several wet days fog
hung thick along the river and rose in gauze-like sheets from the
water. The dry days had the Technicolor brilliance that announces
the approach of fall.

One such day Ian saw Silas cross the fields with a bucket and a
stick. Curious, he wandered down to the river. There he saw Silas
crawling across the top of a flat, house-sized boulder. The stick
was a fishing rod. He held it out from his side. At the end of the
line was a fish about ten inches long. Had he just caught it? Then
why was he crawling towards the water? Ian suspected that it was
best to sit down and watch from where he was, thirty yards away.
Silas crawled right up to the edge of the rock where it overhung
the river. A small logjam adorned its upstream face. He gently
swung the big creek chub just upstream of the logs. It drifted back
toward him. The minnow swam deep, toward the perceived safety
of the waterlogged brush and driftwood.

Suddenly Silas's fishing rod doubled back on itself from the savage
strike of something very powerful. He jumped to his feet, the butt
end of the rod jammed firmly into his belly. He leaned back,
cranking against the reel's screaming drag, as a huge fish steamed
out of its lair under the log pile and headed upstream across the
pool. By now, Ian had climbed up onto the rock. Looking down
into the deep green water he could see a massive dark form
swimming quickly but smoothly across the river.

"Holy shit, that thing's a monster!" Ian skipped the social niceties
of greeting.

Silas reciprocated. "Muskellunge. I noticed him hanging out under
the edge of this rock one day when we were all swimming here. I
didn't figure that he'd leave. They generally pick a home and stay

161

there. They just wait in the shadows and eat anything that wanders too close." The fish made strong runs from one end of the pool to another, fifty or sixty yards at a time. Each run was a little less powerful than the one before it.

Finally, after about an hour, Silas slipped him onto a sandy spot on the riverbank. The musky was probably five feet long. Its mouth had enough sharp teeth to give Ian reservations about ever swimming in the river again. It looked like a barracuda that had bulked out from steroids and pumping iron. Silas bent down and wiggled the big chrome hook loose from its jaw, easing the fish back into the water.

As the fish turned toward deep water, a powerful stroke of its tail covered Silas with cold river water.

Silas yelled at it in mock threat, "Next time I'll filet your slimy ass!" He was grinning ear to ear.

Ian congratulated him. "Incredible fish! Why didn't you keep him?"

"A fish like that isn't anyone's to keep. He's the king of this piece of the river. You've got to respect him. It was an incredible stroke of good fortune to even be able to fight him. I've never gotten one to shore before. Maybe he'd become careless because he was big enough that he had run out of natural predators. Otherwise, he'd have eyed that big minnow with the chrome gizmo sticking out of it and let it swim past. Next time he'll probably do just that."

Ian wondered if Silas was talking about more than fishing. Just as that fish had become complacent so perhaps had the people who Silas saw as his enemies. They were fat and powerful and felt safe from challenge. His recent conversations with Silas about historical mountain battles reminded him of an almost forgotten college research paper on third world warfare he had once authored for a political science course. It was clear to Ian that Silas saw himself as a guerilla soldier.

Ian had written that an effective guerilla warrior is more in touch with the local conditions and populace than the official government. He appears and disappears as opportunities present themselves, often fading back into civilian roles or otherwise mingling with local noncombatants. His battles tend to be ambushes because he is generally outnumbered and poorly equipped compared to his opponents. His meager forces can't afford many casualties. Surprise is his great equalizer. He is absolutely dependent on the support, however covert, of the people among whom he is maneuvering. If he has that support he has a chance of surviving and driving out his enemy. If his opponent underestimates him his chances are that much better. Silas had witnessed the infuriating irrepressibility of the Vietcong. He understood such things on a physical level, probably far better than Ian ever could.

That evening Silas, Kathleen, Ian, and Lori did the fifty-mile trip to the nearest movie theater. They watched an action film about a guy who had lost his land to a conspiracy between corrupt government officials and a big real estate developer. The hero put up a great fight. He was smart, strong and, naturally, morally right, but ended up taking a police bullet in the back. Ian found it more unsettling than he would have a few weeks earlier. They all vowed to do another double date the next Friday night. This time they would let the women pick the movie.

Lori stayed at Ian's that night. In the morning he pointed out his new television set. It had a built-in video tape player.

"Oh, great, we can rent movies," she observed. "I want to get some porn."

"Oh, do we need something to spice up our relationship already?" He asked, giving her the Sideways Glance.

"No, not at all," she assured him. "It would just be, well, *inspirational.*" She giggled girlishly, and quickly flashed one breast from beneath her bathrobe. Ian turned to hug her, sliding both hands inside and under the robe and pulling her breasts against his bare chest. He was marveling at how well his life had been going lately. He was hoping that it was not a last beautiful flourish like the bright leaves of October.

What Ian was really fishing for was some recognition for having successfully installed the television antenna high in the top of the huge white oak behind the house. He had risked his life to get into the uppermost branches of that massive tree. The antenna was at least three times the height of the house roof and was actually able to pick up a few signals, even down in this hole between the mountains.

He turned on the TV. They made love on his battered sofa while a

163

television weatherman babbled about Hurricane Margaret. It had developed over open tropical Atlantic waters into a class five storm and was headed toward Bermuda packing winds of over one hundred and fifty miles per hour.

CHAPTER SEVENTEEN
"They have sown the wind, and they shall reap the whirlwind."

Hosea viii. 7.

"For extreme diseases extreme strictness

Of treatment is most efficacious." Hippocrates

The weekend brought an early frost. Nature was preparing to clean house for the year. All her plants and creatures had enjoyed their opportunity to grow and play. They had created a great teaming, seething, fertile mess. It was time to regroup. The plants got one last sugary hit of autumn sunshine. Animals scrambled for food, a little extra fat would not hurt now. It would be a long winter, very few would actually have the luxury of sleeping all the way through it. Next spring the survivors would get a fresh new start.

Looking out of the bedroom window, Lori saw the white coating on the grass in the shadows between Ian's house and the river. The morning sun had already banished it from the open areas. She commandeered Ian's canvas jacket from his closet.

"What about me, I'm freezing," he protested, throwing an armload of cordwood into the still cold woodstove.

"Hush, chivalry isn't dead until I say it is," came her reply as she wrapped the jacket around her.

The sun soon took full control of the day. Although only a few trees, mostly low-lying maples and shrubs, had begun to turn colors, there was obviously autumn in the air. Even the river ran vividly clear, its rocky bottom gleaming through the aquarium-like transparency. In another two weeks the trees would be at their peak of color. Soon after that the mountains would settle into the muted browns and grays of winter.

Silas and Kathleen came roaring up to the farmhouse's front porch in the old Power Wagon. Cletus ran in front of it barking, then jumped hastily out of the way when his barking failed to slow it down.

"Breakfast in town?" asked Kathleen from the passenger side.

"Sure, let me put shoes on," answered Lori.

"After breakfast, Ian and I had better put up some more firewood," suggested Silas. "There are a couple downed hickories behind the barn. We'll get several truckloads out of them."

Everyone piled into the Power Wagon for the trip to town. Four across the cab was tight and very cozy. Kathleen slapped Silas's hand every time he had to move the gearshift lever, which she was straddling. Cletus barked at squirrels from his vantage point in the truck bed.

At breakfast, Silas noticed three guys sitting at the counter. They were all wearing Preston Powder Company patches on their shirt pockets. Several large white trucks bearing the company logo filled one whole end of the parking lot. He could overhear them talking about the dam. They were saying that a big push was on because construction was well behind schedule.

Lori and Kathleen walked home from the diner while Ian and Silas headed back upriver. There was firewood to cut. Midway through cutting up the first tree, Silas turned off his chainsaw. Ian was carefully pouring gasoline mix into his.

"Did you notice the tanker trucks at breakfast?" Silas asked.

"Trucks, no," Ian responded innocently. They were big enough that he could not have missed them. He just had not paid attention.

"There were three tanker trucks. They belonged to Preston Powder. Probably filled with ammonium nitrate."

Ian still had the look cows give a passing train. He clearly did not appreciate the significance.

"Let me tell you a story," Silas said. "Once, not long ago, in a little local feed store, a clerk received a shipment of ammonia-based fertilizer. This clerk's uncle was behind on his farm payments. He needed to get a good crop out of the land that year or he might lose it. Figuring that the worst that could happen to him would be that he might get fired, the clerk diverted that fertilizer to his uncle's farm.

"Well, unknown to him, the feed storeowner was watching closely for that fertilizer. When it didn't come in on the day he expected it he called the shipper, who reported it as stolen. The next day the whole town was crawling with FBI agents.

"Seems a little crazy doesn't it?

What the clerk didn't realize is that when you mix that stuff with diesel fuel you get a very powerful explosive called ANFO. Ammonium Nitrate and Fuel Oil. ANFO is a workhorse explosive. It is slow, stable and relatively safe. It has to be triggered by another, faster explosive. If you think of dynamite as a thoroughbred racehorse, ANFO is a big load-dragging Belgian. It's the same stuff, basically, that you use to blow the top off a mountain if you're strip-mining coal.

"Or it could make rubble out of a government building. Hence the FBI. It is a Big Deal when a truckload of that stuff disappears. The clerk almost got sent to prison just for being an idiot.

"There were three trucks and three drivers at the diner. I doubt they can actually use that much explosive in one day. My guess is they will empty one truck and all ride back in that truck. The other two will sit at the construction site until there is more blasting to do. That means there could be two tankers full of explosive at the dam site right now."

"What are you getting at?" Ian asked, dreading the answer.

"Nothing yet, but they won't leave that kind of firepower lying around for very long," came Silas's reply.

"Oh shit," thought Ian. He had missed most of what Silas was intending to say because he saw a deep unrest in his friend's eyes. It was like looking down into the steaming crater of a sleeping volcano. Fear might be too strong a word, but it left him uneasy.

The week came and went. Silas was nowhere to be seen. Ian put in some time around his office. He wrote two basic wills for people who did not have much to pass to their kids except a little rocky ground and a few animals. Knowing that their kids would have the land, and the opportunity that it represented, meant as much to those people as if it had been a thousand producing oil wells on a ten thousand acre cattle ranch.

At lunchtime on Monday, Ian was sitting at the counter in the diner talking to Lori. Officer Cletus walked in and took the stool next to him. They exchanged a few social niceties. Sometime after they covered the local weather report and the approach of small game hunting season, they began talking about Ian's role as the town lawyer.

Cletus made the observation, "it must be difficult not being able to choose the people you have to defend."

167

Ian, of course, wondered what he was getting at. Cletus could not effect a smooth transition to a sensitive subject to save his life. Ian played along.

"It's not so bad. All lawyers are taught, early on, that every individual has a constitutionally guaranteed right to be represented by a competent attorney. It's the attorney's job to plead the person's case in the manner most favorable to the client. So long as you do that, the fact that the client's actions may not give you much to work with is just part of the dance."

Cletus shook his head. "I arrested a local punk, Jared Smithers, for shoplifting and possession of a concealed firearm this morning. It's the third time I've grabbed that sticky fingered little bastard. He was about to walk out of Old Man Jennings' gas station with a pocket full of disposable cigarette lighters. He paid for a soda and a bag of cookies but said he forgot about the lighters. And he had a .22 pistol in his pocket. Said he was going camping. I think he's smoked so much dope over the years that he just thinks the rest of us are as stupid as he is."

Ian just smiled and stared at his soup. Hopefully, Jared would get a court appointed lawyer. Some *other* lawyer. Unfortunately, as the only lawyer in town he was likely to be hearing from the court very soon.

Cletus did not let it drop. "He'll say that I didn't Mirandize him before he gave his explanation of why he had the lighters."

Ian could not stand it. He raised one eyebrow. "Did you?"

"Did I what?"

"Did you forget to read him his Miranda rights?"

Cletus did not answer. He just sat there looking frustrated.

"I should know better than talk around a lawyer."

"Well, you know if I get the appointment I'm ethically bound to use anything you tell me that might be helpful to my client in his defense. I don't think I'd worry too much though. As much criminal law as I have practiced in the last ten years, the worst thing that could happen to Jared is getting me for his lawyer."

Ian could not help but think the real reason that boy was sitting in jail was probably because his family had no money for bail, or even a bondsman's ten percent.

Cletus finished his sandwich and left. Kathleen came in and sat on the same stool at the counter.

"Do you know a guy named Jared Smithers?" he asked her.

"Sure, that's Allens' kid brother. I went to high school with Allen."

"Tell me what you know about him."

"Just plain folks. Not much special you can say about them," came her reply, punctuated with a noncommittal shrug of her shoulders. At that point both Ian and Lori leaned over close to Kathleen. Her description had been so bland and uncharacteristic of her that they immediately suspected she was holding out on them. They both stared at her until she realized she was caught.

"Ok, ok, ok," she began, shaking her head in mock irritation.

"They aren't bad people, just real red, if you know what I mean. The kid is a sweet kid, but dumb as a stump. And he's been a little sticky fingered since he was very young. It is his way of getting attention. I just keep my eye on him when he's in the store. On several occasions, I've made him empty his pockets. He just smiles because he knows that you are on to him, and puts the stuff back. It's always little things like nuts and bolts, and blanks for his blank pistol."

"His what?" Ian interjected.

"His blank pistol. He always carries a starter's pistol. He likes the noise. He shoots at birds and rabbits with blanks, just to scare them. He's a little *different*."

"Cletus arrested him this morning for shoplifting and for having that gun on him. He probably never realized it was just a blank pistol."

"I bet Cletus knew it was a blank gun. He's hated that kid for years, ever since the day Cletus thought he saw Jared letting the air out of his cruiser's tires. He couldn't prove it because he yelled and Jared took off. Cletus couldn't move that beer belly fast enough to run him down in a million years and Jared knew it. What the kid didn't realize was that Cletus never forgives or forgets.

"His older brother Allen isn't too much smarter, but he has a good heart and was the best quarterback our high school ever had. I dated him for part of my senior year, but we drifted apart when I went off to college. He's a truck driver these days. I haven't seen him in over a year.

"Is that enough? Do you two want to know any more?"

Ian and Lori seemed satisfied with the expanded explanation. Kathleen turned away from Ian, leaned very close to Lori and whispered softly. "And he is *huge*."

Lori tried to hold back her gasping laugh, which came out as a snort. She quickly turned away from the counter. Ian looked up and raised one eyebrow. He had not heard the comment but Kathleen's delivery was such that it did not take a rocket scientist to figure out roughly what she had said. That, and the fact that she held her hands, palms facing each other, roughly a foot apart as she spoke.

Later in the evening, after the diner closed for the day and the chairs had all been upended on the tables, Kathleen knocked at the glass. Lori let her in. They sat at the counter talking with Emma, the diner's owner and the town's matriarch and sage. After half an hour or so, Emma turned the coffee maker back on and made a pot of coffee. They were talking about men so she knew it would be a long conversation.

"Silas has to be one of the most wonderful men in the world," Kathleen volunteered. It was hardly a casual comment. Something had probably been bothering her all day. "I just can't understand why he is so private. It's like he has some terrible secret."

"Maybe he isn't really who he claims to be." Lori teased, seizing on the feigned mystery.

"I can guarantee that he is the one and only Silas McGraw," proclaimed Emma reassuringly. "His daddy was like that, too. Probably worse. They are old school mountain people. Don't need anyone else, and are damn proud of it. They'd sooner eat bark, ramps and road kill than admit they're hungry. I've known Silas since he was in diapers and that's just the way he is. He's got the hills in him. Of course, those kind of folks really can be harboring a horrible secret and you'd never know it." She shrugged slightly. No telling with the McGraw's. The three generations she had known were all intensely independent and obsessively protective of their little corner of the universe.

"I just wish I could get through," Kathleen continued, shaking her red hair gently as she spoke. "There is so much I want to share with him, but I need to feel like he is willing to share back."

"I bet he *thinks* he's already sharing," came Lori's observation.

170

"Men think they are being *so* open and sensitive whenever they are talking about anything besides sports, mechanical things or their work. Ian tries to be interested in my emotional needs but I can see his mind start to wander before I've gotten half way into what I'm trying to explain. He nearly always fails the 'what did I say?' quiz, though he usually takes a pretty good stab at it. That must be his legal training, he can pick up a good bit of a conversation even though he is thinking about something else."

"Now *those two* are a pair!" Kathleen observed. "How they ever get along so well is an amazement to me. Just what *do* they have in common? I think they must just have a common enemy."

"That would be male pattern baldness and anyone who wants to come up that valley," suggested Lori.

"I only wish I could pick up on Silas's moods like Ian does," Kathleen continued. "It must be a guy thing."

"One thing you will learn about men as you get older," remarked Emma, patting her salt-and-pepper hair back to where it was braided and coiled tightly into a bun, "is that they are just *different* from us. They don't think like us. They don't act like us. If they are looking at the exact same thing as us, they don't even see what we see. A whole separate set of things is important to them. They react differently to things that affect them, and often very strongly, even though we sometimes can't even tell that they are reacting at all. And they respond to things *we* do in ways we don't always anticipate. Yet they have an appreciation of how other *men* will react, and what *they* are thinking. Of course, you must realize, men say just the same thing about us."

She smiled at the thought that such a simple fact would be universally overlooked by each succeeding generation of young women. She could not remember when it finally dawned on her, but it was far too late in life.

"They just ain't us."

"I remember the first time I saw Ian," Lori mused. "He blew into the parking lot in a navy blue Jaguar. It was sooo out of place in this town. He was wearing just-bought jeans and work boots so new that they weren't even scuffed yet. My guess was that he was a doctor on vacation just trying to blend with the locals. The fact that he was self-conscious was obvious. I tried to draw him out, get

171

him to talk. His shyness, or maybe it was just lack of comfort, was kinda cute. I wanted to tell him that it was OK, and that no one cared that he was driving a car worth five years' salary to most of the folks in this town."

She laughed nervously. "Probably best that I didn't say that."

"I already told you guys how I met Silas," Kathleen interjected. "He got a look at The Goods far too early in the relationship. I guess it doesn't much matter now," she noted, somewhat impishly, then shifted the focus of the conversation.

"Alright Emma, how did you meet Omer?" her look demanded a response.

"Now ladies, you have to remember that was over forty-five years ago," she began. "Things were very different then. I just kept running into Omer everywhere I went. If I went to the feed store, I'd see him. Or the hardware store. Or church on Sunday. Finally we decided that if we were going to spend that much time together, we might as well get married."

"So, he was stalking you," Kathleen chided.

"Maybe, sure, they didn't call it that back then. He didn't stop until we had five children."

"That's probably why they have laws against that now." Kathleen threw her hair back and gazed momentarily at the ceiling, grinning. Emma turned the conversation back around. "When are you two going to settle those boys down and have some babies of your own?"

Neither Kathleen nor Lori needed to hear that question. Their biological clocks were ticking loudly enough in their ears already, but Emma's entire generation seemed adept at turning up the volume. Lori and Kathleen looked at each other for a moment to see whether the other was contemplating a serious or cavalier response to the question.

Kathleen dismissed the subject with the simple observation that "having babies could happen in nine months from any time, settling those boys down might take much longer.

"Ian just got unsettled, he's probably not in a hurry to get recommitted," Lori noted. She added, perhaps in jest, "And that Debbie Evans keeps trying to move in on him."

"I don't think I would worry too much about her," Emma assured

Lori. "That biker they call Lucky has been working on getting her undivided attention. They are in here several times a week, always when you are off-shift. I hear he's been staying at her house since Labor Day."

"That girl has been a man-stealin' little bitch since high school. She's never interested in a man unless he is already attached to another woman," Kathleen added.

"Silas is a one women man, but I'm not sure how far or how fast any one woman can move him," she added.

Emma just rolled her eyes. Young women today had no appreciation of their ability to influence their men. It seemed to her that the modern "liberated" woman tried to *demand* the things she wanted, to negotiate straightforwardly with men, like a man. The limitations of that approach were obvious. The art of presenting a woman's needs so that a man felt like he was giving her a gift, or rescuing her, when he met those needs, had been lost to the new generation.

Omer had fallen all over himself trying to win Emma's love and keep her happy. She could never, nor would she ever, have asked him to do all the things he had done for her. Denied the gratification of perceived surprise and appreciation, today's men had lost the urge to be chivalrous. Chivalry had not died. It had gone out of style for lack of interest. This generation of women still *thought* they wanted a prince on a white charger, but had no idea how to find one. In Emma's day knights were made, not found.

"I know it sounds trite coming from an old mountain woman but, if you find a good man, stand by that man. It *will* pay off in the long run. Life is a journey that very few of us really want to take alone."

Lori strolled back into the kitchen. It seemed like a good note to end on and time to lock up for the night. She grabbed the last few bags of trash and opened the side door to throw them in the dumpster. The parking lot was dark but her eyes soon grew accustomed to the faint vestige of illumination provided by the lights of the dining room where Kathleen and Emma still stood talking. A single headlight turned into the lot. It was Silas on his motorcycle coming to give Kathleen a ride home. Almost immediately two more headlights turned into the lot and stopped next to the bike.

Silas was still removing his helmet when officer Cletus walked up to the other side of the bike and bent down as if to pick something up.

"You dropped this Silas," he offered, holding out something that Lori couldn't identify.

Silas looked and chuckled. "Ya sure, Cletus. You can have that. It'll probably do you some good."

"I'm going to have to arrest you, Silas. Just turn around and place both your hands on the bike."

Silas tried to ignore him. He did not even look up. "Get serious Cletus, you know that stuff is yours, not mine."

"Silas, I got you. Don't make me cuff you. Just shut up and get in the cruiser."

"You jackass, this is totally bogus."

"Are you resisting arrest?"

"No, not me." Silas wanted to sucker punch him into the next county, but knew that would only make things far worse. He rolled his eyes. After all these years, Cletus was still pathetic.

Lori starred as Silas quietly got in the back seat of the police car. Her heart beat wildly in her chest and blood thumped dully in her ears. The car pulled out of the lot. Lori rushed inside to get Emma and Kathleen.

"It was like some kind of third world secret police kidnapping," she told the two of them, visibly shaking. Kathleen was furious. "I knew that son-of-a-bitch would eventually pull a stunt like this. It's just like back in high school. He hates Silas and is always trying to get him in trouble. I'm calling Ian right now."

The ringing phone brought Ian up out of deep unconsciousness. He had fallen asleep reading legal journals that he had hoped would help him acclimate to the local court system. They had proven quite relaxing.

Kathleen and Lori told him about the events in the parking lot.

"I can't do anything until morning because there won't be anyone except cops in the courthouse until then, but I will be there first thing."

Coincidentally, Ian had to be in the county seat early the next day to file a divorce for a woman whose husband had developed a

174

habit of coming home drunk and making love to her at knifepoint. The couple's last name, ironically, was Romeo. She was living temporarily with her parents and two very large brothers. No restraining order would be necessary. If hubby came around he would very likely be subject to backwoods justice, and he knew it. When Ian got to town in the morning he walked straight into the Sheriff's Office and County Jail. He asked the Deputy at the window if they had a Silas McGraw there.

"Yes sir," came the crisp reply.

"What is he charged with?"

"Possession of marijuana with intent to sell. Are you his lawyer?"

Ian was wearing a necktie, a dead giveaway in this town.

"Yes, may I see him?"

The Deputy handed Ian some forms to sign and looked at his Drivers License photo. He led Ian through two sets of heavy steel doors painted in dull pastel public-school-and-penitentiary green. Ian found Silas sitting alone at a table in a hallway lined with empty cells.

"You took long enough" came the greeting. Silas seemed to be taking his incarceration in stride.

"Sorry about that, but there wasn't much I could do last night. I am going to go meet the Prosecutor. Before I go see him, we need to talk. What happened?"

Silas still fumed from the events of the night before.

"That little weasel Cletus set me up. He planted a bag of pot on my bike. He made sure it was big enough to get me on intent to sell."

"Do you even smoke pot anymore?"

"I got no problem with people smoking dope, but I haven't had any myself in years."

"Then you'd pass a piss test if they gave you one?"

"Sure, no problem."

"I'm going to talk to the Prosecutor. Just hold tight."

Silas made a frustrated face. "Sure, I'll be right here."

"Oh, by the way, where is Jared Smithers?"

"He was released to his mother's custody yesterday evening, about fifteen minutes after I got here."

Ian walked out of the jail and across the street to the Courthouse.

He was soon ushered into the office of James Dunlevy, County Prosecutor. He introduced himself and explained that he had just opened a law office in Elton.

"Not much work down that way I suspect," Mr.Dunlevy noted.

"To be frank, there's not all that much around here. That is one of the reasons I ran for prosecutor. It's a salaried job. Luckily there isn't much real crime, either."

Mr. Dunlevy was an oddly empathetic man for a prosecutor. Ian had witnessed the prosecutorial mindset on several occasions in the past as local urban prosecutors turned their guns on his clients. He would immediately refer the case to a partner in the firm that specialized in criminal defense. Ian was very aware of his lack of experience in the area of criminal law. This Prosecutor, however, seemed much more relaxed and unassuming than the others. He offered Ian one of two heavily padded leather chairs and sat down in the other.

"Actually I have several clients in your jail right now," Ian replied. "This is something more than a social call." Ian explained Silas's situation in detail. He included background information about the longstanding relationship between Silas and Cletus, including the story of the escapade that had landed Silas in Southeast Asia. He recounted the story of Jared Smithers, as told by Kathleen the day before and of the Deputy's admission that he failed to read Jared his Miranda rights at the time of his arrest. Of course, there was also the fact that Lori had witnessed Silas' questionable arrest from the shadows at the side of the diner, unbeknownst to Cletus.

Mr. Dunlevy leaned back into his chair. He stroked his bushy white mustache. "I've known Cletus Hanley since he was a little boy." There was a moment of silence. He was probably sizing up Ian and trying to decide whether to make his next statement. "Your story does not sound out of character." More silence, perhaps this time for effect. "It would be a real shame if our local sheriff, who just was reelected by the slimmest of margins, were to have his professional reputation sullied by allegations of police misconduct."

Ian nodded his head. He knew where this train of thought was going. "All my clients ever asked for was a little understanding from the legal system."

"Well, I think the system understands."

James and Ian agreed that, assuming Silas could pass a urine screen administered by the county public health nurse for the metabolites of cannabis, prosecutorial discretion should be applied to these circumstances and that any charges against Silas and Jared Smithers would be dropped.

Silas was in Ian's car by noon.

On the drive home from the courthouse, the radio disk jockey was whining about a low
pressure system sweeping south from Canada and the Great Lakes. Looked like the weekend would be a washout. This was actually good news. The rain would head off the late fall fire season. A dry October would have virtually assured that the downed leaves and dry brush would be burning in November.

Things could be far worse. Folks along the Atlantic coast were scrambling for their lives. Hurricane Margaret was feeding on the warm waters carried by the Gulf Stream from the Caribbean. It was intensifying daily. Coastal residents from Savannah to Norfolk were boarding up their homes and getting out of town.

A reporter was interviewing Justin French, an obviously troubled low country hardware store owner, who lived somewhere outside of Savannah, Georgia. Mr. French was busy boarding up his store. He had not been able to get enough plywood from his usual suppliers because the big chain home improvement stores had sucked up all the plywood on the market in anticipation of the pre-storm rush. He had found some in Beaufort, South Carolina, and was just finishing nailing it into place.

He explained to the reporter, in a heavy low country accent, the unrelenting power of the hurricanes that he had seen in the past. "When Hugo came through here a few years ago it pretty much leveled everything. My store lost its roof, but most all the other buildings on this road were blown flat, so I figured that wasn't too bad. Hugo brought tornados with it, and they just smashed through houses, barns, even whole big sections of the pine woods. Tore trees right off the stump. Millions of dollars in damages. Couldn't get a roofer for three months. I sold enough shingles and other roofing material to pay for the damage to the store. Good thing, too, since I didn't have no insurance."

Then he talked about the rain that came with Hugo. "It came down in sheets, a hard, driving rain, as hard as any I'd ever seen, that lasted for several days. The ground couldn't hold any more, but this land is flat enough that it couldn't run off. Eventually the roads became impassible from the standing water. The power was out and the town water plant was half under water. The water was unfit to drink for weeks."

Ian could already hear the wind whistling around the reporter's microphone. There was no doubt they were in for a storm.

CHAPTER EIGHTEEN

"Fire in the lake: the image of revolution." I Ching

"We are dancing on a volcano." Napoleon Bonaparte

The evenings were getting shorter now. Ian spent a few with Lori, doing honey-do things around her little hillside house. He impressed himself with the skills he had picked up over the years. Never a real domestic guy, he was surprised to find that he could still handle a paintbrush, a hammer, and a screwdriver. He had not used these skills since adolescence. Even some basic electrical stuff, like rewiring her lamp, came back to him without much hesitation. Lori's memory, it seemed, was similarly reliable. She reminded him that he and Silas had promised to take Kathleen and her to the movies on Friday night.

The evenings he was not at Lori's, he worked around the farm. As the summer's heat faded into the cool crispness of fall, Ian was reminded that winter was on its way. There were many jobs that needed tending before the first snow. Rural land demands attention, no, *devotion* from those who would live in harmony with it. These were not the first endeavors that he had tackled around the farm. Projects, already years overdue, awaited him the day he moved in. He threw himself into them, aware he had a great deal to learn about country life.

Shortly after meeting Silas, Ian had asked him about the old apple trees planted in rows behind the barn. They were well past their prime and in desperate need of a severe pruning. Silas could remember the old man planting them, but he was a young child at the time. He cautioned that it was already too late in the year to cut them back, or even thin their wild foliage, but he explained to Ian what types of apple they were, what they were good for, and when they would bear fruit. The tallest trees were Golden Delicious, which Silas said was the type of apple that grew best in these hills. Some smaller trees were Rome apples. Silas thought they were semi-dwarf trees, artificially grafted to roots that would keep them from growing too large. A few other trees Silas remembered as Yellow Transparent. He noted that they were cooking apples with smooth delicate skin and would be the first apples to ripen, possibly even before the end of summer.

He was right about the trees. Months later, they had all borne bushels of fruit. Some of it was misshapen or bug eaten, but next year the trees would be pruned and sprayed. Even this year's crop had given Lori plenty to work with. Ian had eaten more apple pies and cobbler this season than he had in his entire life. There was enough canned applesauce and apple butter in the pantry to last a decade. Ian was considering buying an apple press so he could make cider.

Above the trees was a gentle east-facing knoll. Thickly overgrown in sumac, locust, and sassafras all laced together with interwoven honeysuckle vines, it was once a hillside pasture for hogs. It was now in the process of being reclaimed by the forest.

Earlier in the summer

Ian went down to the hardware store where Kathleen pointed him toward a Stihl® chainsaw with a sixteen-inch bar. She assured him that it was a good all around tool for normal farm duty. Now, chainsaw held high like the star of a c-grade horror movie, Ian waded into the tangled brush swinging the screaming saw in a wild arc ahead of him.

His intention was to clear land for more apple trees, which he would plant early next spring. He would buy good modern nursery stock. This knoll was obviously a nice location for an orchard. It was high enough to be above the late frosts that would lay thick in the river bottom on still spring mornings. It got good sunlight, especially in the morning through mid-afternoon, and the soil was remarkably workable for hillside land in these parts. Perhaps the hogs had helped that.

Ian had made it maybe thirty feet into the tangled vines when he heard Cletus yip as if startled. He barked weakly and ran around the side of the house. Ian felt a weight on the top of his foot and looked down to see a fat brown copperhead sliding across it. For an instant, his blood ran cold. The snake disappeared silently back into the brush. Then Ian spotted another snake, smaller than the first, sitting on a downed tree limb only ten feet to his left. Yet another copperhead appeared out of the dense honeysuckle only to crawl across a small log and disappear back into the vegetation.

180

Even though he had never had an experience like this before, he strongly suspected that he had stumbled upon a snake den. He had heard similar stories down at the diner. Somewhere under those vines was shelter, perhaps a pile of old lumber or fieldstone or well casing, something that the snakes could den in. He thought about getting his "snake gun" but realized that he could not shoot what he could not see. The dense honeysuckle probably hid lots of the venomous little bastards, but looking for them would be more dangerous than leaving them alone. Worse yet, that yelp may well have been Cletus getting bit.

Ian carefully retraced his steps back to the closely-cut grass near the barn. He walked over to the house where he found Cletus curled up on the porch, apparently alright. Ian decided to watch him closely for the rest of the day. Neither of them went near the brushy knoll again.

When Ian told Silas what had happened, he advised patience. "Just wait until cold weather when they hibernate. Clean up the area then. Without food and cover, the snakes will move on. Like politicians."

Ian vowed to wait until winter. Then he would cut that hill bare and burn the brush. Next spring it would be his orchard.

Ian checked Cletus that evening and found him favoring his leg just a little. He called Lori at work early the next morning. She cornered the local veterinarian when he came in for breakfast. The vet said that if the swelling was minimal it was either a very small snake or had not injected much venom. If the dog was doing alright this long after being bitten, about all he would recommend was to keep an eye on him and keep him away from the snake den. The first recommendation Ian was already doing. The second was not a problem. Cletus had no interest in being anywhere near those snakes.

Even after he was driven off the hill by snakes, Ian found plenty of uses for the chainsaw. Thunderstorms had left several downed trees in their wake. He started keeping the chainsaw behind the seat in his truck. A major part of the firewood he would need for next winter was already sitting beside the house. It came from two red oaks, a tall hickory, and a large hollow beech tree. They had fallen across the road and, since he had to cut them up to move them anyway, they became firewood. He also had some more hickory from the two trees that had fallen behind Silas's barn.

He especially liked splitting the wood with the heavy iron maul that Kathleen had also recommended to him. It made him feel very strong and self-reliant. It was a good, solid manly tool.

By the end of summer, Ian was not the man that had fled the city less than half a year before. He even looked very different. Lori's cooking had put a good ten pounds on him, but hard physical activity had distributed it well. He had not cut his hair the whole time. He could bind it into a short bushy ponytail. At the firm, he would have never dreamed of growing a beard, but he had one now. Well-trimmed and flecked with gray, it made him look distinguished in a woodsy sort of way. It felt nice. Natural.

His previous life seemed very distant. His mother now kept in touch with regular letters and an occasional telephone call, but he had not heard from anyone else, including Cynthia or her family, in months. Regardless, he had never felt stronger.

Friday after work, Cletus met the truck a quarter mile out the road from the house. He had been doing that for months. Ian figured that he could hear the truck as it made the sweeping turn around the hillside over three quarters of a mile down the valley. Sound carries up a river valley, especially on a still fall evening. Cletus escorted the truck back to the farmhouse then greeted Ian as he stepped out. Tail held high, he trotted up the steps and waited at the door for Ian. It was dinnertime.

Cletus was wolfing down his dog food when the telephone rang. It was Lori. She said that she and Kathleen would be at Silas' house about six-thirty. Ian should just walk over to his place about then. They'd all go to the movies in her car. Fine with him.

He threw on a pair of semi-clean jeans and a sweatshirt. His old Nikes® and a Route 50 Truck Stop hat completed the night-out ensemble. It was just beginning to get dusky when he headed out toward the neighbor's farm.

Ian stepped onto Silas's front porch to find him sitting in an old cane-backed chair with his feet up on the porch railing. He was dressed in coveralls and army surplus camo jungle boots.

The women pulled up in front of the house. When they got out of the car, Ian was immediately impressed by one of many man-

182

woman differences that had slipped his mind during his recent flirtation with bachelorhood.

The women were stunning. Kathleen wore a short black leather skirt and a body-hugging red sweater. Lori had tight black jeans and a sheer white blouse over a bra nearly as sheer. Men go to the movies to relax or actually see a movie. These women obviously interpreted this as a *date*. They were dressed to impress their men, and anyone else who might see them while they were out.

Silas looked uncomfortable. Kathleen probably had not given him many details on the evening, though he surely knew from earlier conversations tonight was supposed to be a movie night.

"I'm sorry folks but I can't go anywhere," he announced. "That big red heifer over there is about to drop a calf and I'm afraid it might be a breach." He pointed to a very wide and wobbly looking cow just visible around the side of the barn.

Kathleen pouted. "Damn it Silas, we set tonight aside two weeks ago. What are your cows doing calving at this time of year?"

"Honey, that bull is in with the cows all year long. Calves can come along at any time. My father did things that way, so do I."

He appeared unperturbed. An October birth was really no big deal. It was much better than the inevitable coldest-night-of-the-year deliveries that the family cows always seemed to require when he was a kid. In those days, he would stay up all night with his father and a kerosene heater. They huddled in a corner of the barn trying to keep the new calf from freezing to death before the sun came up.

"Why don't you two go to the movies together. I'd appreciate it if Ian could stay to help me in case we have to turn that calf around to get it delivered."

Ian agreed to stay and help, although he had no bovine obstetrical experience. The thought of having rubber gloved hands bicep-deep inside the southern end of a north-facing cow did not really appeal to him. Kathleen looked a little annoyed, and Lori a little disappointed, but they got back in the car and headed out the road.

"Tonight's the night," Silas remarked as he turned and stepped into the house. Inside, on the kitchen table, sat the drywall compound buckets that Ian had seen in the basement weeks before.

"Is that cow really going to deliver?" Ian asked weakly.

183

"Oh, probably, but old Red could spit a calf out standing on her head. She doesn't need us." Silas continued. "I've been going up to the dam every day. They have two full tankers of ammonium nitrate and a tanker full of diesel fuel sitting up there right now. In each of these buckets, I have gel explosive, caps, a motorcycle battery and a timer. These are the detonators for the ANFO. We carry these up there, blow a hole in the dam, and get back here before dawn."

"You of course realize that any monkey business with explosives will have this entire county crawling with police, ATF and probably FBI." Ian reminded him. Fear sat in the pit of his stomach like a hot-cold block of dry ice.

Silas did not hesitate, his mind was long since made up. He was ready.

"Let 'em come. If you want out, I'll understand. This is something I have to do. It's not your fight." Silas responded.

Ian thought for a moment. About Junior and his family. And about Sam, a rough-hewn and crusty logger he knew from a score of breakfast conversations at the counter in the diner. Sam's story was not unlike Junior's, but with a wood-hick twist. And Kathleen, Lori and a dozen others who saw the Big Laurel valley as a last refuge from a world gone just a little mad. They had, in the short time that Ian had been in town, already grown closer to him than anyone he had left back in the city. He wondered whether the diner's owner, Emma, local *mother superior* and daughter of a coal miner who for much of her childhood had been black-listed by the coal companies for union activity, would ever be happy catering to the summer-condo-by-the-lake set.

"No, six months ago this would not have been my fight. Now I can't deny, even to myself, that this *is* my fight," Ian grimaced. "What do I do?"

"Grab a bucket. Here's a light. Don't use it yet," Silas said, handing Ian a six-volt flashlight. Out the back door they went, headed for the trail up the river. It became dusk, then darker, as they walked. The air was heavy and damp. A steady drizzle settled in. As their eyes adjusted, they took visual clues from vestiges of light filtering into the gorge. The last light of day streamed over the canyon rim. Soon spot lights from the construction site gave them direction. An hour after dark they stood on the edge of the clearing at the dam.

There did not seem to be anyone around. The crews were off for the weekend. It was going to rain all weekend anyway. Silas pointed toward a lighted construction trailer on the far side of the dam. "There is supposed to be a security guard in that trailer all night to watch after the site," he said. "Except they hired Stanley Coombs. He can not stand to miss a party. They should have hired a guard to watch him. I have come up here every evening. He leaves thirty minutes after the last of the construction crew. He has been down at The Stand shooting pool every night this week. He will get back here after last call. That gives us about seven hours to do the job."

They kept to the shadows until it was clear that Stanley had already gone to town. Once they determined that they were alone, they began to work in earnest. Silas and Ian trotted over to the fuel truck.

The keys were in it. Why not? It was parked under the watchful eyes of twenty-four hour security. Ian started to climb up onto the truck. Suddenly Silas waived him off. Ian's foot touched the running board of the cab and he pushed away.

"Don't touch it," he warned Ian.

Too late, Ian had grabbed the door handle. Silas threw him a red cotton handkerchief.

"Wipe that handle off real good." Then he added, "Let's check the tankers first, the ANFO may be premixed."

Silas almost flew up onto the first tanker and opened the hatches on top of the tank. It was nearly full of what a friend of his father's used to refer to as "Satan's kitty litter." The sweet familiar smell of #2 fuel oil rose from the hatch, too potent for even the steadily rising wind to sweep away. He did the same check on the second tanker. It too was full. He never said anything, but the premixed explosive had allayed one of his worst fears. He knew that the odds of getting a perfect 94% fertilizer, 6% diesel fuel mix were very slim if he had to try to do it by just pouring fuel into a truckload of fertilizer. The other common procedure in these parts was to use trucks that automatically mixed the fuel oil with the ammonium nitrate as it was being augered into boreholes in the rock to be blasted.

185

The truckload of fuel was for the dozers and other heavy equipment, not for mixing with fertilizer.

After he inspected the second tanker, Silas jumped back down to where Ian stood with the two buckets. Pulling the lids off of the buckets, Silas hooked the wires to the batteries and set the timers for thirty minutes. He climbed back up and dropped one bucket into each ammonium nitrate tanker.

"We have thirty minutes until these blow, barring short circuits or other shitty luck," he announced. "Find me two concrete blocks or large rocks."

With that, he swung up into the cab of the first tanker and cranked up the big diesel engine. Then he did the same to the other. They settled into patient, rolling idles. *Locked and loaded*, armed and dangerous. Ian found a stack of concrete blocks next to the office trailer and ran two of them over to the trucks.

"Put one on the passenger seat of each truck," Silas directed. By now, they had both long forgotten about their initial concern with leaving fingerprints. He hopped into the first truck as soon as Ian placed the block in it. Throwing the shift lever into low gear, Silas pointed the rig out across the top of the dam. At the far end, fast against the massive timeless sandstone of the cliffs that used to guard Mink Shoals, lay the diversion tunnel. This carried the river around the great rubble plug that was being constructed in its path. When the dam was completed, the tunnel would be closed and water would slowly drown the river valley for fifteen miles upstream.

The formerly dreary night was now ablaze with lightening. The wind, almost calm two hours ago, lashed the top of the dam with forty mile-per-hour gusts. Sand and bits of debris swirled in the headlights as Silas hit second gear. "Nasty thunderstorm coming," he thought.

Silas reached for third gear. He was on the dam looking for the turn that would take him down the upstream face of the rock pile to the mouth of the tunnel. Suddenly there it was. He locked the brakes and the truck slid toward the river. In mere seconds, the tunnel opening loomed in the darkness. A cement tube at least twenty feet in diameter, it was the biggest damned culvert he had ever seen. The river poured casually into the darkness.

186

Silas brought the truck to a stop at the water's edge. This would be the crux move. He had to send the truck down the drain without going with it.

The water pouring into the tunnel, although it looked slickly calm, was deceptively powerful. To land in even a foot of that water would be to get his legs washed out from under him and enjoy a one-way trip to Hell. The truck, and the truck only, was to be swept deep into the dam until it was finally stopped by the tunnel's giant valve structure. He took a length of bailing twine from his pocket and ran it from the brake pedal to the steering wheel.

He gunned the motor, slammed it in gear, dropped the concrete block on the accelerator pedal, and jumped as far from the cab as his legs would propel him. Hitting the ground hard, he felt a sharp rock cut deeply into his knee, but jerked up to his feet immediately to be sure that he was not in the path of the rear wheels of the tanker.

It tracked straight into the tunnel as if it were running on rails. Silas was sprinting again. He noticed a red stain already marking the front of his coveralls, but chose to ignore it. Running faster than he had run since his high-school football days, he headed back across the dam to where Ian stood next to the second truck.

"Run after me!" he shouted to Ian as he climbed up into the truck. "We need to run across the dam, over the tunnel and up the hillside."

Gunning the motor and sidestepping the clutch, he felt the second truck lurch toward its final destination.

At the water's edge, he reenacted the drill. Stop, bailing twine, concrete block, *jump*. This landing was better. The second truck followed the first into the abyss.

Back in town, Lori and Kathleen had gone to Lori's house. With Lori's blender and a fifth of tequila, they made a few margaritas. Because they managed to get polluted well beyond all legal and practical intoxication safety thresholds, they realized that a long drive to the movies was out of the question.

"How about a short walk to a game of eight-ball?" was Lori's alternative suggestion.

It was still early, even by local standards, when they came through the front door of The Stand. There were already about thirty people in the place, mostly guys having a few beers and waiting or hoping for some women to show up. Every eye was fixed on them. Lori was not too drunk to get that baitfish-in-a-school-of sharks feeling, but she *was* drunk enough not to care. Kathleen, even if she had been dead sober, was never going to be intimidated by these yokels. Hell, she went to school with a fair number of them. They put their quarters on the nearest pool table to the door, sat down at the bar, and ordered a couple of margaritas. It was only a few minutes before the players ahead of them finished their game. Kathleen went to the wall rack and carefully selected a cue.

She turned to the victor from the previous game. "Find yourself a partner. My friend and I will play teams, eight-ball."

He motioned to the guy he had just beaten, a tall, wiry, hungry looking unemployed logger named Jason. Jason picked a stick off the wall and quietly, but with a slightly threatening tone said "I'll break."

At that instant Silas McGraw crested the dam. He looked out across what was intended to be a deep still lake someday. Now it was just a deep rocky gash in the earth liberally peppered with tree stumps. Surrounding it were high dark hills silhouetted in cold white light. Multiple flashes of lightning crisscrossed cloud-to-cloud and cloud-to-ground.

He could feel the ghost of Jeremiah McGraw reaching down into his boot for the knife.

Ian stood in the middle of the rock-strewn road that led back to where the trucks had been parked. He handed Silas one of the flashlights. Silas shouted over the thunder and wind.

"My watch says we have ten minutes to get as far from here as we possibly can. I have no idea how big an explosion we'll have, but I'm betting pretty fucking big. If we don't get far enough, I'll be seeing you on The Other Side. Run with me, we're going right over the tunnel and up the mountainside. Don't stop running 'til you feel the blast, then take cover anywhere you can. There's likely to be flying debris."

"Debris?"

"You know...dirt and rocks..."

"Rocks?"

"Yes. Rocks. Likely big enough to take your head off."

They ran. As hard as two middle aged guys could run.

By now the storm was upon them. The roaring wind and driving rain was at their backs. The sheets of falling water absorbed the beams from their lanterns, but the wind scooted them along faster than they could ever have imagined running without it. Frequent bolts of lightening illuminated their path far better than their puny artificial lights.

At the end of the dam, directly over the tunnel where the two giant bombs patiently awaited the signal to do their jobs, was a rutted bulldozer track that led up the mountainside in the general direction of the trail home. Ian and Silas headed for it. The climb was steep and slippery, but the intense tailwind seemed to be sweeping across the valley and almost lifting them up the hillside. The massive amounts of adrenaline flooding their bloodstreams did not hurt either.

Kathleen and Lori were drawing plenty of attention back at The Stand. Stanley Coombs was sitting at the bar with Lucky Sonovich, who was buying him round after round of Jack Daniels® and Coke. They had both turned their barstools to watch the women shooting pool.

Stanley asked Lucky if he knew "the tall one," meaning Lori.

"No, but the redhead is Silas McGraw's girlfriend," Lucky responded.

Stanley winced. Silas was something of a legend around town. Stanley remembered him from high school and, even after all these years, did not care to risk antagonizing him. So much for the redhead. Even her friend, the tall one, was probably trouble.

"Just kick back and relax," Lucky counseled. "It's going to be a long night. Have another drink. Nights like this one are too few and far between."

Bernie leaned over the bar and whispered something to Stanley. Stanley became visibly agitated. He turned back toward Lucky.

"Shit...Bernie says he just heard over the scanner that Cletus Hansen is heading up to the dam site to check on me. I wonder why the hell he picked tonight of all nights to think I need his damn company." He began to get off his barstool. Lucky stopped him.

"You can't beat him up there now. Who knows how big a head

start he's got."

"Then what can I do? He'll rat me out to the project manager for sure. I can't afford to lose that job, I got bills to pay."

"Give me a couple of minutes. Where's the payphone?"

Stanley pointed to a cubbyhole on the far side of the bar near the restrooms. Lucky headed in that direction. He was back in a few minutes.

"Whadya do?" asked Stanley.

"Don't worry about it. Trust me. It's *taken care of.* I'll explain later."

Stanley and Lucky settled back. Bernie brought them a couple fresh drinks.

Kathleen was still feeling the tequila. And she *did* enjoy tormenting the local boys just a tad. She reached, almost theatrically, for a long shot, her back to the men seated at the bar. Her leather skirt slid high enough up her thigh to reveal a glimpse of the lacy trim at the top of her nylons.

"Stretch for that ball Kathy!" blurted Stanley. He had already forgotten about Deputy Cletus.

She stood up from her shot, turned to face Stanley (who she disliked ever since he "accidentally" grabbed her breast at a high school dance fifteen-plus years before), and gave him a long hard look intended to have the same effect as a bucket of ice water on his crotch.

"Its KATH*LEEN*," she corrected him, poking his sternum with the cue stick and leaving a blue dot of chalk dust on his khaki work-shirt, then punctuated the exchange as she turned back toward the table with a muttered "dickweed."

Lucky nudged Stanley in the ribs and made an exaggerated hold-ing-back-a-laugh face.

"Dickweed?" Stanley whispered, incredulous. "They got names for women like that."

Kathleen made her shot, and the next shot. Two cushions and into the side pocket. Only two balls left. And the eight ball, of course. Ian and Silas were well above the dam now, running rain soaked and adrenaline supercharged down a small trail through the mountain laurel and rhododendron. They could feel the Devil's breath at their backs. Waiting for the anticipated horrendous thump, fearing that it might be too great, or their distance from it too little. Would this be the last thing they ever do? Or worse yet, would *nothing* happen, leaving two trucks full of explosives and covered with their fingerprints lodged in the dam's diversion tunnel?

Kathleen missed. But so did her opponent.

Lori cleanly dispatched the eleven and thirteen balls with her first two shots. The eight ball lay only inches from the corner pocket nearest the bar. The cue ball sat almost exactly between the two side pockets. An easy shot. A choke shot. She draped herself across the felt and lined the shot up carefully. Her blouse had lost a strategic button, providing the boys at the bar with yet another subject for conversation and speculation.

Her breasts strained at her skimpy bra as she pulled the cue back and smoothly stroked the cue ball. It found its mark, but what it had in accuracy it lacked in velocity. The eight ball moved slowly across the green, oozing toward the pocket. Lori leaned down on the table, dragging her nipples across the felt, feigning that she would blow the eight ball into the pocket.

Stanley thought to himself, "thank you God for drunk chicks."

For a moment it looked like it would stop at the very brink. It seemed to hang there for an interminable expanse of time. Lori lifted her breasts off the green felt. The friction left her nipples noticeably erect. Stanley was transfixed. Then the eight ball dropped.

Ian tripped, or maybe just fell to one knee, at the moment of detonation. The ground shook. There was an immense deep bass double percussive *whomwhomp*. Vapor clouds poured from both the upstream and downstream ends of the tunnel. A fissure opened directly above the point where the trucks had lodged in the pipe. A geyser of pulverized rock shot skyward from the rift. One truck had blown first providing containment for the second blast, or perhaps setting it off.

Silas and Ian were in genuine and immediate mortal danger. It was literally raining boulders from the size of marbles to the size of watermelons. Suddenly a light appeared not ten feet from the trail. It startled Ian. Were there witnesses to this vandalism, this felony in progress? An oddly familiar voice directed them to follow the light.

"Boys, you had better get under here fast," it said, then continued. "Those rocks *will* kill you."

They turned and dove into the soft dirt under a deeply undercut and overhanging sandstone outcrop. Boulders crashed through the trees and brush just a few feet away.

The dry and sheltered area beneath the rock was as big as a suburban living room. Seated on a block of stone, next to a sky blue panhead Harley®, was a guy who Ian had seen before. Somewhere a long time ago. Well, not *that* long ago, in fact it had been only a few months, just seemingly in a different life.

"Father?" came Ian's greeting. How odd it was to run into the heavy-tipping strip club patron out here in the middle of nowhere. Although it *was* his weird set of directions that had, in a sense, led him here.

"Yes, Ian. I see you remember me. It's been a while." He smiled broadly and with great ease. He seemed very comfortable with the situation. His clothes were dry, as was his bike, despite the wind-driven rain that soaked the ground only a few feet from his seat.

"I've watched you two all evening." He waved his hand slowly and reassuringly, as if he read their minds, to dismiss their obvious concern. "No need to worry, your secret is very safe with me. Be assured, however, this place *will* be crawling with police and investigators by morning. I doubt they will find much of use to them. The explosion and water will see to that." He shook his head disapprovingly, almost sadly, and gazed out at the driving rain. He pointed casually toward the construction site.

"Dams like that one are such an arrogant exercise. All they really prove is that men don't have much more sense than beavers. Beavers' accomplishments are only slightly more short lived and insignificant. In a couple of generations, even these structures crumble and fail. Nature will inevitably demonstrate the futility of this sort of engineering nonsense."

He again gestured toward the dam. "That one won't last the night. Maggie's coming for it," he said, flicking his fingers as if to dismiss the massive structure as inconsequential.

"Maggie?" asked Silas.

"Hurricane Maggie. This rain is what's left of her after crossing several hundred miles of land. She's weaker now, but can still kick up a pretty fair deluge." Father sat back and rested one leg upon the other. Ian and Silas sat in the dirt at his feet like curious children.

"It is a strange little ball game man insists on playing with Nature." Father stared into the darkness. "Funny thing about ball games with Nature," he noted without turning back toward them until he finally held up one finger. His eyes glowed just a bit, as if amused. "Nature always bats last."

Outside the shelter it was now raining only torrents of pure cool water. The men peered into the darkness. Lightening displays still intermittently illuminated the dam site in brief bursts of intense stark whiteness. The flank of the dam where the diversion tunnel had been was noticeably slumped. The blast had shattered the tunnel's lining and a big chunk of the rock that formed the adjoining mountainside. The weight of the overlying rock had collapsed the tunnel. A large crater had been blown half way down the dam's face where it met the native rock of the gorge. The rest of the dam itself appeared basically intact. With the tunnel gone, water already pooled, slick and darkly moribund, behind it.

"I really expected a bigger blast. I don't know if we even breached that damned thing," observed Silas.

"By morning you'll know differently," came the old man's reply. "The softest things in the world overcome the hardest things in the world." The old man winked knowingly. "Soft things like rain."

"Lao-tzu?" asked Silas, vaguely recollecting readings from long ago. He had an overwhelming sense of déjà vu. It permeated this entire interlude.

Father nodded slowly. "Well, actually his gardener, but he generally gets credit for that quote. But now, you gentlemen must get yourselves home and get cleaned up. Come morning, be sure to go about your business normally. The agents of the law will pay you multiple visits. You are on their lists, so be introspective and humble and don't give them anything to work with. Oh, and don't start your motor vehicles until after the first law enforcement scout has come and gone."

Silas looked puzzled and clearly intrigued but jumped to his feet, turned toward the night, and took off. The old guy waived Ian to follow Silas. They were both once again running hard into the night.

Silas heard the panhead fire up. Then he heard the engine rev through first gear far faster than he would ever accelerate on a muddy road, especially in the driving rain. Suddenly the woods flashed again in white brilliance. The crash of thunder was immediate and deafening. Another lightening strike roared close behind them. The air was thick with ozone. Ian turned to look back out of fear that the old guy might have been hit. A sheet of rainwater ran in his eyes. Although he strained to see, there was no visible sign of Father or the bike.

CHAPTER NINETEEN

"When a man wants to murder a tiger, he calls it sport:

When a tiger wants to murder him, he calls it ferocity.

The distinction between crime and justice is no greater."

George Bernard Shaw

"There is no limit to the good that can be accomplished

if no one worries about who gets the credit." Anonymous

"Answer a fool according to his folly." Proverbs xxvi. 5.

Hurricane Margaret narrowly missed the Outer Banks. The meteorologists were projecting that she would take a northeasterly path and dissipate harmlessly in the North Atlantic. Suddenly, apparently influenced by the low-pressure system stalled over the central Appalachians, she veered sharply to the west.

Roaring over the piedmont, she slammed into the mountains sending bands of intense thunderstorms over steep high country watersheds. In the dendritic tributaries of the upper Big Laurel Fork, over a dozen inches of rain fell in a couple of hours. Gurgling pastoral mountain brooks metamorphosed in minutes into wild roaring monsters, ravenously devouring everything in their paths. Hundred-year-old hemlocks were uprooted and hurled toward the sea. Five hundred years worth of streamside vegetation and debris, including whole laurel thickets, old logjams, camping trailers, chicken coops, cars, and pieces of highway were suddenly pouring downhill in a liquid avalanche. Mother nature was piloting her runaway train.

The torrents scoured mountain hollows right down to their ancient stone foundation and bulldozed tons of rubble downstream. Witnesses could hear the sound of the riverbed boulders rolling down the naked bedrock, being driven toward the valleys by the irresistible hydraulic force.

While they had no way of knowing it, the floodwaters had crested what was left of the dam before Silas and Ian had gotten half way home. The river began eroding the now-vulnerable rubble insult, starting at the site of the collapsed diversion tunnel. It would not take long to sweep it far and away downstream.

Silas and Ian ran full bore to within a mile of his farm but finally had to slow to a walk. Silas's coveralls were soaked with a mixture of mountain clay and blood from an ugly gash below his right knee. He had ignored it as long as possible. There were plenty of other things happening to help take his mind off of his leg. The inevitable endorphins had helped.

When they got back to the farm, Silas limped toward the barn to check on his cow. Ian went home to get cleaned up.

Back at The Stand, Bernie had just ushered his last inebriated patrons out into the night and locked the doors. Kathleen and Lori went to Lori's to sleep off their buzz. Stanley Coombs nodded to Lucky and started back to his office at the dam site.

"Oh, by the way. What did you do about Cletus?" he asked.

"Called the dispatcher and told her that Johnny Adkins had flipped his car into the ditch up Sugar Creek Hollow. Cletus covers this whole end of the county. She said he had turned around and was headed downriver. By the time he gets down there and looks for that car, it will be impossible for him to get back to the dam before dawn."

Stanley stood in the doorway and looked up into the pouring rain. "Who is Johnny Adkins?" he asked.

"I don't know, but I am sure he will appreciate the help."

The answer did not make sense to Stanley, even after drinking all evening.. Regardless, he threw his head back, snorted a brief drunken laugh, and headed out into the night to get his truck.

Stanley had never seen it rain like this. A fast flowing stream of mud and debris rushed down the middle of the main paved road out of town. After he got to the turnoff, it took him three and a half additional hours to work his way down the washed-out dirt road to the dam. Luckily, he had a chain saw in his pickup, as he had to cut through at least ten downed trees to get there.

What he saw upon arriving at the dam made his blood run cold. Losing his job was the least of his worries. The river had breached one whole side of the dam and an angry tidal wave of muddy water, uprooted trees, and huge floating piles of debris was heading downstream. He bolted into the office trailer and called the sheriff's office.

When the night dispatcher answered he bellowed, half drunk and on the verge of tears, into the receiver, "the dam has broken, evacuate anyone near the river *immediately*!"

The dispatcher sensed a prank. Stanley repeated his message four times, each time more frantically than the time before. He identified himself three times before the dispatcher finally believed him and sent out the bulletin. She said Cletus, the usual deputy on this end of the county, was all the way down on Sugar Creek. No deputy was within twenty miles of Elton. With the condition the storm had left the roads in, it would be dawn before any of them reached town.

Ian stepped out of the house shortly after first light. The sky in the East was beginning to show small patches of brilliant blue. The first rays of the morning sun were shooting through the holes in the clouds, illuminating the tops of the mountains, and streaming across the valley. Hurricane Margaret had made a relatively surgical strike on the Big Laurel watershed and moved on quickly to the northeast. A few adjoining watersheds had some minor flooding. Margaret backed up the sewer systems of several major cities on her way back to sea but she claimed no lives. Ian could see Silas on his front porch in different clothes than the night before.

Ian had started toward Silas's house when he cast a glance at the river bottom pasture. What he saw froze him in his tracks. There was no field, only a large muddy lake with tall crashing waves on the far side where water poured out of the Big Laurel's upper gorge. As the huge brown waves rose then collapsed upon themselves, they sent deep bass thumps and hisses reverberating across the bottom and up to the house. It sounded to Ian like men talking in distant low muffled tones. Perhaps Silas's ancestors.

A single large hawk circled high above the deluge.

Silas was also standing stone still and gazing intently toward the bottom when Ian got there. He was holding a cup of coffee but could not take his eyes off the river.

"You know this means the dam let go." He seemed surprised. "Hear those waves breaking? The river is talking to us." He glanced briefly toward Ian, his brow furrowed. "Thank God Almighty we

197

are free at last." Martin Luther King, Jr. from the "I have a dream" speech delivered August 28, 1963 in Washington D.C.

He looked away. "I just pray that no one gets hurt. This flood is going to kick the living shit out of town."

"I can't imagine a force of nature quoting a young Baptist minister," Ian quipped.

"Can you imagine a young Baptist minister quoting a force of nature?" Silas replied. "When Martin Luther King used those words in his famous 'I Have a Dream' speech, he was quoting an old African-American spiritual . Heaven only knows what event originally inspired the song. In that same speech, he quoted the Bible, Amos 5:24, proclaiming the fight would continue until 'justice rolls down like waters and righteousness like a mighty stream'."

"Mighty stream, indeed! It is amazing that the river could come up that much," Ian mused. "That lake wasn't half full."

"Floods in the mountains are particularly impressive because there is no place for the water to go. It just gets deeper and a lot faster until everything in its path is swept away."

"At least that hawk is well above it."

"Back when the old boys around here would shoot every red tail they saw…they claimed they killed their chickens and ducks…my father would never hurt one. He claimed they reminded him of his grandfather. His grandfather, my great grandfather, was a true wild mountain man. Great Grandpap built a string of primitive little one-room log camps in various spots around this drainage. Here, in this meadow, he kept a cabin for his wife and my grandfather, but was often gone for weeks at a time while he hunted and ran his trap lines.

"My father swears that he had a sixth sense. If he was needed at home, perhaps someone would get hurt or sick, he would appear almost as if out of nowhere and bring half a deer or a couple of wild turkeys, wild fruit and some furs to sell for cash. He would stay until things normalized. When the smokehouse and root cellars were full, he would restock with gunpowder and tobacco, and disappear into the wilderness. 'Gone on the wind,' my father would say.

"My father loved the voice of a hawk and the way it carried across this hollow. He said the sounds that animals make, like the sounds of the wind and water, are the earth's way of talking to us. He saw thunder as a warning and the scream of the hawk as a victory cry." Silas looked out upon the flood as a single startlingly clear scream drifted to their ears. A small chill rushed up Ian's back.

Lori and Kathleen awoke two hours later to the sound of police sirens on the street below. Cletus and the other deputies were telling people to evacuate their homes. No one had any idea when the flood would crest. So far, only one row of buildings was under water. None of them were homes. They all belonged to the cement company. One was Ian's office.

Kathleen looked out the window. She could see that the family's hardware store was getting a little too close to the river for comfort. She tried to remember whether her father had purchased the flood insurance she told him might be a good idea. He had resisted, stating that the building had been there for sixty years without being flooded.

Too late to worry about it now. As she watched, most of the town's residents just milled around in the street and stared at the water as the river washed over the bridge at the center of town.

Dozens of floating logs and trees began to pile up against the bridge. The structure started to tremble, then visibly bounce, with the current surges. About that time, even the adolescent boys who had been standing on the besieged structure, abandoned it in favor of more solid ground. A few more trees piled on.

The bridge shook, heaved once more, and was gone. Even the concrete abutments disappeared into the flood, though they would later be found inches from where they fell. They had been undercut by the current and merely toppled over, out of sight under the churning waters.

The crowd gasped in awe.

By now, all of the cattle were in the backyard. They looked lost, as if wondering what the hell was going on. The big red heifer had delivered a healthy, still clumsy, calf without human assistance.

Ian and Silas had each taken a short nap, made breakfast, bandaged Silas's leg twice. They were back to drinking coffee on the front porch of Silas's place when Deputy Cletus arrived. It was almost noon. He pulled into Ian's driveway. Silas ran for his binoculars.

They watched as he went to Ian's door.

His approach was slow and halting. This was due no doubt to the growling presence of his namesake, who then strolled over to the patrol car and pissed on the front tire. Realizing that Ian was not home, the deputy walked over to Ian's truck and placed an open hand on its hood.

"The SOB is checking to see if your engine is warm. He wants to know if you've been anywhere recently. He's a little late for that ploy, but I guess better late than never." Silas lowered the binoculars and rolled his bloodshot eyes.

"Cops just don't trust anybody."

Soon the patrol car was headed toward Silas's place. The deputy got out and gave a practiced "Good Morning."

"'Mornin' Cletus," responded Silas. "What's up?"

"That flood yonder," he pointed to the muddy lake that was once pasture, "That's no ordinary flood. Stanley Coombs, the security guard up at the dam, says it was sabotaged last night."

"Are you telling me that we are in danger of having a dam break all over us?" Silas inquired, attempting to sound concerned.

"No, our most recent reports from the dam are that the river has pretty much cut its way back to the level of its old channel already. The lake had never been filled in the first place because the dam wasn't finished yet. Once the water from last night's rain washes through, it should start to recede." Cletus officially assured them.

"That was quite a storm last night, wasn't it?" Ian remarked, figuring the weather was a safe topic.

Silas, however, wanted to talk about the dam.

"What makes Stanley think it was sabotage?" interrupted Silas, careful to use Cletus's characterization. He was only a little concerned about his lack of sleep making him say something he might regret. He was hoping to hear Stanley's story.

"He says two tanker trucks of explosives disappeared. We're calling the FBI in on this. They'll figure it out. The shame of all this is that word is already out that there may not be any money to rebuild the dam."

There was a fleeting but uncomfortable moment of silence.

Neither Ian nor Silas moved to start up the conversation again. Cletus finally resumed his monologue.

200

"But, from what I hear, you'd probably like that. You've never been real fond of that project, have you?"

Silas was not biting at the bait. "Cletus, you know that I really don't give a shit about what's going on seven miles away. I mind *my* land and *my* business." He just smiled innocently. But then, he had to ask. "Where was Stanley when all this was going on?"

Ian knew that Silas was not above walking on thin ice. He found it a bit annoying, however, that walking was not enough for Silas. Father's admonition to keep humble echoed in Ian's ears. It would be best to just let Cletus go away. The more they engaged him in conversation, the more likely that one of them would say something Cletus could use in his investigation. Or pass along to the FBI. Ian was aware that Silas could not refrain from taking a shot at Stanley, who he considered a major dickweed.

"He says that the rain on the roof of the office trailer put him to sleep," Cletus tossed his head slightly and raised his eyebrows. "Must be nice to sleep that soundly."

"It's the mark of a clear conscience." Silas observed with a smug grin.

"I guess," Cletus gave the two of them one last long looking over. They both tried to appear nonchalant.

"You all take care." He backed down the steps and stood next to the Power Wagon, which was parked in the yard.

Placing a hand on its hood, ostensibly for balance while he looked at the mud on his previously shiny shoes. But he really wanted to feel for any heat that it might be emitting. He called back to Silas and Ian, "Let me know if you hear anything more about any of this."

Silas waived goodbye dismissively.

Cletus got into the cruiser and was gone.

There were a few minutes of silence. Ian spoke first.

"If you insist on skating on thin ice, can you at least resist the urge to dance?"

"What?" came Silas' simple reply. He had already become mesmerized by the rhythm of the water rolling across the fields.

"You were messing with Cletus, and Stanley in absentia. The longer Cletus hung around the more likely he was to notice something not right. Like that quarter-sized blood spot on your jeans that wasn't there when he first arrived."

"Shit, I never was much of a doctor."

"You might need stitches."

"No way, I've been cut worse peeling potatoes."

"Remind me not to eat potatoes around here."

"Hey, I think we deserve some credit for getting old Cletus out of here without him getting any nosier than he was," Silas admittedly was glad to see him leave.

"And perhaps some credit for last night?"

"Nope, no credit for that. Not now, not ever."

More silence except for the sound carried by a soft morning breeze up the hollow to the house, of waves crashing in the river bottom.

"There is virtually no limit to what can be accomplished if people don't worry about who gets the credit," Ian reflected.

"You mean the blame?" Silas replied, his mouth half full of coffee.

"Same thing, just different perspective," Ian noted. He watched a giant oak tree that had been torn from its foothold upstream, drift peacefully across the muddy lake. He knew it harbored the un-flinching kinetic energy of a bulldozer.

"You have probably ruined the day for a lot of influential people with your irresponsible little act of vandalism," he taunted Silas.

"This is just a small deal in the great scheme of things," Silas responded, picking up on Ian's diminutive characterization, "Fuck 'em if they can't take a joke.'" It was one of Silas's favorite expressions, but he saved it for when it was especially ironic or under-stated. "Montani Semper Liberi." Silas added.

"Say what?" Ian thought he recognized a Latin phrase, but was surprised at its source.

"That's Latin for 'Mountaineers are always free.' It is the state motto of West Virginia."

Ian smirked. He liked that expression. Inexplicably, considering his new status as felon-at -large, he felt the best he had felt in years. Empowered, liberated, a little dangerous. Maybe he was just a victim of his environment. Part of a bona fide two-man militia. Maybe he could blame his actions on a diet too high in refined sugar and simple carbohydrates. Naw, he'd been eating better than that.

They toasted with strong black coffee to vandals and freemen.

Ian reflected on recent events. "You know that if that dam project stays dead, maybe I have a chance to legally get three old men out of those sad little trailers and back on their land." He smiled. He mused that it was an illegal smile. "I had a professor back in law school who used to say the law respects self-help. I am not sure, however, that this is exactly what he had in mind."

Silas started to speak. "Back in Sunday school."

He looked over toward Ian, laughed, and answered the unasked question. "Yes, I went to Sunday school. Twice. My aunt made me go with her. She thought my father a heathen because he didn't subscribe to organized religion. She was very wrong. He was a deeply spiritual man." He continued. "There was this teacher who used to say that the Lord helps those who help themselves." He looked out across the floodwaters to the far mountain. It was ablaze with fall color. The events of last night still troubled him just a bit.

"Who was that guy under the rock?" he finally asked Ian. "And how did you know him? How did he come to be there at that time? That seems way too strange for coincidence."

"I can certainly appreciate the strangeness, but as to how he got there, I haven't a clue."

"You knew him? Is he from around here? Guys don't just take their bikes out for a ride in a hurricane."

"I met him in a titty bar roughly six months ago. He gave me directions here, though I never really told him where I wanted to go."

Silas raised an eyebrow. "I thought you said you just stumbled onto this place."

"I did, but somehow he encouraged me to come this direction. I had no idea where I was going. I could have ended up almost anywhere. Somehow this place just sort of fit."

"He looked familiar," Silas continued. "But the only place I can place him would be a physical impossibility." He gazed back at the flood and spoke without turning his head.

"When my grandfather was dying, and this was when I was just a boy, probably thirty-some odd years ago, I went to his room. It was in this very house. The room where I sleep now. It's also the room where I was born.

"A man was standing over my grandfather's bed. The guy under that rock looked just as I remember that man. Of course, that was a long time ago and that friend of my grandfather has no doubt long since gone to his reward. That man told me that my grandfather was going away but that he would be in good hands. He also told me that we all have a job to do in life and that my grandfather's job was done but that mine had just begun. I remember thinking that I was too young to have any job at all.

"Funny thing though, that guy rode an old blue Harley. When I came out of the house, it was parked in the yard. Later it was gone, but I never saw him leave. My grandpappy died that afternoon."

Ian did not respond. The whole story left him a little uneasy. He found himself thinking about his own mortality. The impermanence of things, including the universe, always made him feel strangely weak. He made himself move on to another subject. They drank their coffee and watched the bright midday sun of Indian summer glint off the muddy tide swirling across their fields. Rafts of shattered trees circled the relatively calm waters of the broad bottom. Some would be sucked back into the flow and be whisked to town and beyond. Others would stay eddied out and be grounded in the fields as the waters receded. There would be a lot of cleaning up to do all along the river after the flood.

That evening, once the Big Laurel had clearly peaked and begun to recede, the town had a spontaneous survivors' party at The Stand. The beer was free, the music was loud, and by ten o'clock Debbie Evans and both her younger sisters were drunk and dancing topless on the bar.

Omer Strickler sat at a corner table drinking Jim Beam® with his grandson. Jimmy Strickler was, at twenty three, the manager of a sawmill and one of the more eligible bachelors around town. They were watching the Evans women dance.

"What do you think 'bout that Gramps?" asked Jimmy, elbowing the old man.

"Same thing you're thinking boy," came the reply.

Jimmy looked puzzled.

"Just remember this, son." Omer's eyes twinkled slightly, perhaps from the whiskey. "The body may grow old, but the mind never changes."

204

By eleven o'clock the sounds coming from Silas's old truck, which was parked in the shadows near the raging but slowly quieting flow, would have made a veteran madam blush. In the morning Kathleen had to Windex her footprints from all over the inside of the windshield and both side windows.

Nothing like surviving a natural disaster to confirm that it is great to be alive.

EPILOGUE

Thanksgiving dinner was at Ian's that year. Lori made him tidy up
the place to the point that she felt it was at least minimally present-
able. She even sat in a lawn chair in the backyard and directed his
efforts at brushing a fresh coat of tar on the old metal roof. They
both knew she was really there to drive him to the hospital if he
fell. The roof became a two-day job when Ian discovered that the
ancient sand mortar in the chimney had weathered back into plain
sand. He gingerly disassembled it down to the roofline then
mortared it, brick by brick, back into place. Add masonry to the list
of new skills he had acquired this year.

Ian borrowed some folding chairs from the restaurant and a big
table from the volunteer fire department bingo room. Lori,
Kathleen, Silas, Ian, Ian's mom, and Kathleen's father, all said they
would be there. The weather was supposed to be classic late
autumn, clear and crisp with just a hint of chill in the air. Firewood
sat stacked by the stove just in case.

There was plenty of firewood. When last month's flood receded, it
left the entire bottom strewn with driftwood. Huge oak, sycamore,
hemlock, and poplar logs lay piled or scattered like the pick-up-
sticks Ian used to play with as a child. Silas and he had spent the
better part of a week, and half a dozen saw-chains each, cutting up
the driftwood jams. They had enough wood for several winters.
The small debris they loaded into Silas's truck and piled on the hill
where Ian's new orchard would be located. It would make an
incredible bonfire some cold night. And perhaps bake some snakes.

Lori even wrestled Cletus into the tub and gave him his first real
bath. It was not well received. He would periodically lunge for
freedom only to be tackled and grappled back into wet submission.
By the time it was over it was difficult to tell who had bathed
whom. Both Cletus and Lori were soaked to the bone. She turned
him loose, prematurely it turned out, before escorting him out the
door. He shook the water from his fur while standing in the middle
of the living room, dousing Ian, the walls, and Lori again. Score:
Wolfdog 1, Humans 0. Then he went outside and rolled in the dirt.

On Thanksgiving Day, Ian's mom showed up first.

"Old ladies always get up early," she apologized. "We are supposed to drive slow enough that getting up so damn early doesn't matter. I guess I don't drive that slow yet." She laughed.

She, of course, had a million questions. It was great to see her again. Ian marveled that someone who had been able to go for years without any contact at all now had such an intense interest in how he was doing. Yet he did not doubt her motivation or sincerity. She just had a great deal of mothering to catch up on.

"How'd you all fair after the big flood?" She wanted to be sure she had not missed any developments since she last spoke to Ian. She had called only a day or two after the actual flood, just as soon as the phone company restored her telephone service. It had failed in the storm, as had her electric power. High winds and raging creeks undercut or knocked down roadside power poles all over the area. It was weeks in some cases before the utility companies got them back in place.

Lori laughed. "Are you kidding? Your son doesn't even know a natural disaster when he sees one. Kathleen and I were in town when the flood hit. The river flooded the whole first row of buildings down near the river, including his law office. Luckily, it crested before it got into Kathleen's hardware store. The bridge in the middle of town collapsed right before our eyes. I called Ian but there was no answer at his place, and Silas doesn't have a phone. We hopped in the car and drove downstream as fast as we could to try to find a place to get across the river to come check on these guys. The next intact bridge was at Ten-mile Creek. It was shaking from the force of the water as we crossed it.

The old dirt road up the other side of the river was washed out in places. We were able to get through, although we scraped and dragged the underside of the car a bunch of times. At Ginseng Hollow the creek was so high that it was lapping over the bridge. Kathleen and I held our breath and drove across. I could see the water cascading powerfully through the rocky chasm below the road. Who knows how far it would have washed us if the bridge had collapsed. We might well have been killed. Deputy Cletus was sitting in his car on the other side of the bridge waiting for the water to recede. Even *he* had the sense not to cross it the way it was.

"Oh, and you'll love this," she looked toward Ian. "As we crossed the bridge, Cletus was watching us with that half leer that he uses when he thinks that he is invisible. As we got close, the part of the cruiser's windshield that was in his field of vision suddenly went opaque. I heard a scream and looked up. In the tree, twenty feet above him, was a great big red tail hawk with its wings and tail feathers spread wide. It looked quite pleased with itself. If we hadn't been there, I believe Cletus might have taken a shot at it with his service revolver. As it was, he just turned his windshield wipers on and started squirting washer fluid everywhere.

"We left him there, just sitting in his cruiser, annoyed and waiting. It took us about an hour and a half to get up here from town. When we arrived, the two of them were sitting on Silas's porch drinking coffee and shooting Silas's .22 rifle at a milk jug floating around in the flood water down in the field. That whole bottom was under water. Neither of them seemed concerned at all. Silas did say that he took a head count of his cows. And Ian said Cletus was safe and sleeping on the porch. Of course, neither of them called to check on Kathleen or me."

"Men have a fascination with natural disasters. That was the one thing Ian's father would watch on television. He'd sit and stare at any news story on floods, hurricanes, tornadoes, earthquakes, anything like that," Alma noted in partial explanation.

"Our phone was out," Ian offered in his defense though he looked a little sheepish. Granted, failing to check on Kathleen and Lori was a serious faux pas.

"We knew that you two could take care of yourselves." He offered weakly in further inadequate justification. "And we figured that if we drove out of here to a phone, your phone lines would be down anyway."

Silas and Kathleen walked through the door.

"Welcome," exclaimed Ian. "I'm glad that you're here to save me from the abuse I'm about to take from these two."

Silas wrinkled his brow questioningly. He naturally had no idea what Ian was talking about. Ian introduced his mother to Silas and Kathleen. They all busied themselves getting the table set and the meal ready. Soon Kathleen's father wandered in and triggered another round of introductions.

He looked a little apprehensive. Not a very social man to begin with, he had become accustomed to solitude since his wife left him and moved to Charlotte half a dozen years earlier. At first, he shadowed Silas, who he had grown very close to over the last year. It bothered Kathleen a little that they seemed to understand each other as well as they did. Maybe she feared that they understood each other better than she would ever understand either of them. They talked hunting, fishing, motorcycles, cars, motors, cams and pistons, plumbing, wiring, carpentry, cattle, and other manly things. At some point Ian followed the smell of food into the kitchen. He was driven out with flamboyant gestures utilizing large kitchen utensils, as the women exercised dominion over the preparation of dinner. The men circled the woodstove, accepting of the fact that one or all of them would almost certainly be later accused of sitting in the other room and drinking coffee ("were idle and useless") while the women worked ("downloaded and conspired") in the kitchen. Not one of them gave it a second thought.

They *did* at least build a fire in the woodstove in anticipation of the inevitable, "Honey, why do you keep it so cold in here?" Then they kicked back in the folding chairs, which were far enough from the table that they would not interfere with the dinner preparations. Kathleen's father told a story about a man who had traveled the world on a religious pilgrimage of sorts.

"He visited some of the world's great cathedrals and churches. In several he found, far in the back rooms away from the view of casual visitors, 'hot line' telephones purporting to be able to put the caller directly in contact with Heaven. The cost of such a call was usually at least many years' salary for any man of normal means. He had dismissed it as a mechanism for fund raising by the Church. A way to tap the high rollers.

"Some years later, near the end of his pilgrimage, he stopped at a little white frame church way up a hollow in a place not far from here. In one of the back rooms in the downstairs part of the building, in a room usually reserved for Sunday school classes, he saw one of those telephones. The sign on it explained that it was a direct line to Heaven. It said, 'to call, please deposit 35 cents.' The traveler was, of course, flabbergasted and immediately brought the telephone to the attention of the wiry old preacher. He said, 'I've seen these phones at other churches around the world, but they have always charged tens of thousands of dollars to place a call. This one is only 35 cents.'"

The old preacher looked at him, surprised by his apparent excitement.

'Well, naturally,' the reverend noted, 'from here it's a local call.'"

After the smiles had faded, Kathleen's father was quiet for a moment then asked Ian and Silas if they had gotten a visit from the FBI.

An agent named Samuels had been to the hardware store to ask whether there had been any recent purchases of a number of items such as watches, electrical components and batteries.

"I showed him my records, but he didn't seem to think there was anything unusual in there. He sat in my office and looked through them, but didn't take any, or ask for any copies. He seemed satisfied with what he saw."

"He stopped out here about a week after the flood," Silas ventured. "He caught me down in the bottom restringing wire where the flood had flattened all of my fences. There were all sorts of questions, but he asked them in a friendly enough way. He never even asked me to stop working, though I don't think he liked getting his hands dirty when I asked him to hold a couple muddy locust posts steady so I could tamp them back into place. Did I know anyone around here who had explosives experience? I said sure, a bunch. I named all the blasters I'd known in the mines since childhood and said he'd have to also include my name on that list. He asked me if I knew what ANFO was. I laughed and reminded him that my name was on his list. He just sort of shrugged that one off. For a Fed, he really didn't seem very pushy."

"Yeah, he got me too, about that same time," Ian added. "Caught me dragging muddy furniture out of what was left of my office. He wanted to know where I was that night and when I first noticed the floodwaters. I reminded him that it was storming hard all night. I had spent until the wee hours of the morning with Silas, waiting for that big red heifer of his to calve, but ended up telling Silas that I would be in bed if he needed me. When I got up in the morning, the bottom was full of muddy water. Silas was standing on his porch drinking coffee, and the calf was wobbling around the paddock in front of the barn. Same deal, he seemed satisfied and headed down the street toward the diner."

Lori was setting plates on the table and overheard the conversation. "He stopped in the diner and talked to me, too. He wanted to know where the four of us had been. I told him that Kathleen and I had been at The Stand and that the two of you were delivering a calf."

"He got to me, too," Kathleen chimed in from the kitchen. "Thorough guy."

"That's what he's paid for, Honey," responded Silas.

"It's his training," added Ian. "They are all over this one. Probably because ol' Stanley was so sure that it was some sort of act of terrorism."

"Like he'd know terrorism if it bit him on the ass," Kathleen responded from the doorway. "He spent the night sitting on a barstool trying to look up my skirt or down Lori's blouse. A terrorist could have planted a bomb on him. Unless it was in his shorts he never would have noticed it."

"Just don't get smart mouthed with the FBI darling," her father advised.

"They want someone real bad, which makes them very dangerous. They might even resort to trying to pin this on some innocent fool who gets too cocky with them," Ian advised. "I know that they have talked to a lot of people around town, including everyone who was at The Stand that night."

Everyone except Lucky Sonovich. Lucky had vanished. No one around town had seen him since that evening.

Kathleen's father spoke up, "You know, word in the paper is that the dam project is dead. The state congressional delegation says that the cost-to-benefit ratio is too low to justify appropriating any more money for it. It has been suggested that the fact that the dam actually burst without loss of life or really serious property damage was proof that it was never needed in the first place. That's probably true, but the flood sure had me sweating bullets for a few hours. The water rose to within a foot of the back door of the hardware store. That building has been there since the thirties. It's been through plenty of floods, but that's the closest the river's ever gotten to it."

"It's not every day that a dam breaks," Silas reminded him. "I suspect it's probably pretty safe from normal floods."

That reminded Ian of a promise he once made. "You know, if the project is finally dead, I should be able to pry Junior Harper's farm back away from the government. His buddies down in those trailers, which by the way almost got swept away in the flood, will want theirs back, too. It won't be easy getting the land back. I'm sure the government guys will trot out some lame justification for keeping it. But I think that without the project I can maintain that they don't have a legitimate governmental purpose to hold onto it. The project was a condition precedent to their having any right to it."

"You might want to call Congressman Randy Young," Lori suggested. "He knew my Dad. He also ran on the get-government-off-the-back-of-the-little-guy ticket." He might see this as an opportunity to keep some campaign promises.

Ian nodded. Probably a good idea.

"Who wants to carve the bird?" The question came from Ian's mom, who walked in from the kitchen, twenty pound turkey held high on a white china platter.

Kathleen's father, who had requested at their introduction to, "please call me Scott," leapt to his feet to help her with the turkey. He placed it on the table and began the process of rendering it into thick, serving-sized slabs.

As they all gathered around the table, Ian couldn't help but think that they looked like a couple generations of solid traditional American family. Yet they had come together relatively recently from people blown by fate and fortune like the dry late fall leaves. Kathleen was thinking that the scene needed some children.

Silas offered to say grace. Kathleen cringed imperceptibly. She hoped it would be a serious prayer because she really did not know how Ian's mother would take it if he started getting blasphemous. "Dear God," he began. "Thank you for bringing us all together for this dinner in celebration of your generosity. It has been a year of changes for all of us. We've lost some very precious things, and found treasures previously unimagined. Your hand was in all of it. Thank you for bringing Ian and Lori to our town and into our lives. Thank you for being kind to our homes and businesses and to my cattle, which have been fat and healthy. Though it presented us with challenges, we understand that the recent flood was a necessary thing. Thank you that it didn't take any lives. We are grateful to be blessed with your green lands and free flowing waters and promise to always respect them. Give us the strength to love and protect that which you have blessed us with, both inside and outside of our houses. Lastly, thank you for this food and for letting us share it with Alma and Scott, for without them we would all be living in a very different world. Amen."

Ian was touched. So was Lori. Kathleen was relieved. Ian's mom and Kathleen's dad were eyeing each other over the cranberry sauce. Cletus waited patiently under the table, a devotee of the trickle down economic theory.

After dinner, during cleanup, Lori and Kathleen were in the kitchen. Kathleen leaned close to Lori and whispered "I think they like each other. They're so cute." A warm, mischievous smirk stretched across her face. Her green eyes sparkled.

"Well, you're never too old you know."

On the far side of the county two motorcycles pulled into a gas station at a lonely intersection on a long winding stretch of country blacktop. The riders, wrapped in layers of wool and leather, both appeared to be weathered veterans of the open road. They silently filled their old motorcycles, a sky-blue Panhead and a black shovelhead Superglide, with high-test.

After they had kicked their bikes back to life and settled into the saddle, one bike pointed east and one to the west. They looked face-to-face across the pump island at each other and nodded. The older rider spoke first.

"Good work, Lucky"

"Always a pleasure, Father."

"Lucky, I'd appreciate if you would look in on the place from time to time."

"Anything in particular?"

"Whatever comes naturally."

"Consider it done, Father. Give my best to Mother."

"I will," Father beamed. "She sends hers as well. Take care."

Father cast a passing glance up to the roof of the old concrete block building that had once been an automobile repair business but now sold soft drinks and junk food. A large hawk stared back at him. In one powerful motion, it spread its wings and flew straight up to a height of several hundred feet above him. Father's gaze followed it for a few seconds. He grabbed the clutch lever and tapped his motorcycle down into low gear.

The big bird cut a high arc and headed upriver.

The men once again exchanged nods as they began to roll in opposite directions.

Brown leaves scattered as they accelerated hard into the November twilight.

www.ingramcontent.com/pod-product-compliance
Lightning Source LLC
Chambersburg PA
CBHW031308120626
46554CB00001BA/340